BY ELISSA SUSSMAN

Funny You Should Ask
Once More with Feeling

Stray
Burn
Drawn That Way

ONCE MORE WITH FEELING

ONCE MORE WITH FEELING

A NOVEL

ELISSA SUSSMAN

DELL
NEW YORK

A Dell Trade Paperback Original

Copyright © 2023 by Elissa Sussman

Published in the United States by Dell,
an imprint of Random House, a division of
Penguin Random House LLC, New York.

DELL is a registered trademark and the D colophon
is a trademark of Penguin Random House LLC.

LIBRARY OF CONGRESS CATALOGING-IN-PUBLICATION DATA
Names: Sussman, Elissa, author.
Title: Once more with feeling: a novel / Elissa Sussman.
Description: New York: Dell, [2023]
Identifiers: LCCN 2022060550 (print) |
LCCN 2022060551 (ebook) | ISBN 9780593357378
(trade paperback) | ISBN 9780593357361 (ebook)
Subjects: LCGFT: Romance fiction. | Novels.
Classification: LCC PS3619.U845 O53 2023 (print) |
LCC PS3619.U845 (ebook) | DDC 813/.6—dc23/eng/20230112
LC record available at https://lccn.loc.gov/2022060550
LC ebook record available at https://lccn.loc.gov/2022060551

Printed in the United States of America on acid-free paper

randomhousebooks.com

2 4 6 8 9 7 5 3 1

Book design by Elizabeth A. D. Eno

This book is dedicated to Prozac and Jelly Bellies.
I couldn't have done it without you.

"Theater is a verb before it is a noun,
an act before it is a place."

—Martha Graham

"I've always said I had more guts than
I had talent."

—Dolly Parton

ONCE MORE WITH FEELING

TOP 100 MUSIC SCANDALS OF THE PAST 50 YEARS
#14: KATEE ROSE DESTROYS RYAN LANEVE'S HEART (AND HER CAREER)

It will make you feel old as dirt to realize that there are youths today who are completely unaware that Ryan LaNeve, movie star, was once Ryan LaNeve, teen sketch show cheeseball. The short-lived *Show N Tell* was a launchpad for many a star, including his former flame, Katee Rose. LaNeve and Rose first met on the set when they were teens, but their relationship was thrust into the spotlight as they both gained popularity—her as a solo act and him as one-fifth of CrushZone, the hottest boy band of the time.

Their reign as the prince and princess of pop ended abruptly when LaNeve revealed that Rose had been unfaithful. Although it was never confirmed, the scandal gained even more traction when it was implied that Rose had been cheating on him with none other than fellow CrushZone member Calvin Tyler Kirby.

In a case of life imitating art, LaNeve left CrushZone to take a star-making role in *Kiss Me First,* as the sad-sack husband who watches his marriage dissolve when his wife prostitutes herself, in a loose remake of *Indecent Proposal.*

As for Katee Rose? The nasally performer had already been on the way out, and the scandal was just the final nail in the coffin of her career.

◇ OVERTURE

It was trial by fire, musical theatre–style.

Once our bags had been unpacked, instead of the first-day bonding activities I was accustomed to at my usual Jewish summer camp, everyone had been herded into the theatre and told we'd be auditioning for the end-of-summer showcase.

Right. Now.

Camp Curtain Call was not fucking around.

Most people would be shaking in their boots, but I wasn't. I was more than up for the challenge. I was ready.

It was exactly the reason I'd wanted to come here in the first place.

I had it all planned out.

Step one: Convince unsupportive parents to spend bat mitzvah money on expensive, exclusive theatre camp.

Step two: Astonish everyone at said camp with my talent, charm, and can-do spirit.

Step three: Perform—to a standing ovation—at the end-of-summer showcase, impressing an audience full of agents, managers, and other theatre powerhouses.

Step four: Theatrical domination.

I sat in the back row and observed my competition.

Even though I'd anticipated step one to be the hardest to pull off, I knew the rest wouldn't be a Sunday walk in the park. There was talent here—plenty of it—but that didn't discourage me. There was no pride in being the best of the subpar. If anything, this would make my triumph all the more glorious.

Auditions were being conducted alphabetically, so I had the advantage of watching everyone with last names from A to Rosenberg go before me. We were an hour in, and I'd already changed my audition song twice, after watching the front row of instructors sigh at yet another rendition of "I Dreamed a Dream" and "Don't Rain on My Parade."

Luckily, I'd prepared at least a dozen potential performances, ranging from the expected to the more obscure. Right now, I was debating between "If I Were a Bell" and "Lion Tamer." One was funny, one was wistful. Most singers were leaning toward the latter, so I was leaning toward the former. Luckily, I was excellent at both.

It was essential that I stand out.

The next camper stepped onstage.

"Rachel James," she said, her hair thick and shiny, her teeth perfect.

There was a soft groan next to me. I glanced over to find a face scrunched with disdain behind big, round glasses.

"It's a stage name," she said when she caught me looking. "Her real name is Rochelle Illowski."

A stage name. I was probably going to need one of those.

Though, when I imagined receiving my (first) Tony Award, it had always been "And the winner is Kathleen Rosenberg!"

I could tell, from the way the instructors leaned forward, the way the whole room went quiet, and the straight line of her shoulders, that Rachel knew what she was doing.

And she did.

Her voice was gorgeous. Crystal clear and emotive.

We weren't supposed to clap after auditions, but half of the campers did anyway. No one stopped them.

"She's good," I said.

"She's been on tour," the girl with glasses said.

I was unspeakably jealous. And a little nervous.

"Wow," I said.

"She's a bitch."

I looked at my new friend, surprised and delighted by the outburst. She shrugged.

"She put pine cones in my bunk last year," she said. "And stole my signed Rent playbill."

"That bitch," I said, and meant it.

"I'm Harriet," she said. Her box braids were pulled up away from her face in a towering twist.

"Kathleen," I replied.

We shook hands.

"First summer?" she asked.

I nodded.

"Fourth," she said.

"You must know everyone," I said.

She shrugged, but with a pleased smile.

"It is very nice to meet you," I said.

I meant that too. A Rent fan and someone who knew the ins and outs of Curtain Call? It was as if the patron saint of musical theatre—Stephen Sondheim—was smiling on me.

Perhaps.

"What do you sing?" I asked.

"I'm an alto," she said.

Lucky indeed. A new friend that I didn't have to compete with.

"But I mostly write songs," Harriet said.

"You write your own songs?" I asked.

She nodded.

It was like she'd just confessed to having a superpower.

"You're my new best friend," I said.

"Okay," she said.

Harriet knew everyone and everything about them. At least the important things, like how many summers they'd been attending, if they'd been featured in the showcase, and if they'd ever performed professionally.

"That's Courtney," she'd say. "Six summers. Was only in the showcase once and it was an ensemble role."

Or "That's Shauna. Only her second summer, but she had a duet last year."

Or "Corina wasn't here last summer, but she was the summer before. I think she was in the chorus."

It was a little like being with my dad when he was reciting baseball stats. Only actually interesting.

"Who. Is. That?" I asked.

My attention was completely captivated by the most beautiful man I'd ever seen. And considering that he looked at least sixteen, he was definitely a man. He had floppy hair cut like a curtain in the middle of his forehead and a puka shell necklace, and I couldn't stop staring at the way he'd looped his thumbs into his cargo shorts as he rocked back and forth on his heels. He had nice legs too. Strong and tanned.

"*Calvin Kirby,*" *he said, standing center stage.*

Every hormone in my body went off like overheated lightbulbs. Pop. Pop. Pop.

He was a baritone.

I was in love.

NOW

'd made a terrible mistake.

Well, *two* terrible mistakes.

The first was agreeing to the lunch. The second was not insisting that Harriet and I arrive together. We would have been late, because Harriet was always late, but it would have been better than being early, which I was because I was always early.

Cal too, apparently.

He was already seated when the waitress escorted me back. He glanced up as I approached.

Three mistakes.

The grainy headshot that the trades used whenever he was mentioned was at least five years old, and now that he was here, eyes locked with mine, it was clear that photo hardly did him justice.

He stood and seemed to go up and up and up. Had he always been this tall?

His clothes fit well. He had a five o'clock shadow that had arrived just in time. His hair was artfully tousled. I imagined him wearing mirrored sunglasses while driving through Brooklyn in a convertible, causing everyone to stop and stare.

"Kathleen Rosenberg," he said.

And then there was his voice. I'd forgotten—worked hard to forget—just how fucking good it was. How deep and resonant.

God. I felt it in my toes and my fingertips.

"Well, well, well," I said. "If it isn't Calvin Tyler Kirby."

His cheek twitched, but his polite—fake—smile didn't falter.

He hated being referred to by all three names. Which was exactly the point.

Cal should consider himself lucky that I wasn't using his even more loathed nickname.

In fact, he should consider himself lucky that I showed up here in the first place. The last time we'd seen each other, he'd called me a "mistake" and I'd told him to get the fuck out of my life.

He'd obliged.

My feelings about him hadn't changed, but circumstances had. And I'd promised Harriet I'd hear him out.

"It's good to see you," he lied, holding out a hand.

"Come now," I said.

Placing my hands on his shoulders, I leaned up and gave him two loud, obnoxious air kisses. His muscles tensed beneath my palms. His cologne—like an orange grove—wrapped around me. I ignored how good all of it felt, let go, and stepped back.

"Shall we?" He gestured toward the table.

We sat.

It was like being in a sauna of awkwardness. I could feel it in my pores.

"It's been a while," I said. Understatement of the century.

Cal raised an eyebrow but said nothing. His menu was apparently fascinating.

I was fairly certain, despite his unruffled exterior, that Cal was doing exactly what I was doing—which was recalling the last time we'd been in a room together, exchanging barbs. We'd both said some unkind things.

How long had it been? Ten years? Fifteen?

It didn't really matter. I could still remember the disgust and disappointment in his eyes. How he'd turned away, not looking back as he left me alone to deal with the consequences of our shared actions.

I wondered if he felt bad about it now, or if he still thought I'd deserved what happened.

The complete lack of apology seemed to indicate he had no regrets.

Well, that was fine. Fucking fine.

Because it wasn't like I was about to accept an apology, even if he had offered one. *Sorry* wasn't enough to repair what had been broken.

My career. My spirit.

I knew I was being dramatic, but I was quite certain Calvin Tyler Kirby wouldn't expect anything less.

"Harriet's always late," I said, even though I was sure he knew that.

"I'm in no rush," he said, still examining his menu.

I wanted to reach across the table, rip it out of his hands, tear it into a million tiny pieces, and force him to look at me.

"Fantastic," I said through clenched teeth.

I should have turned my attention to my own menu but found myself staring at him instead. At all the ways time had changed him. I tried imagining his younger self superimposed over this one, contrasting the gray in his hair and the lines around his eyes with my memory of him with frosted tips and eyeliner.

Had he done the same to me when I walked in?

I would deny it if pressed, but I'd put extra effort into my appearance today. My hair hadn't been blond since my Katee Rose days, but I'd taken the time to tame and style it, resisting the urge to dye my own multiplying grays.

The weather was that charming in-between of winter and spring, when days had an equal chance of being floral and bright or chilled and slushy. It had been nice when I left my apartment, but there was no guarantee that it would stay that way. I'd worn jeans and a lightweight sweater, but I knew for a fact that Cal had noticed the fit of both since his gaze had darted downward—just for a moment—when he first saw me. It was gratifying to know that the boobs that had earned me the moniker "Titty Rose" from the tabloids continued to maintain their stage presence after all these years.

"Is there something on my face?" Cal asked.

He hadn't even looked up.

"Just your eyes, nose, and mouth," I said sweetly.

If he was trying to catch me off guard, he was going to have to try a lot harder. I was ready for him. Crouched, with tail twitching, just waiting for an opportunity to attack. I might have gotten softer and rounder since he last saw me, but I'd sharpened my claws. Donned some armor. If he thought he was dealing with the person I'd been back then, he was going to be sorely disappointed.

Katee had trusted him.

Kathleen knew better.

"I've heard the grilled octopus is good," he said.

"It is," I said.

He finally lifted his eyes to meet mine.

"How good?" he asked.

He was asking about the octopus, but also, he wasn't.

"Best you've ever had," I said.

He smiled at that.

I'd forgotten about his stupid fucking dimples.

"Sorry I'm late," Harriet said.

We both started at that. I hadn't even seen Harriet approach. In fact, for a moment, I'd completely forgotten that she was the reason I was here in the first place.

I wanted to blame the dimples.

Cal rose to greet Harriet, giving her a hug. I did the same.

"Give him a chance," she said in my ear.

I sat, and the smile I offered was all teeth. Sharklike.

"Kathleen was just telling me how great the grilled octopus is," Cal said.

"Life changing," I said.

That earned me a sharp kick from Harriet under the table. It stung, but not as bad as learning that my best friend had been cavorting with my archenemy for months behind my back.

Okay. Cavorting wasn't quite the right word.

Plotting. Collaborating. Scheming.

We ordered—Cal got the octopus—and once the server had gone, Harriet's gaze bounced between the two of us as if she were waiting for a bell to go off and one of us to take the first swing.

It wasn't going to be me.

"I appreciate you taking the time to meet with me," Cal said. "Thank you."

I hated how polite and formal he sounded. I'd thought it would be awkward enough seeing him again after everything we'd been through, but it was somehow worse to sit here and pretend that none of it had happened. To playact that we were strangers. Professional strangers.

Well. If that's how he wanted to play it.

"Oh no," I said. "Thank *you*."

There was a pause and Cal cleared his throat.

"*Riveted!* is a very special show," he said.

Last week when Harriet had asked me to meet her for dinner, I had braced for the worst. She'd been distant for months, canceling plans at the last minute and making ridiculous excuses, like that she was busy because she was training for a marathon.

The only thing Harriet had ever run for was Shakespeare in the Park tickets.

We'd gone to our favorite place, Aardvark and Artichoke, and I'd focused on my drink while going through a mental list of all the worst-case scenarios for why she'd been avoiding me. She was sick. She was moving. She was back together with my least favorite of her ex-girlfriends.

It was worse than all those things.

And better too.

"I'd been searching for the right show when Harriet approached me," Cal said.

"It's so crazy," Harriet had told me last week. "He called. Completely out of the blue."

I raised an eyebrow and looked at Harriet.

She stared at her water glass.

"How fortuitous," I said, but knew there was a reason she'd lied.

I couldn't even blame her for the subterfuge.

Riveted! wasn't the first musical Harriet had written. It wasn't even the fifth. Or the tenth.

When we met at fourteen, she'd written at least two dozen songs—and a handful had been quite good. By the time I was touring worldwide as Katee Rose, Harriet had albums of excellent material. She had been on the verge of success, of becoming the kind of songwriter that was in high demand. The person that everyone wanted to work with.

Instead, she was practically anonymous, stuck writing the occasional tune for made-for-TV movies or C-list one-hit wonders. Once in a while, it would seem like she'd be getting another chance, another break, but it always fell apart before anything could happen. She deserved better.

And all I could do was watch and feel guilty all over again.

"*Riveted!* is fresh, yet familiar," Cal was saying. "It walks that line between nostalgia and innovation."

"It's brilliant," I said.

"It's brilliant," Cal echoed.

At least we could agree on that.

"I want to do a workshop here in New York," Cal said. "Then out-of-town tryouts. Maybe the Globe or the Orpheum, or even somewhere closer to home. And then, if all goes well—and I plan on it going well—we'll be taking it to Broadway."

He said all of this with such confidence that it was hard not to feel hopeful.

But hope was a dangerous, capricious thing. Especially connected to Cal Kirby.

"And you'll be directing it," I said.

"Yes," Cal said.

This wasn't just Harriet's show. Yes, *she'd* written the all-female musical based on the iconic Rosie the Riveter, but one of the three leading roles, Peggy, had been created for *me*. It was tailor-made to emphasize my known talent—dancing—and also my lesser-known ones, like the fact that I actually had a pretty decent voice under all the auto-tuning management had done to my albums way back when. And even though I hadn't recorded anything in a decade, I knew that auto-tuning happened even more frequently these days. The last record before my forced retirement had been especially egregious—I had barely recognized myself when I'd heard it.

This time if I went back onstage it would be on my terms. With my voice. My name.

I'd tried for years to love something else the way I loved performing.

Money wasn't the problem—I'd been smart *and* lucky—I had enough to live on, especially since my life wasn't especially extravagant anymore. And there were always residuals from my songs, which still got licensed. In lean times, I taught dance, but mostly I did that to fill the days.

That was the thing I'd had to get used to after my career ended. All the time I had. And all the time I had to myself.

Boredom had been a novelty at first—once the depression lifted—but a novelty that quickly faded.

I took up all kinds of hobbies, trying to find something else that would provide the feeling of being in the spotlight. Listened for sounds I loved more than applause. Sought the good kind of nervousness that happened right before a curtain went up. Hungered for the pleasure that came from hitting that perfect note and holding it . . . holding it . . . holding it . . . and letting it go.

But I couldn't escape who I was.

"When would the workshop begin?" I asked.

"There are a few other things we need to discuss before we get into schedules," Cal said.

I was gratified that Harriet also seemed surprised by this information. As far as I'd known, this meeting was mostly to make sure that Cal and I could be in the same room without ripping each other to shreds.

Signs were pointing to *no*.

"What other things?" she asked.

"Casting," Cal said.

The implication was crystal clear.

I pushed back from the table.

"Look," he said, "it's complicated."

"No," Harriet said, "it's not. Cast whoever else you want for other roles, but Kathleen *is* Peggy. The part was written *for* her. *With* her." She turned to me. "I told him that. From the beginning. From day one."

I knew she was telling the truth. I was a part of the show. A package deal. One that *some* people might see as a benefit to sales and marketing.

"This is why I wanted to meet with both of you," Cal said.

"Of course," I said. "Much better to see the damage when you do something like this in person."

He ignored me, which was good because I was ninety percent sure I could kill him with my gaze if I tried hard enough.

"I'm beholden to the producers," he said. "And they have opinions."

"I've heard those are like assholes," I said.

Cal met my gaze, and I was surprised to see anger simmering there. What the fuck did *he* have to be angry about? He was the one with the power. He was the one in control. He was the one holding our hopes and dreams in his hand.

If anyone should be furious, it was me.

And I was.

"Will you let me explain?" he asked, jaw tense.

I gestured for him to continue, though most of me had gone numb.

"The producers are nervous," he said. "About Katee. Her . . . reputation."

I. Was. Going. To. Kill. Him.

"*My* reputation?" My throat was tight, and the words came out with a squawk. It wasn't the most flattering sound, but I didn't really care.

Because *Cal* was the reason for my so-called reputation. Because it had happened over a decade ago. Because I was a different person now. Because Katee Rose didn't fucking exist.

The whole thing was just an excuse to get me out of the way.

"I won't do the show without her," Harriet said.

I hadn't expected anything less, but it didn't matter. I knew what Cal was doing. He was forcing her to choose.

It was cruel. That's what this was. A cruel punishment to get back at me for what happened. As if he were some innocent bystander caught in my destructive, slutty path. As if *he* were the wronged one.

I should have expected it. Should have anticipated it.

And I couldn't even say that I didn't deserve it.

I just didn't think he'd be low enough to drag Harriet into it.

But that was my fault too. Because old Cal? Sweet, thoughtful Cal from back then would have never done anything like this.

I was the reason he wasn't that kind of person anymore.

"We have options," Cal said.

I looked over at Harriet, saw our shared dreams of Broadway and opening night and the Tony Awards dissipating like smoke.

I'd killed her dreams once before. I wasn't going to let that happen again.

"Do it without me," I said.

"What?" she said. "No."

"You'll find someone else," I said. "Someone better."

Fat chance. That role had been written for me. It was perfect for me. I'd be amazing.

But this was Harriet's opportunity.

Maybe it was better this way. When Harriet had told me that Cal wanted to direct the show, the thought of being in the same room as him, let alone working with him for months on a show I cared deeply about, letting *him* direct *me*, made me nauseous.

I'd imagined that he was probably relishing the chance to put me through the wringer. To punish me. Again. And again. And again.

Apparently he preferred a clean kill.

Harriet sat there, looking at me, looking at Cal, and then looking at her hands. She took a deep breath. Let it out. She stood.

"I'm sorry," she said to Cal. "I won't do the show without Kathleen."

I grabbed her arm, pulled her back into her seat.

"Stop," I said. "Don't be ridiculous."

For the first time since arriving in the restaurant, I turned and faced Cal head-on. No overly dramatic cheek kisses, no gritted teeth, no angry glares. I didn't smile and I spoke evenly. Slowly.

"Harriet is a genius," I said.

"I agree," he said.

"She deserves this," I said.

"Yes," he said.

"Good," I said. "Then it's settled."

"Kathleen—" Harriet said, but I held up a hand.

"Comp tickets whenever I want," I said. "That's the deal."

Her eyes were brimming with tears. I passed her a napkin, biting the inside of my cheek so I wouldn't cry as well. Because there was no way I was letting a single tear fall in front of Cal.

He wanted to hurt me? Fine. Mission accomplished. But he wasn't going to see me cry. Not again. Never again.

"Not so fast," Cal said.

Harriet and I both went still.

"Excuse me?" I asked.

"I said there were options." He leaned back in his chair, arms folded. Smug.

"Options," I repeated.

"No need to martyr yourself before you hear them," he said.

Harriet put her hand on my knee, which was a good thing because if she hadn't, I might have leapt across the table and throttled her director.

"What are the options?" Harriet asked.

Cal looked at me.

"You audition for the role," he said.

"Audition?" Harriet repeated.

"For you," I said.

"For the producers," Cal said.

"For you," I said.

"To make sure it's the right fit," Cal said.

"Excuse me," I said, getting up from the table. "I need to use the restroom."

It was thankfully empty, dark, and cool. Mirrorless. I swept away the first damp quiver of tears from my lashes and took a deep breath.

I knew this feeling far too well.

The tight vise around my heart, the way it felt like a hand was squeezing, squeezing, squeezing, the shortness of breath, the helplessness of it all, was an anxiety attack. Learning that these feelings had a name—had a diagnosis and solutions—had been a revelation after years of muscling through something I'd thought was normal.

There was medication. Therapy. Meditation.

But there were times when I couldn't control the way my body reacted. I hated it. Hated the reminder that there were certain things I couldn't overcome by sheer nerve and stubbornness and willpower.

I took a deep breath. And another. And another.

Audition.

I wasn't opposed to auditioning as a concept. I understood and respected the purpose of the exercise, and there had even been a time when I reveled in any opportunity to show off. To perform. When that giddy, nervous energy could sustain me for days.

The problem was that I'd be auditioning for Cal.

Auditions were an opportunity to show exactly what you were capable of. To showcase not just your talent but the innate nerve required to be an artist—an unshakable confidence in your own skills. You needed to believe that you were great—that you were exactly what they were looking for.

Some might call it arrogance.

Either way, there was a time when I'd had that—and more—in spades.

It wasn't completely gone, but I'd be lying if I didn't admit that the past decade or so had landed some brutal blows to my ego.

So now the thought of auditioning filled me not with excitement but with dread. And disappointment.

Because there were a handful of people on this planet that knew exactly what I was capable of. Harriet was one of them.

Once upon a time Cal had been too.

Obviously that had changed.

He was either fucking with me or didn't trust that I could do it.

Both options made me furious.

It would be so easy to walk back to the table, pick up my glass of water, and throw it right in his smug face. He probably wouldn't hold it against Harriet. He'd probably be expecting it. Might even be hoping for it.

Just proof of my so-called reputation. The perfect justification for why I couldn't be cast in the show in the first place. A self-fulfilling prophecy.

But I wasn't that girl anymore.

I didn't have the luxury of saying no. Of walking away.

And I didn't want to.

This was my chance. And I knew, from experience, that I might not get another. I was lucky to get this one.

I wanted this part. Needed this part.

And I loved myself more than I hated Cal.

So, I put some cold water on the back of my neck and walked out of the restroom, back to the table. I sat down across from Cal. I patted Harriet's hand when she put it questioningly on my knee.

"All right," I said. "Name the day."

THEN

CHAPTER 2

They were still screaming my name.

I felt like I was vibrating, the sound of the crowd like a rung bell throughout my entire body. I kept waiting to get used to it, but it hadn't happened yet.

"You were incredible, babe!" Ryan said as he swept me up in his arms, not caring that I was slick with sweat and coated with body glitter.

He spun me and the room blurred around us. When we stopped, he kissed me. He tasted like sour candy and chewing gum. Familiar and welcome. I couldn't believe he was here. That we were together again.

Everything. Was. Perfect.

Mostly.

Maybe.

The truth was, I'd been starting to think that it was time for us to break up.

But that was just because the long-distance thing had

been getting to me. That was over now. We were fine. We were great.

"It was good?" I asked.

"Good?" Ryan pulled back and let out a low whistle. "They love you!"

I'd killed it tonight and I knew it. My feet, my back, my knees, would all be hurting by tomorrow, but that wasn't anything a hot bath and a long massage couldn't cure.

Right now, I couldn't feel a thing. I was floating on air. My first big stadium show, and I'd packed the place. Two hours on the stage in front of thousands of screaming fans, who all knew the words to my songs and sang along. I still hated that management, aka Diana, had decided it would be better for me to lip-sync, but I understood that it kept me from huffing and puffing into my mic. Because those dance moves were not easy.

"I think I messed up a few steps during 'Kiss Me Now,'" I said.

Ryan shook his head. "If you did, no one even noticed."

But I had. Which meant I needed to practice that routine again before the next show. Before we took off.

"I can't believe the tour starts next week," I said.

Ryan put his arm around my shoulders, pulling me close and planting a kiss on my temple. I felt kind of icky, with the sweat beginning to dry on my skin, but he didn't seem to notice.

"I can't wait," he said. "This is what we've been dreaming about."

"A whole year together," I said. "All around the world."

When the tour had first been announced, I'd been disappointed. I'd already toured the United States, stopping only to record a few new singles and shoot a cameo in a movie that was coming out next year. The pace had been grueling, and the thought of continuing at this speed, not just new cities every few nights but new countries, had been overwhelming. Then they told me who'd be opening for me.

"You gotta come meet the guys," Ryan said.

"They're here?"

"They're here!"

His hand in mine, I was pulled away from the stage.

The last six months had been the hardest, with Ryan at boy band boot camp in Florida. Even on the rare occasions when we got to talk, we were both so exhausted that we'd fallen asleep on the phone multiple times.

"Did they see the show?" I asked.

Ryan nodded. "They're big fans," he said.

I ducked my head. It was still awkward and a little embarrassing to have "fans." Especially when they were my peers.

"Should I change first?" I asked, pulling my sweat-soaked costume away from my body.

It suctioned back to my skin with a juicy *thwack* when I let go. Ew.

But Ryan was already pulling me into the VIP area. We were immediately swarmed, but across the room, I saw four guys rise—almost in unison—from a couch. Clearly the boot camp had worked.

It took some maneuvering, but Ryan managed to get us through the crowd of people to the other side.

"Katee," he said, "this is CrushZone. My band."

"*Your* band?" one of the guys asked. He had a charming Australian accent and sounded amused, not annoyed.

Ryan laughed. "You know what I mean," he said. "This is Wyatt."

I shook his hand.

"This is LC and Mason." Ryan gestured to a blond guy with brilliant blue eyes and his visual contrast, a guy with dark almost blue-black hair, eyeliner, and thick strong eyebrows.

"I'm a big fan," LC said. There was a faint twang to his voice.

"We're all fans," Mason said.

He had a great smoky voice. I was betting he was one of the front men, along with Ryan.

"And this is Cal State," Ryan said.

Seeing him again was like getting air blown right in my face. And down the back of my neck.

"Cal," he said.

Still a baritone.

"Hi," he said.

I stared.

He'd dyed his hair.

"Oh my god," I said. "Cal Kirby?"

He grinned at me. "Hey, Kathleen," he said.

I stepped forward, about to hug him, but Ryan had already wrapped his arm around Cal's shoulders and was messing with his hair. Cal pushed him off, his eyes still focused on me.

"I wasn't sure you'd remember me," he said.

"How could I forget?" I asked.

God. Those dimples. That voice. If anything, both had gotten better with age.

"A girl always remembers her first . . ." I cleared my throat. "Her first duet partner."

I'd wondered, over the years, what had happened to him. If he still thought about that summer. That last night. That moment on the roof.

The smile we shared—knowing and sheepish and a little bit naughty—indicated that he had. I felt all tingly inside.

"You guys know each other?" Ryan asked.

Cal looked away. I looked at Ryan.

"We went to camp together," I said.

"When we were kids," Cal said. "The first thing she said to me was that I'd been flat during my audition."

"That's not true!" I said, outraged.

"No?" He gave me a look.

"It wasn't the *first* thing I told you," I said.

"Second thing, then," he said.

"Well, you were," I said.

He laughed. Ryan didn't. I cleared my throat.

"He knows Harriet too," I said.

"You're still friends with Harriet?" Cal asked.

I grinned. "She's writing songs for my next album," I said. "She'll be coming on tour for a little bit too."

"Cool," Cal said.

"Yeah," Ryan said. "It's cool that you guys all know each other."

I recognized the tone in his voice. Luckily, I knew how to defuse it.

"Hey," I said, wrapping my arms around his waist. "I missed you."

He was so cute, his nose scrunched up as he debated whether to be jealous or attentive. I gave him a squeeze.

"I missed you too," he said.

"How did you guys meet?" LC asked. "We've been asking Ryan, but he keeps telling us something different every time."

I gave Ryan a look, but he just grinned at me.

"What?" he said. "We *could* have met at the blackjack tables in Vegas. Or while swimming with sharks."

"The midair skydiving story was a little suspect," Mason said.

"Well, I guess in comparison to that, it's not quite as interesting," I said. "We met on *Show N Tell*."

The teen showcase had lasted only a few seasons, but it had completely changed my life. Not just meeting Ryan—which had happened while he was a main cast member and I was a lowly dancer—but it had connected me with Diana, who became my manager and helped create who I was today.

"I watched her audition," Ryan said. "And told the producers that they *had* to cast her."

I always pretended that I liked this story, but I didn't. I didn't like how Ryan made it sound like he was responsible for my career. Like *he* was the one who made all of this happen.

"My hero," I said.

Ryan looped his arms around me, and this time the kiss wasn't as chaste as the one he'd given me before. It felt like his tongue went *all* the way down my throat.

The guys coughed.

"Guess we should give you some privacy," Wyatt said.

"Yeah," Ryan said, and leaned in to kiss me again.

"Yeah," I said, leaning back.

"Nice meeting you," LC said.

"See you on tour," Mason said.

"I can't wait," I said.

"Me neither," said Cal.

NOW

The year after everything fell apart was still a bit of a blur. I'd slept a lot. Twelve hours. Fourteen. Eighteen.

Part of it was the fact that I'd been working nearly non-stop since I was a teenager. The other part was the heavy, bone-deep weariness that came from the reality that the entire world knew you were a big old slut who had cheated on your beloved boy band boyfriend.

My last concert had erupted in boos, and even though Diana said that she and the rest of my management were just taking a break, that they were just stepping back to give me time, it was clear to all of us that my career was over. That no one was going to buy albums by or tickets to see someone who had smashed Ryan LaNeve's heart into a billion tiny pieces.

He'd even shed a tear—a single tear—in one of his many, many interviews. He *couldn't stop talking* about our breakup. About how *betrayed* he felt. How *blindsided* he was by the whole thing. All the while sitting right next to Cal, who said nothing.

It wasn't until CrushZone broke up that the rumors connecting me with Cal began circulating. It never got added to my Wikipedia page, all official-like, but it became a "common knowledge" pop culture thing. I suspected that was Ryan's work as well, but it didn't seem to hurt Cal too much. Nope. Everyone was happy to blame me.

I didn't do press. I didn't do interviews. I stayed inside.

Even if I'd wanted to go anywhere, I knew the paparazzi would follow, all hoping to get a shot of me looking my worst. Which would have been easy since I'd rather have slept than showered in those days.

They would sometimes camp outside my apartment, but as time went on, and other celebrities drew their attention, I was able to take walks at night. Sometimes Harriet would join me—she was my lone connection to the outside world, though even she disappeared for a while when my next album was officially canceled. I couldn't blame her. I didn't want to be around me either.

Eventually the price on my head dropped and I didn't have to worry about getting photographed every time I left the house. I wasn't worth the effort or the time, and even though I was relieved, I knew what it meant as well. It was over. Everything. All of it.

I was a has-been before my twenty-fifth birthday.

I really should have known better. Even Sondheim killed off the Baker's Wife when she fucked Cinderella's Prince. Mr. "Charming, Not Sincere" got away scot-free, while the wanton slut got what she deserved, crushed under a giant's boot.

* * *

The week before the audition, I kept having stress dreams.

I knew that some people had nightmares about being on-stage. About forgetting lines or not even knowing that they were supposed to be performing. My anxiety didn't manifest in that way. Instead, I dreamed about being on tour. About leaving one place and finding, as I tried to pack my bags, that my belongings had multiplied, and I no longer had room for all of them. The longer the dream went on, the more drawers or doors or rooms I discovered that were full of things that I was terrified of leaving behind.

It made sense, my therapist said. The transient quality of that time in my life had always been disorienting. It was something I'd never felt I could complain about because even though it was dizzying and exhausting, I also knew that flying around the world to perform in front of thousands and thousands of people was the kind of life that others would kill for. That fourteen-year-old me had dreamed of.

The last thing I wanted to be was ungrateful.

But I'd never had those dreams when I was on tour. The weird thing about them was even though I woke up feeling stressed and exhausted, I also felt nostalgic.

Which wasn't a bad mood for today's audition, so I let myself lean in to it.

The role I was auditioning for—*my* character—was a woman with one foot in the past and one in the future. When Harriet had told me about *Riveted!*, she'd pitched it as *Newsies* meets *Nine to Five*. Peggy was the Dolly of the trio of leads. Blond, busty, oversexualized, and undervalued. She was Glinda and Elle Woods and Marilyn and Katee Rose. Men loved her, women envied her, and her hair was big and full of secrets.

I knew Peggy. I *was* Peggy.

I sat in one of the chairs lining the hallway, wondering why the holding pen for auditions was always somewhere with the most unflattering lighting. Fluorescents flickered above, making me feel both dizzy and overly alert. A perfect state of mind for the situation at hand.

Harriet had helped me practice all weekend. I knew the audition song backward and forward, but that wasn't good enough. I had to be so incredible that whoever was on the other side of that door would be unable to say no to me. I had to erase all existing perceptions of my talents, abilities, and reliability. I had to transcend my *reputation*.

And even if I did, even if I blew their fucking socks off, there was still a chance they'd say no. Still a chance that they were going to say no all along, and this was just some exercise in futility. Or cruelty.

I didn't want to believe that Cal was the kind of person that would set up an entire audition process just to hurt and embarrass me, but the truth was I didn't know him anymore. I had no idea what the past several years had done to him—how our shared past might have crystalized him into someone sinister and unkind.

My jaw kept tensing up on me, my foot wanting to do a jig beneath my chair. I inhaled through my nose and let the breath out slowly. I felt like I had to pee while also being extremely thirsty.

At the end of the hall, the door opened. I sat up straight, music on my lap, hands folded demurely on top. I hated that I could feel them trembling.

I expected Cal or his assistant, but it was neither.

"Well, isn't this a surprise," Rachel James said.

Her hair was still shiny. Her teeth still perfect.

Her smile—a real "cat caught the canary" one—indicated that this was not, in fact, a surprise. At least to her.

What was she doing here?

Rachel was on that list of people—like Cal—who I checked in on once in a while. Just to see if karma was real. So far, all signs pointed to *no*.

Not that Rachel was the big, famous Broadway star she'd—*we'd*—always wanted to be, but she *had* been on Broadway. She was a professional actor, sometimes a featured performer, most often in the chorus, but she'd headlined a couple of national tours.

"Rachel." I stood, and towered over her.

How did she know about the show? It hadn't even been announced yet.

I knew there was no way in hell that Harriet would allow her—*our*—summer camp nemesis to be a part of this musical.

Would Cal?

"I just stopped by to say hello," she said.

I looked at the sheets of music tucked under her arm.

"In what key?" I asked.

She laughed. It was fake.

"It's a good show," she said. "And a very good part."

I knew she was fucking with me, but why did she have music? Why was she here? Now. Today.

It was enough to make the vicious, slimy worm of doubt begin to burrow into my confidence. Which, honestly, had been on shaky ground for the past decade or so.

"And it's always nice to see Cal when he's in town," Rachel said.

I crossed my arms. "You've been in touch?"

"Well, we were *such* good friends at camp." She gave me a look. "Not as close as you and he became later, or so I've heard."

Subtle.

"Great seeing you," I said.

"Likewise," she said. "And hey, I'm sure we'll run into each other again."

"Don't count on it."

She smiled. Toothy.

"It's a small world," she said. "You never know what opportunities are around each corner. What doors will open"—she gave me a long once-over—"and which ones will close."

Speaking of doors, the one at the end of the hall opened again. It wasn't Cal, but thankfully wasn't some other unfriendly ghost from my past.

"Ms. Rosenberg?" the young woman asked. "They're ready for you."

"Good luck," Rachel said.

That bitch.

There was a crunching sound and I realized I'd been crumpling my music into my fist.

I quickly smoothed it out and followed the assistant, resisting the urge to cast one last look over at Rachel. She might have gotten to me in the moment, but the second I walked into the audition room, I planned to forget her. I planned to forget everything except what I'd come here to do.

Impress.

Astonish.

Enthrall.

There was a table on one side of the room. There was an older woman in a suit, a guy in jeans and a T-shirt, and two much, much older men. Both had gray tufted hair and sour expressions—a real-life Statler and Waldorf.

I assumed they were the money. The ones who were worried about my reputation. The ones I had to impress.

At the end of the table was Cal.

He was looking at his phone.

I offered my biggest, brightest smile anyway.

"Kathleen Rosenberg," the assistant said.

"Thank you for having me," I said.

Cal put his phone down. There was no reaction from the two old Muppets, but the woman in the suit smiled, as did the guy in jeans. He also took a long, unsubtle look at my body.

I didn't need to wonder what he thought, the way his smile faded into a frown as if he'd been hoping for my twentysomething pop star self to show up.

Instead, he had me—nowhere near my twenties, gray in my hair, and a body that was way wider and squishier than it had been back then. I tried not to care. I tried to tell myself that once I started singing it wouldn't matter. I tried to tell myself that I was fine exactly the way I was.

Harriet and I had agreed that there was only one option for me to sing—the eleven o'clock number, "I've Never Been Seen"—the one she'd agonized over for months before coming to me with what I strongly believed was the best song she'd ever written. And I sounded fantastic singing it.

The accompanist started playing and I knew from the first note that came out of my mouth that I was going to nail it. And I did. A song about dismantling your own image, about getting lost behind blond hair and fake smiles, about wanting to be seen—truly seen—was a song I connected to on a visceral level. And I put all of that into my performance.

When I was finished, my audience sat there, stone-faced, arms crossed.

Good thing I hadn't been expecting applause. I knew better than that. Auditioning was like playing poker—you gave nothing away.

They had me read a few pages from the script and I killed those as well. Because I knew this part. Knew I was perfect for it—not just because it had been written specifically for me by my best friend, but also because I was a *good* performer.

I'd just never been given the chance to show it before.

"Well," one of the older gentlemen said, "I think we've seen enough."

And just like that, I knew I wasn't getting the part.

After all, this asshole wouldn't even look me in the eye. I doubted he'd given me a second of his attention, even when I'd been singing my heart out for him.

Cal was once again looking at his phone.

"Thank you for your time," I said.

I wanted to curl up in a ball on the floor.

"Hold on," Cal said. "Could you do one more song for us?"

I had already bent to get my bag, but I straightened warily.

"Of course," I said, feeling like I was going to regret it.

Cal walked over to the piano, flipped through some sheet music, and brought it over.

"Here. Give this a try."

I stared at the song he'd handed me.

Are you fucking kidding me? I wanted to ask.

His request combined with Rachel's unexpected presence made me all the more unsure about what was going on and what his intentions were. Was this all some sort of sick game? If so, it was very involved. It had *layers* of meaning. A veritable onion of vengeance.

"Not a problem," I said.

"Do you need a moment to go over it?" he asked.

Was he actually trying to help or was this just another way to embarrass me? Because this wasn't how auditions worked. The actor brought in their music, their song choice. I wasn't performing at a wedding or a bat mitzvah—I didn't take requests.

And this song . . .

"No," I said, regretting it immediately. "I know it."

I did, because anyone who knew anything about musicals did, but I couldn't remember the last time I'd sung it. Well. That wasn't entirely true. I knew exactly when I'd sung it last. No doubt Cal did as well.

Still. It had been years. Years upon years. The smart thing to do would be to go outside, run through it at least once— maybe twice—and then come back.

But I wasn't feeling very smart. I was feeling like I'd been backed into a corner and now everyone was watching, wait- ing for me to do something that justified their decision not to cast me. And I tended to do very dumb things when I felt that way.

"Are you sure?" Cal asked.

I couldn't tell if he was antagonizing me or giving me an actual out.

"Absolutely," I said, not taking it.

I didn't trust what he was doing—didn't trust him—but I wasn't going to let him see me hesitate. I wasn't going to let him see me doubt myself.

Unfortunately, I did have to ruin poor T-shirt guy's image

of me even further by taking my reading glasses out of my bag. I knew the song, but I didn't trust myself to remember the lyrics. I'd have to follow along with the pianist. It wasn't ideal, but then again, none of this was.

I could already hear Harriet's outrage.

"They made you sing *what*?"

At least I could count on her popping open a bottle of wine for me when I told her.

"Ready when you are," I told the accompanist.

I started off too quietly.

Anyone who knew anything about theatre would advise *against* doing "Memory" for an audition. It was too well-known, almost to the point of cliché. And it was *hard* to sing. Not just on a technical level; it didn't work if you couldn't pull up the emotion to bring it home. And that wasn't easy to do without any preparation. I didn't understand why Cal was having me do it.

It was a song that built, but I knew almost immediately that I'd put myself at a disadvantage. Beginning where I did, in a rasp of a whisper, meant that I was going to have to climb that crescendo in bigger leaps and bounds than I usually did.

When I was fourteen, I'd brought the house down with this song. I'd had nothing—and everything—to give. My voice was my ticket, my chance.

But I hadn't understood the song. Not really.

I'd pretended back then—and I'd done a good job of it—but *this*? This was real. This was true. I felt the song. Felt it in my bones. The despair, the regret, and beneath all of that, the hope that remained, despite everything.

Closing my eyes, I let the room fall away, let the audience, Cal, the whole reason I was here, disappear.

I sounded good. Not perfect, but good. Honest.

I reached my favorite lyric—"Touch me, it's so easy to leave me"—and really put my teeth into it. Unfortunately, as my voice found that final, reaching note, it cracked.

Cracked.

And that was the final nail in the coffin of this audition.

There was almost no point in continuing, but I did. Because I could.

And I did it with a fucking flourish.

As the song reached its crescendo, I released my grip on the piano. Stepped forward. Flung my arms open and let my voice carry me to the end. As the song ended, the final notes plinking away in complete silence, I opened my eyes.

I scanned my audience.

Nothing.

"Thank you for your time," Cal said. "We'll be in touch."

And just like that, I was dismissed.

CHAPTER 4

I didn't relax until I got home.

Armed with ice cream, an edible, and my favorite Chinese takeout, I dumped my mail onto the table in the hallway and prepared for an evening of self-pity and wallowing.

It was amazing how drained I felt. All I'd done was go to Midtown, sing two songs, and come home. Of course, it wasn't as simple as that—I'd been thinking, worrying, preparing for the audition for weeks, focusing all my energy into making sure I blew the producers away. I'd kept my nerves at bay largely by working, by rehearsing, and now that I was done, everything seemed to slam into me at once.

I put the ice cream in the freezer, popped the edible, and grabbed an egg roll. I was too tired to even plate the rest of my food, instead back-flopping onto the couch in a move that would have gotten me very low scores from the Russian judge.

At least it was over.

I chewed my egg roll and stared at the ceiling.

The apartment was the only remaining proof that there had been a time when I'd been wealthy and successful and famous. It had been one of the first things I bought, after paying off my parents' mortgage and pouring money into my sister's college fund. At the peak of my career, I'd owned several places, but this was the only one that had ever felt like home.

It was the only thing I owned outright.

There was a slight jingle and then Fish leapt onto the couch arm before descending to sit on my stomach and stare at me. Well. The second thing I owned outright.

"You don't eat egg rolls," I told her, which was, of course, a lie.

If I didn't go and put the rest of the Chinese food away, there was a strong possibility that she'd nudge a carton off the counter with her nose, causing it to fall and therefore spill its contents all over the floor in a feast fit for the smartest, cleverest, most annoying cat in all five boroughs.

As a distraction, I ate the rest of the egg roll and gave Fish a scratch under her chin, which was her favorite place to get scratched. Soon enough, she was purring and pressing her face against my palm, focused more on affection than food. For now.

"Maybe I'll start teaching dance again," I said.

I'd turned the basement unit of the brownstone into a dance studio and would offer private lessons or kids' classes whenever I felt like the days were way too long and empty.

I always advertised as "Kathleen Rosenberg" but for the most part, students—or their parents, depending on the age—would figure out who I was pretty quickly. I didn't mind, as long as they weren't dicks about it. And if they weren't, but they were clearly fans, I usually spent the last class teaching them some of my more famous dance moves from music videos or performances.

If they were dicks about it, I took them off the mailing list and wouldn't let them reenroll. I hated discovering who were dicks about it.

I'd put a lot of my emotional well-being eggs into the basket of Harriet's success as a composer and lyricist. And now I couldn't even get a part that had been specifically written for me.

I really wished the edible would kick in soon because I could use some manufactured levity.

Fish meowed, but I could tell she didn't really care about my woes. As long as I fed her, she didn't care how I spent my time.

"Don't worry," I said. "I won't let you go hungry."

She rubbed her chin against mine.

At least I had the apartment. When I first bought it, I'd filled it with the kind of expensive, uncomfortable, beautiful things that a star like me was expected to have. Things that looked good on *MTV Cribs*—which I'd been featured on.

But after everything went to hell, I sold most of those things off—annoyingly, for a fraction of the price—and replaced them with stuff that I actually liked. Almost none of it had been new, and definitely not at the same price point as my previous furniture, but it was comfortable and cozy and mine.

It all showed a little wear and tear these days, but I kind of liked it that way. There was a chair in the corner with a pillow over the seat because there was a huge rip in the cushion. I'd moved an end table over one of my larger rugs when I'd spilled wine on it. And the bedspread in my bedroom was in desperate need of a revamp, but I kept putting it off. Sure, it was starting to fray at the edges—thanks to Fish and her claws—but it was soft and familiar and warm.

It was a metaphor for my life.

I let out a sigh deep enough that Fish dug her claws into my chest as it heaved her upward.

Underneath me, I felt my phone buzz with an incoming call.

I'd texted Harriet when I got out of the subway, a simple thumbs-down emoji, so I knew she'd want to know exactly what I meant by that.

"I didn't get it," I said as I picked up the phone. "Cal made me jump through these stupid fucking hoops and I'm pretty sure it was just to see me sweat. They were never going to give me the part."

There was a silence.

"Well," Cal said, "if that's how you feel."

Fuck. Me.

I jackknifed up, displacing Fish, who leapt off me with a yowl loud enough to be heard down the street.

"What was that?" Cal asked.

"My cat," I said.

Unfortunately, the movement also seemed to jolt the edible into action, so I was both panicked and high at the same time, the room dipping dizzily around me.

"You have a cat?"

"I didn't mean it," I said.

"You don't have a cat?"

"I do have a cat," I said. "I didn't mean . . . the other stuff."

"About me making you sweat?"

The tone of his voice was annoyingly suggestive. I couldn't tell if that was purposeful or if the edible was making me horny as well.

It *had* been a long time since I'd gotten sweaty. In a suggestive way.

Not the time to be thinking about that.

"I didn't sweat," I said.

What was wrong with me? I needed to be apologizing—profusely—not arguing. But apparently I couldn't help it.

"You did a little," Cal said.

Asshole.

"And you could probably stand to take a few voice lessons," he said.

I gritted my teeth.

"Make sure that you're singing in the right key."

As if he hadn't just sprung that song on me at the last minute.

"I have a few names I can give you," he said. "People who can help you with control."

He meant my voice, but also.

"Cal," I said.

"Yes?"

What the fuck do you want?

"Can I help you?"

He let out a soft chuckle. It was the first time I'd heard him laugh since . . . since forever.

It shouldn't have given me a warm, cozy feeling—he had *just* been insulting me—and yet . . .

"I hope so," he said. "I'm calling to offer you the part."

I pulled the phone away from my ear to stare at the screen. I wasn't sure what I was looking for, but I also couldn't trust my own hearing.

"Hello?"

"Hi," I said.

"Are you drunk?"

That condescending prick.

I mean, I *was* high, but that was beside the point.

"No," I said. "Just . . . did you say you wanted to offer me the part?"

"Yes," Cal said. "If you want it."

If. I. Wanted. It.

"I want it," I said.

I wasn't even going to pretend to play hard to get. Even if he deserved to squirm a little.

"Great," he said. "We start rehearsing for the workshop next month. Mae will send you the details."

"Mae?"

"My assistant," he said. "You met her at the audition."

"Right," I said.

I was definitely high. I closed my eyes, wishing I'd waited a little longer before taking that edible. God, it had kicked in quickly.

"Okay," Cal said. "I'm going to hang up so you can call Harriet."

"Okay," I said.

"Okay," he said.

But he didn't. And I didn't.

"Cal?" I asked.

"Yes?"

"Why?"

"Why what?"

"Why did I get the part?" I asked.

Stupid, stupid me. I sounded so pathetic, so desperate for praise. I blamed my loose, vulnerable tongue on the weed, but I knew it wasn't just that. I needed to hear it.

"Because it was written for you," Cal said.

"But you made me audition," I said.

"Of course I did," he said. "I hadn't seen you perform in years. I had to make sure. But you're the only one who's auditioned for this role. I meant what I said about convincing the producers."

"You made me do *that* song," I said. "Why?"

"Because," he said.

What the fuck does that mean?

"Just take the win, Kathleen," he said.

I didn't like how smug he sounded, but I was probably going to have to get used to that.

"Fine," I said. "Thank you."

I hadn't said that yet. But I meant it.

"You're welcome," he said.

There was a long silence.

"Can you believe we're doing this?" he asked.

It disarmed me. Not just the question but the way he asked it. Like we were kids again. All whispered and hushed and holy. Like making a wish.

One that had come true.

"It doesn't feel real," I admitted.

It was that rare sensation of hope and excitement and joy. A second chance. It was hard to believe it.

"It's very real," he said.

I pinched myself.

"Ouch," I said.

"Did you just check?" Cal asked. "If it was real?"

"No," I said.

He laughed, and that sound, all low and warm and familiar in my ear, made me feel a certain way. And made me think about Cal in a certain way too.

Not just the warring emotions of anger and lust that he inspired, but a wistfulness. Because in this moment, the two of us, just voices at opposite ends of the city (or so I assumed), it was easy to fall back into memories of how things had been.

"It's going to be amazing," Cal said.

I wanted to believe him. Wanted his words to be prophetic, not just encouraging. But I'd learned long ago that no one could make—and keep—promises like that.

"I hope so," I said.

Fear and anxiety flattened my tone.

"Trust me," Cal said.

But that was the problem. I didn't. I couldn't. Not after everything that had happened.

It was as if I'd said it out loud.

"I'm hanging up now," he said, his voice dull. "Go call Harriet."

"Okay," I said.

And that time he did. And so did I.

THEN

CHAPTER 5

Harriet joined us in London.

She arrived with a massive list of things she wanted to do and see, but I only had one afternoon off before we moved on to Bristol, so we settled on spending the day at the Victoria and Albert Museum.

I invited the guys, but only Cal and Ryan were interested. Though, when we arrived, it became clear that Ryan wasn't so much interested in the museum as he was in spending time with me. Which was sweet. Mostly.

"Do you think anyone will recognize us?" he asked.

I'd already been recognized—and pap'ed—arriving at the hotel, so I had no doubt that we'd get some stares. This was my first European visit, but I was popular here, and the tour was nearly sold out. I just didn't know if Ryan and Cal—or any of the CrushZone guys—were at that point yet.

But they would be soon enough.

"Maybe," I said.

I was kind of enjoying being incognito for the moment. Just enjoying my friends and the museum and a new country. It was one of the best perks of the job—getting to see the world with the people I loved.

Cal and Harriet walked ahead of us, Harriet's hands flying, Cal's laughter floating back to tickle my ears as they explored.

"I'm obsessed with these jackets," Harriet said.

"The hats are pretty cool," Cal said.

"Maybe I should start wearing hats," Ryan said. "That could be my thing."

The guys had been told to each work on developing an individual style, or persona. Mason had already claimed the bad boy slot, with his penchant for leather bracelets and black eyeliner. LC was the good southern boy, and Wyatt was letting management shape him into the wacky one, wearing loud, bright clothes and experimenting monthly with hair color and style.

"You look good in hats," I said.

"Maybe they'll put Cal State in glasses or a pocket protector or something," Ryan said.

Cal had been dubbed "the smart one," which I knew irked Ryan. But it made sense. Not only *was* Cal smart, but he was also the only one of the group who had gone to college.

Even though he was several feet in front of us, I could still see Cal's shoulders tense at Ryan's nickname. I knew he hated it, but I also knew that telling Ryan that would only result in him using it more frequently.

Ryan could be kind of a butt sometimes.

"The Lumber Jills were the British equivalent of Rosie

the Riveter," Harriet was telling Cal. "They were part of the Women's Land Army during World War Two."

We were wandering through the exhibit that Harriet had been the most excited to see—Working Women's Fashion in the Twentieth Century. Dozens of mannequins were dressed and posed alongside vintage photographs and miscellaneous items. Being friends with Harriet was like getting a degree in history. Or so I imagined. Probably better because Harriet knew all the interesting, random, salacious facts that they never seemed to teach in school.

The mannequin Harriet and Cal had stopped in front of was wearing overalls and a collared shirt and had her hair pulled back in a kerchief. Resting on her shoulder was an axe. Even though she didn't really have a face—just a smooth egg-like globe—the pose and the sharp object made her look extremely badass.

"That would be a great Halloween costume," I said.

"Or onstage costume," Harriet said. "You'd look great with an axe."

I laughed. "Can you imagine?"

Harriet blinked and I could see that yes, yes she could. Very clearly.

"A row of dancers with axes," she said. "Like *Seven Brides for Seven Brothers,* but women instead."

"That is a complicated dance number," Cal said.

"What's *Seven Brides for Seven Brothers*?" Ryan asked.

"A musical," the three of us said.

Ryan sighed. "Right."

Despite his claiming to love all kinds of music, I'd been unable to find the musical that Ryan would tolerate, let alone enjoy. He just kept telling me how dramatic and unrealistic they were. I tried to explain that realism wasn't the point, that it was about feeling things fully, and how sometimes they were so big and overwhelming that you had to sing about it.

He didn't get it.

But it was okay. Most guys didn't. Most straight guys.

"Are there any World War Two musicals?" Cal asked.

Harriet and I stared at him.

"Uh, *Cabaret*," I said.

"*Carmen Jones*," she said.

"*Sound of Music*," I said.

"*Pacific Overtures*," she said.

Cal raised his hands in defeat. "Sorry, sorry," he said.

"You should be," I teased.

"Guess you need to brush up on your history, Cal State," Ryan said.

I saw a muscle in Cal's jaw clench.

"Someone should make a timeline," Cal said. "Not when the musical was written but when it takes place."

Harriet's eyes lit up. "Like a musical history lesson."

"Or a musical marathon," Cal said, "through time."

Ryan groaned. We all ignored him.

"Ooh." The wheels in my head immediately began turning. "What would be the first one? *A Funny Thing Happened*?"

"What about musicals that don't take place at any particular time?" Harriet asked. "Or something like *Assassins*, that covers a bunch of different time periods?"

"*Assassins* would definitely go with other musicals taking place in the sixties," I said.

"Why not the Civil War?" Cal asked.

"*Because,*" I said. "If you put it that early, the rest of the story lines would be spoilers."

"You can't have spoilers for history," Cal said.

"Yes, you can," Harriet said. "You have no idea how little people know."

"See?" I gestured toward Harriet, feeling triumphant. "I'm right."

Cal rolled his eyes. "We literally just invented this system."

"I'm still right," I said.

"You guys are such nerds," Ryan said.

He seemed pretty annoyed. I guess I couldn't blame him. We were discussing one of the few topics he had absolutely no interest in—and that Harriet, Cal, and I had both interest in *and* experience with. It couldn't be fun to be left out like that.

"Sorry, babe," I said, putting my arm through his and resting my cheek on his shoulder.

"I'm tired," he said. "Can we go back to the hotel?"

I could tell that Harriet wasn't ready to go. That she wanted to see more. With me. I was torn. I was tired too, and we were at the very beginning of what was going to be a long, exhausting tour.

But we were going to be traveling together for the next year, and Harriet was only going to be with us for a month or so. And who knew when we'd be able to be in London together again? She was going back to New York and starting a real job and wouldn't be able to just come on tour with me.

"I want to see what else is here," Cal said. "If you guys want to go back to the hotel."

I couldn't tell if Harriet was disappointed, or if she was

glad to spend time with Cal one-on-one. I couldn't tell if I was jealous.

I was pretty sure I wasn't. Because Harriet was my best friend and Cal was . . .

Well. I had Ryan, so it didn't even matter what Cal was. He was Ryan's bandmate.

"You guys can go," Harriet said. "I'll bore Cal with all my nerdy historical tidbits."

"Are you sure?" I asked.

Did I want her to say no?

"I'm sure," she said.

"Come on, babe," Ryan said, his arm around my neck, his nose nuzzling my cheek. "I feel like I haven't seen you at all."

It *had* been a while.

"Okay," I said. "If it's really all right with Harriet and Cal."

"It is," she said.

"Yep," Cal said.

"Omigod!" A voice behind us echoed through the quiet museum. "It's Katee Rose!"

Suddenly we were surrounded.

"Is it her?"

"It is! Katee! Will you sign my brochure?"

"Will you sign my arm?"

"Will you take a picture with me?"

I put on my best Katee Rose smile, a little surprised that it had taken this long to get recognized. I'd tried for inconspicuous, hair back, a baseball cap pulled low, and my least showy pair of jeans. There were barely any rhinestones on them.

At least it wasn't a large group and since we were in a

museum, they were polite and all but formed a line on their own to get autographs and pictures.

I looked up halfway through the makeshift meet and greet to find Harriet taking pictures of her own—like *she* was my mother or publicist—and Cal standing with his arms crossed, bemused but with a slightly nervous look on his face. No doubt he was imagining his future.

I could tell that Ryan was doing the same, only he looked happy and eager.

"Want a picture with us?" he asked a large group of young girls.

One of them looked at him, confused.

"Um," she said.

"We're CrushZone," Ryan said.

He got a wall of blank looks in exchange.

"We're big in America," Cal said. Dryly.

They *would* be, but I saw Ryan's face fall.

"This is Ryan LaNeve," I said. "He's a member of Crush-Zone *and* my boyfriend."

Immediately everyone's eyes lit up, and Ryan was soon surrounded. He beamed at the attention.

"Sign this!"

"Can we get a picture?"

"Are you and Katee going to get married?"

My eyebrows rose, and I caught Ryan's eye over the crowd.

"Maybe," he said.

"Oh really?" I said.

We hadn't discussed it.

"Oooooooooo," the crowd said.

Ryan grinned and I saw a few girls swoon. Yeah. This anonymity wouldn't last long.

"Don't forget Calvin Tyler Kirby," I said, gesturing toward Cal. "He's in the band too."

He shot me a look, but cleared it away with a smile as he was approached with cameras and Sharpies.

"What about you?" someone asked Harriet. "Are you also in the band?"

"Uh, no," she said.

"She's my best friend," I said.

That was good enough for my fans. They wanted autographs from *everyone*.

"We have tickets to see you tomorrow," one of the girls said.

"We're opening for her," Ryan said.

"They're great," I said.

"Are you going to do 'Miss Me, Kiss Me'?" someone asked.

That had been on my first album, which hadn't done as well as the following one. It had been more moody and lyrical, not upbeat and pop-y, which is what I was now known for. More dancing, less crooning.

"Maybe," I said.

I wasn't.

"It's my favorite song," she said.

"Mine too," Cal said.

I rolled my eyes at him, unable to tell if he was teasing. This fan was an aberration. No one liked the early stuff. But it was still nice to hear.

"Which one is that?" Ryan asked.

"Let's go back to the hotel," I said quietly.

"Can we get one of you together?" someone asked.

"Of course," Ryan said.

Interacting with my fans—especially when they were as

sweet and complimentary as this group—was one of the things I loved the most about what I did. It usually invigorated me. But today I was feeling the weight of jet lag and struggling not to yawn after each picture. I knew I had to be careful. It was too easy for an unsmiling picture of me with a fan to spread across gossip sites. I'd be called "ungrateful" or "unapproachable," and Diana was very clear about needing people to think I was just your average teen girl who had gotten very lucky.

Which was true, but also, a lot of work sometimes.

But Ryan seemed to thrive under the attention. I was happy for him—and he was good with fans, generous and friendly. Eager to pose for photos and autograph whatever was shoved into his hands. He made it look easy and effortless.

A glance at Cal, who had moved away with Harriet, indicated that he was less excited about being in the spotlight.

Well. He was going to have to learn how to deal with it, just as I had. Because I knew, in my bones, that he and the guys were about to become very, *very* famous.

NOW

CHAPTER 6

First days were always that riotous combination of excitement and fear. First day of school. First day of camp. First day on set. I'd had many first days, but this one felt more momentous than any of them. And far more terrifying.

"I can't wait for you to meet everyone," Harriet was saying.

"Hmm?" I'd been lost in thought, staring down the approaching building like we were playing a game of chicken.

One that I'd lose because, well, it was an immovable object.

"We didn't fight about a single cast member," she said. "I think that's a good sign. We agreed on everyone."

It had been determined that it wasn't necessary for Harriet to sit in on my audition, but Cal had her deeply involved in every other part of the process.

Still, I was only half listening.

"Uh-huh," I said. "Great."

We were waiting for the traffic to slow, one more street before we got there. The cars cleared and Harriet crossed, but I stood there, frozen on the sidewalk, eyes fixed on the glass and chrome monolith where we were due in thirty minutes.

Harriet darted back to me.

"Kathleen?"

I blinked at her, startled back into reality.

"Oh wow," she said. "Come on."

I let her tug me into a coffee shop.

"Matcha tea," she told the barista.

"Something caffeine-free," I corrected. "I'll be bouncing off the walls."

The last thing I needed was a burst of energy right now.

We sat down at a table toward the back.

"Are you okay?" Harriet asked.

"I don't know," I said.

I'd spent my entire life hoping for an opportunity like this. A road map to Broadway, full speed ahead. Now that it was here, now that we were about to start the workshop, I was suddenly wishing things would slow the fuck down.

It was all happening so fast. Hadn't it been yesterday that we met with Cal in the first place?

"You're going to be great," Harriet said, her hand on my arm, giving it a reassuring squeeze.

I wished I could believe her, but I couldn't. I was terrified. Near paralyzed with fear.

Anxiety—that bastard—had my heart rattling like a paint mixer. I felt like I wanted to peel my own skin off and run around Manhattan naked in my bones. Definitely not a moment for caffeine.

Every part of me said that I couldn't do this. That I was going to fail.

I'd been so confident when I was younger. Never thought for a minute that I wasn't going to do exactly what I wanted to do. Maybe I should have been a little more fearful back then. More careful.

"This is a mistake," I said.

"No," Harriet said, her voice firm. "This is not a mistake."

I looked up at her and I could *feel* the desperation visible in my eyes. It seemed to radiate out of me.

"Stop it," Harriet said. "You're psyching yourself out."

"Don't tell me what to do," I said.

She grinned at me. "That's the Kathleen I know and love."

I glared at her, but she had managed to chase away the fear, if only for a moment.

"Look," she said, "you're ready. You've been rehearsing with that vocal coach, right?"

"Right," I said. Annoyingly she'd been one of the recommendations from Cal.

"Working with that dance teacher?"

"Mm-hmm."

Everything was rusty. I was in shape, but not eight-shows-a-week shape.

"You know the show."

"Sure," I said. "As much as someone knows a show that's about to be workshopped, taken apart, and then reassembled."

"You're going to be fine," Harriet said as she stood up to get our drinks.

I was pretty sure I was never going to feel ready. Because I was never going to *be* ready.

I'd had my moment and perhaps it was dangerous and foolish to think that I could try again.

Harriet plunked the tea down in front of me and we both ignored the way my hand shook as I lifted the cup to my mouth. I had to use both hands for good measure, like a fucking child.

There was no point in telling Harriet I couldn't do this.

And I was a lot of things, but I'd never backed out on a commitment.

Well. Except that one time.

"I'm nervous too," Harriet said.

I blinked. I'd been so caught up in my own anxiety spiral that I'd totally ignored the fact that today was a big day for Harriet as well. It was probably *bigger* for her. She was about to hear the musical she'd written, spoken and sung out loud with a full cast, for the first time.

Reaching over, I put my hand on hers. Sure enough, it was trembling too.

"The show is incredible," I told her.

Harriet smiled down at the table. She didn't meet my eye.

I felt a twinge of guilt. I knew it had to be hard for her. For most of our friendship, I'd been in the spotlight—or working toward it—and she'd been in the background, cheering me on. A real *Beaches* of a situation, minus the tragic illness.

"I'm so proud of you," I said, feeling like it was probably long overdue.

I hadn't seen much of her during the audition process. I'd assumed it had been because of schedule and timing, but now I was wondering if I should have been checking in more. Should have been more attentive to my oldest friend, rather than entertaining my anxiety at all hours of the day.

I made a mental note to focus more on Harriet going forward.

"Are you ready?" I asked.

"Are you?" she countered.

I wasn't.

"Yes," I said.

The rehearsal space was bright and big and open. High ceilings, mirrors on every wall, except for the one with floor-to-ceiling windows. I was pretty sure they were tinted, but it still gave me fishbowl feelings.

People were milling around, unwinding scarves from their necks—it was chilly today—and greeting familiar faces. I was grateful for Harriet and resisted the urge to reach out and take her hand. I wasn't someone who got nervous meeting new people, but this situation felt different and unique and one thousand times scarier than anything else I'd experienced.

Cal looked up when we entered—he was standing over by the piano with a young woman who had impeccable eyeliner.

"You're here," he said.

Even though I'd just been thinking about bolting, I still didn't appreciate his surprise.

"Looking good, Mr. Director," Harriet said, and I was gratified that Cal got a little pink-cheeked, even though he tried to hide it by looking down at his clipboard.

"This is Taylor," Cal said, referring to the woman with the eyeliner. "She's our stage manager. Taylor, this is Kathleen and Harriet."

I squared my shoulders and gave her my best Katee Rose smile.

"I have it on great authority that Cal only works with the best of the best," I said, "which tells me that you're an incredible stage manager."

I could hear myself overcompensate—lean too far into grand diva. A turban and foot-long cigarette holder wouldn't have been out of place from the way I rolled my R's in "incredible."

Over her shoulder, I saw Cal let out an aggrieved sigh. I didn't blame him; I was cringing at myself as well. If I wasn't careful I'd start complaining about how it was the pictures that got small, not me.

"You're *all* very talented," he said.

"Oh," I said, "I know."

Goddammit. *Shut. Up.*

Thankfully Taylor just grinned.

More people began to arrive. I saw in their expressions what I had long grown accustomed to—first the sense of unplaced familiarity, then the search through the mental Rolodex for my face, followed by the realization that I wasn't a long-lost friend or co-worker but in fact someone who had once been very famous. And then, depending on how much they'd loved Ryan LaNeve, I could count on anything from mild judgment to utter disdain.

Today was mostly expressions of total shock. Like they weren't just surprised that I was there but surprised that I was still alive.

That was followed by wide-eyed rubbernecking, stares darting between me and Cal.

Bad enough that I'd broken Ryan's heart, but cheating with a member of *his own band*? Well, that was some high-grade villainess shit. I wasn't just a slut but a temptress slut. The most dangerous of the slut varieties.

Casting announcements had listed me as Kathleen Rosenberg. I'd expected some people to make the connection, but apparently my reputation had *not* preceded me.

"Hello," I said to the cast members that passed. Thankfully I did it like a normal person, not Norma fucking Desmond.

I wondered what they were thinking. Probably that they could look up the definition of "stunt casting" in the dictionary and find a photo of me.

Statler and Waldorf arrived, along with Cal's assistant, Mae. There was a row of chairs along the wall for them, while the rest of us had music stands to place our scripts and music on.

Everyone else arrived, and I got a couple more double takes. I offered little finger waves to everyone who stared, trying to ignore the way my anxiety was disconnecting me from my body. I took a couple of deep breaths, focusing on my feet on the floor and my butt in the seat.

I felt unbelievably awkward and out of place. Not just in the room but in my own skin. I was sweating and freezing at the same time, my knees chattering. I pressed my palms flat against the script in front of me, all but bracing myself for what came next.

Cal stepped to the front of the room.

"Welcome," he said.

He didn't look nervous at all. He looked great, actually. Hair looked great, clothes looked great. Smile? Great.

But then I looked down at his hands and saw that they were trembling. Just a little.

He was still human.

For whatever reason, it didn't make me feel any better.

"Now, who recognizes me?" he asked.

Everyone in the room looked around at each other, clearly not expecting the question.

"You were at our auditions," someone said.

Cal laughed and it spread through the space.

"Fair enough," he said. "I guess I should have clarified. How many of you recognize me from something else? Something, let's say, a decade or so ago?"

A few tentative hands lifted into the air. I rolled my eyes and put my own hand up. I had no idea what he was doing.

"Oh, come on," Cal said. "Really? You don't remember this?"

He struck a truly ridiculous pose, one arm propped on the other, hand under his chin, lips in a broody pout. Any CrushZone fan would have recognized it from the cover of their first album, *Shore Leave*. All that was missing was a sailor hat.

Someone started whistling the title song from that album. I looked around. It was Harriet.

"Thank you," Cal said, pointing to her. "Let's just get this all out in the open, okay? I was a member of CrushZone."

There was a smattering of applause—I could tell that everyone still didn't really know where he was going with this.

"And I'm sure you all recognize the woman in the front over here." Cal pointed to me.

The fuck?

I wanted to sink into my chair and disappear through the floor. Unfortunately, the laws of physics were still very much in place.

"You will all learn to know her as Kathleen Rosenberg, our Peggy," Cal said. "But she too once graced the pop star stage as the legendary Katee Rose."

I thought about throwing my script at him. My aim wasn't great, but the book was big and I was pretty sure I could probably scare him into shutting up.

At least the applause was a little more robust for me. I turned and gave a little wave, before shooting a glare toward Cal.

Did he really need to single me out like this? On our first day?

I kept my spine straight, hoping my face wasn't as red as it felt.

"I won't speak for Kathleen," he said. "But as much as I loved being a member of CrushZone, that's in the past. You're all here because you love the theatre, because you want to be a part of this very special show. You're professionals. You're the best of the best." He put a hand to his chest. "I'm here to create something magical. Something important. Something new."

Cal paused, taking a moment to look around the room.

"This is a brand-new show," he said. "We have the unbelievable gift of bringing something to life for the first time. It's an honor to be sharing Harriet's incredible music and lyrics with you."

It was hard not to be captivated by how earnest he sounded.

I very much wanted to believe him.

"I believe in the power of starting anew," he said. "Every show, every role, every performance, is a chance to start fresh. Every day is a new opportunity for success. I don't plan on judging anyone for what you did yesterday, or the day before, or the year before."

The room seemed to be holding its breath.

"And I hope you will extend me the same courtesy," Cal said.

Well. If I wasn't so annoyed at him for putting an unwelcome spotlight on me on our very first day, I might have grudgingly admitted that his speech had been pretty damned masterful.

In a few sentences Cal had managed to address both of us elephants in the room while preemptively chiding anyone who had been thinking about asking about our previous lives.

I applauded politely along with the rest of the crew. But I could still feel dozens of eyeballs trying not to look directly at me. Whether or not Cal's gambit would prove successful long term was to be determined, but at least I wasn't going to get swarmed during our lunch break and asked what really happened between me and Cal and Ryan.

Not today at least.

"All right." Cal clapped his hands together. "Let's introduce ourselves and get started."

I took a deep breath.

And. Here. We. Go.

CHAPTER 7

I made it through my first day without throwing up or passing out. We read—and sang—through the show, and while I was certain I didn't wow anyone, I didn't fuck anything up too horribly either. There was no doubt in my mind that the majority of those present, myself included, considered my casting as nothing more than a gimmick. A way to get attention.

It wasn't the worst place to start from. Expectations were extremely low, so I could only improve from there.

Or I'd just embarrass myself in front of them, and the Broadway community.

At least I knew from experience that embarrassment wasn't fatal.

Not yet.

"Excellent work, everyone," Cal said.

He'd mostly sat and listened—too early in the process to actually start directing us—and I had to fight the impulse to go over to him and ask for a detailed breakdown of how I'd done.

I both wanted to know and knew that it was better that I didn't. Because this was just the beginning, and I knew that getting input on something I already knew wasn't good enough was a great way to build the kind of crippling self-doubt that could linger.

That could tank a performance.

I needed to do everything in my power to keep those feelings at bay. It was already a struggle. Last night, I'd stared at myself in the mirror for a good hour, looking for Katee Rose. Because I knew that's what everyone else would be doing.

Katee Rose had been beautiful and perfect and manu-factured. Until she wasn't. Then she'd been sad, sloppy, and embarrassing.

The woman in the mirror last night had wrinkles and sun damage, and of fucking course, a zit on her chin.

Kathleen Rosenberg was imperfect. She was fine. She was alive.

Usually that was enough to keep the demons at bay. The voices that whispered that I wasn't what I'd been and wasn't that just so tragic? Wasn't it sad that I'd gained weight and had bad skin and frizzy hair? Wasn't it just so completely embarrassing that I wasn't perfect anymore?

Therapy had helped me see myself as more than the alter ego that had been thrust on me. It had allowed me to be more than Katee Rose. Allowed me to stop dieting, stop ob-sessively working out, stop worrying constantly about my body and my face and how it looked and how I looked.

But now? Anyone with a brain knew that if this show went to Broadway, it would help to have Katee to sell tickets.

And that knowledge was like catnip to all my insecurities. I'd had a salad for lunch today. A fucking salad, when what I really wanted was a chicken parmesan sandwich covered in ooey-gooey melted cheese. And fries.

Instead of listening to my actual needs, I thought of my waistline and my skin. And went hungry.

Stupid, stupid girl.

I was going to grab a slice of grandma pizza on my way back to the apartment and eat it without mopping up the grease. Take that, zit.

I packed up my things, trying to avoid my reflection in the floor-to-ceiling mirrors that took up one wall. Mirrors were what had gotten me in trouble in the first place. Visions of the past.

Still, I couldn't completely avoid myself. Usually it was when I stopped looking that I caught glimpses of Katee. We had the same eyes, after all.

"Good work today," Cal said as he passed me.

I should have just said thank you. Instead . . .

"You might have given me a warning," I said.

Cal stopped. Turned.

"A warning?"

Don't say anything, I ordered myself. *Walk away. Go home.*

Instead, I lowered my voice to a poor approximation of his.

"*She too once graced the pop star stage as the legendary Katee Rose,*" I intoned. "You could have asked if I wanted you to do that. Or given me a heads-up."

Cal raised an eyebrow. "Why? Would you have prepared a splashy intro number?"

"Yes," I said. "With fireworks and cancan dancers. Or

maybe I would have preferred to remain somewhat anonymous."

"You really thought people wouldn't figure it out immediately?" he asked.

That wasn't the point.

I scowled at him. He sighed.

"Just thought it would clear the air," he said. "Can't say I didn't try."

"I don't trust you," I said.

Well. It was nice to know that my self-destruct button was still intact, and I was just as itchy as ever to press it.

Why am I like this?

He narrowed his eyes at me.

"Is this your version of an olive branch?" he asked. "It might need some work."

"It's *my* version of clearing the air," I said. "Just get it all out there before it poisons everything."

He nodded. "Fair enough," he said. "I don't trust you either."

"You're arrogant," I said.

He mirrored my stance, arms crossed. "You're dramatic."

"You're condescending."

"You're inexperienced."

"You're pushy."

"You're inflexible."

"You're stubborn."

"Likewise," he said.

The truth was that with each barb, we could easily be talking about ourselves.

"You're also so fucking good that I can't look away," Cal said.

My breath escaped me. I stared at him, and he shrugged.

"Honesty, right?"

"Right," I said.

There was silence.

"It wouldn't kill you to say something nice about me," he said.

"It might," I said.

A wrinkle appeared between his eyes. I'd hurt him. I told myself that I shouldn't care. He'd hurt me far worse.

It's not a competition, my therapist would say.

And I was being an asshole. A stubborn, dramatic, inflexible asshole.

"Sorry," I said. "You're . . ."

"Don't strain anything," he said.

I glared at him.

"You're in control," I said. "You know what you're doing. You have a clear vision. And it's a good one."

Red tinged his cheeks.

"Thank you," he said.

"Honesty, right?" I asked.

"Right," he said.

"I still don't trust you," I said.

"We'll work on that," he said.

I didn't appreciate the surety in his voice.

"Let's just focus on getting through the workshop," I said. "Cordially."

"The workshop and the out-of-town tryouts and a Broadway premiere," he said. "Can you survive that long being *cordial* to me?"

"I can if you can," I said.

We both started walking toward the door.

"Do you really think we'll go to Broadway?" I asked.

"Yes," Cal said. No hesitation.

I'd been that confident once. I missed it.

Harriet was waiting for me out on the street. She raised an eyebrow at the sight of me and Cal leaving together, but he just lifted a hand in acknowledgment and walked away from us.

"It's nothing," I said when she hit me with a questioning look.

Neither of us had made any plans for after the workshop. In fact, I'd spent the last few weeks so focused on this one particular day that I realized I hadn't really thought about everything that would be happening next. All the work and stress and energy that was going to be required of me. Of all of us.

Suddenly I was exhausted.

I expected Harriet to say something, to suggest we go somewhere to discuss how the reading had gone, a postmortem on the first day, but the two of us just walked to the station, waited for our train, and then sat side by side, silently, heading to Brooklyn.

Her stop was first. As we pulled into the station, Harriet turned and gave me a hug. Held me tight.

"It's really happening, isn't it?" she asked.

"It really is," I said.

She shook her head as if she still couldn't believe it.

"See you tomorrow," she said, and got off the train.

CHAPTER 8

Today was the day I was looking forward to the least.

One-on-one with Cal.

We'd be discussing character motivation, rehearsing my solos, and practicing choreography. Of course, his assistant would be there—and a pianist too—but I still couldn't shake the nervous, itchy feeling that this was a bad idea.

My therapist thought I had some unresolved issues with Cal.

I thought, *No shit, Sherlock.*

The problem was that I didn't really want to resolve those issues. I wanted to stay angry at him. Because in some ways, it felt more dangerous to forgive him.

I had to remind myself of what he'd done. Or rather, what he hadn't done.

I'd lost *so much.*

Cal . . . had not. He was fine. Better than fine, in fact.

The unfairness of it was hard to swallow. But that was

okay. I preferred that bitterness sitting in the base of my throat, instead of a nostalgic lump quivering with hope.

"Morning," Cal said.

"Morning," I said.

Polite. Calm. I could do this.

"I thought we'd discuss Peggy and her motivations first," Cal said. "Then work on incorporating those insights into her solos and movements."

"Sure," I said.

It wasn't that I had a problem talking about my character. I knew Peggy. I loved her.

But there was something about discussing her with Cal that made me feel eggshell vulnerable.

"She's got a lot going on, our Peggy," Cal said.

"Yes," I said.

"Lots of hidden depth," he said.

"Yes," I said.

Cal's assistant sat there, taking notes, the tip-tapping of her computer keys comforting and distracting. It was easier to be cordial when we had an audience. I *was* a performer, after all.

With his arms crossed, Cal leaned back in his chair, giving me a long look. I sat at the edge of my seat, hands folded like I was waiting for afternoon tea.

"Feel free to jump in whenever," he said.

I didn't appreciate his tone. That "Did you even *do* the reading?" tone. The "I went to college and you didn't" tone.

Polite. Calm. *Perform.*

"She's strong," I said. "Tough."

"On the surface," he said.

"She's not faking it," I said.

"I didn't say she was."

"She's been through a lot," I said.

"Let's talk about her coping mechanisms," Cal said.

"She's good at compartmentalizing," I said. "All aspects of her life are separate from each other and that's the way she likes it."

"Does she like it?" Cal asked. "Or is it necessary?"

"Same thing," I said.

Cal tilted his head. "Is it?"

"For her," I said. "She doesn't have the time—or energy—to enjoy things for the sake of enjoying them. All that matters is survival."

"Hmm." He actually rubbed his chin as he leaned even farther back. "Hmmm."

"What?" I asked.

It was sharper than I had intended, but I'd sensed some judgment in those "hmmms." I didn't like it.

"Nothing," he said. "You just have an interesting perspective on her."

"Interesting?" I repeated. "Or correct?"

"I don't know if there is such a thing when it comes to character," he said. "It's all up for interpretation."

That was incredibly not helpful. I wanted to be right. I *was* right.

"Why don't we try going over some of her songs?" Cal asked. "See if we can infuse some of this information into your performance."

We worked with the accompanist for an hour, stopping and starting, discussing lyrics, analyzing intent. How much of what Peggy said was honest and real, how much of it was a façade.

"She loves her double entendres," Cal observed.

"Who doesn't?"

"It makes her hard to pin down," he said.

"Not if you ask nicely," I purred.

He looked at me. I looked at him. The pianist let out a choking little laugh. I would have done the same, but the way Cal's eyes had dropped to my lips silenced me.

I couldn't help looking at his mouth too. His jaw. His throat.

I watched him swallow. Hard.

My legs felt a little wobbly.

"As Peggy would say," I managed.

"Right," Cal said. "Of course."

The silence stretched out between us.

"I guess I walked right into that one," he said.

"Mm-hmm."

"Why don't we take a break?" he asked.

"Sure," I said.

Come on, Rosenberg, I thought. There has to be a way you can communicate with Cal that isn't via passive-aggressive comments or suggestive replies.

I left the studio and walked around the block, trying to clear my head and calm my libido. There was something gratifying about Cal's reaction, but I didn't like how aggressively I was careening between feelings of complete resentment and knee-knocking lust. Neither was helpful, both simultaneously was even worse.

The accompanist was gone when I returned to the rehearsal space, and Mae was staring at her phone, her forehead furrowed with worry.

"What's wrong?" I asked.

She jumped. "Oh"—she put her phone away—"nothing. It's fine."

"What's fine?" Cal appeared behind me.

Mae burst into tears, surprising all of us.

"I'm sorry," she said. "It's nothing."

"Obviously that's not true," I said.

I didn't really expect Cal to do anything—in my experience, men were ill-equipped to deal with emotions of any kind, and they usually ran from weeping women as if a few stray tears might melt them.

My father, Ryan, and all other boyfriends had always responded to my emotions with a firm pat on the shoulder and a stilted "There, there," while remaining focused on their phone or the TV or whatever else was more worthy of their attention.

But Cal immediately gave Mae a hug and made some comforting *shhhh, shhhh* sounds as she wiped her nose on her sleeve. Right. He had sisters.

"What's wrong?" he asked when she'd calmed down some.

"She's fine," Mae said, "but my cousin fainted at work today. She's a teacher in Washington Heights."

"Oh my god," I said.

"She's at the hospital," Mae said. "But she's okay. They said she'll be okay."

"Let's get you a cab," Cal said. "You should go be with her."

"But"—Mae gestured at the rehearsal space—"I have to take notes."

"Don't worry about that," Cal said. "Your cousin is the priority right now."

I could tell that Mae was torn, but she let Cal pack up her things and get her a ride to the hospital.

"Call me when you can," he said as he walked her out. "But only to update me on how you're doing—everything else can wait."

I began to put away my own things.

"She'll be okay," Cal said, coming back into the space. "Are you leaving too?"

I paused. "I just thought . . . without Mae . . ."

The two of us alone will murder each other. Or . . .

"Yeah," he said, rubbing the back of his neck. "Sure."

"You wanted to work more?"

I wasn't sure I trusted myself.

"I don't know if we'll be able to find another time to focus this much attention on Peggy," he said. "But it's been a long day."

It hadn't, not really. I was tired, but not drained.

I could stay. I could keep working. Just the two of us. Together. Alone.

It was fine. I was being dramatic. I was an adult. A professional. Cal was too.

I put my bag down. "Okay," I said. "Let's keep going."

"Are you sure?" Cal asked.

I gave him a look.

"Okay," he said. "Great. Thank you."

"I should probably thank *you*," I said, albeit reluctantly. He raised an eyebrow.

"For caring this much about Peggy," I said.

"I care about all my girls," he said, clearly referencing the way our fully adult female characters were often categorized as "girls" within the show.

The rehearsal space, which had felt normal-sized and accommodating thus far, suddenly seemed to shrink. All I could smell was Cal's cologne. Oranges everywhere, and yet,

I still had the urge to put my face against his throat and really breathe in.

Bad idea.

Remember how much you can't stand him, I ordered myself. Remember that he's condescending and smug and he completely, utterly threw you under the bus to save his own ass.

"Let's go over Peggy's walk," he said.

He'd mentioned that he wanted her to have a specific gait—one that immediately, visually set her apart from the others. Because even though the audience would be introduced to each character in their everyday clothes—Peggy's being a sexy nightclub number—for the majority of the performance, everyone would be dressed in identical coveralls, with the pattern of their head coverings as their main identifier.

"I'm not cutting the heel off one of my shoes," I said.

It was rumored that was how Marilyn Monroe had gotten her signature wiggle walk.

"I was more thinking Catherine O'Hara at the end of *Best in Show*," Cal said.

I stared at him.

"Joking," he said.

"Ha," I said.

"Why don't you just go with your gut?" Cal suggested. "Give us a few options."

He made it sound so easy. Like I could pull a distinctive movement—one that was noticeable but not laughable—out of my ass on command. And not just one, but several different versions.

"I don't suppose you have any ideas," I said.

He *was* the director, after all.

Cal circled me, chin pinched between his thumb and pointer finger. Even when he passed behind me, I could still see him in the mirrors that lined the wall, so it felt like I was well and truly surrounded.

"Okay," he said.

He waved for me to get out of the way. I didn't have to be asked twice.

Leaning up against one of the mirrors, water bottle in hand, I watched Cal's process.

He started by walking back and forth in his usual way. Then he started swinging his hands. Then his hips. The whole thing was extremely exaggerated and patently ridiculous, but I didn't laugh. I watched as he let the walk grow more and more outlandish, crossing his feet like a high-stepping horse, shoulders jutting forward with each movement.

Then he began to pull back each element, piece by piece. His stomping steps began to look more like a glide, his hips shifting as if he were moving in water, slowly, carefully. The walk was both cautious and seductive.

"What do you think?" Cal asked, one hand on his hip, the other trailing along his side.

I didn't answer, instead began walking behind him, attempting to mimic what he was doing.

"It helps to start big," he said, when it was clear I wasn't quite getting it.

We probably looked ridiculous, the two of us walking back and forth, back and forth, knees high, hips swinging. But he was right—it was easier to soften the movement than to build up to it. After a while, Cal dropped out of our two-person parade and stood aside to watch.

"Your right side is a little weak," he said.

I'd heard that before. He was correct, of course, but I was loath to admit it, just as I had been back then.

"Better," Cal said.

I could feel it—the way my body adjusted to the rhythm of Peggy's walk—it added something to the character. This was a woman who knew she was being looked at, but instead of shrinking away from the attention, she leaned into it. She made you *want* to watch. Because if you were watching, she was in control. And Peggy was all about control. It connected me to her, even more than I'd already been.

"Let's try incorporating it with some choreography," Cal said.

Right. Because it wasn't enough that I had to walk like this—I had to make it work with my dancing as well.

"Let's try 'With or Without Them,' " he said. "We want to make sure you stand out."

There had been a time when all I wanted to do was stand out. Now, my feelings about getting the spotlight were a little more complicated.

"I thought this was an ensemble number," I said.

"It is," Cal said. "But each of you needs to feel specific."

He went to the middle of the room and started walking through the choreography.

"Step, step, turn, hip, hip, arms," he directed.

I followed, trying to meld his directions with Peggy's style of walking. It wasn't easy.

"Okay," Cal said after I'd fucked up enough times.

He came and stood in front of me. I waited for him to yell. To berate me for getting his precious steps wrong.

Part of me wanted it. Wanted his anger. His fury. Because *that* I could match.

"Let's try something," he said.

Instead, he looked sympathetic, which was worse.

"This dance is kind of like a couples' dance," he said.

"Only without a partner," I said dryly.

"Exactly," Cal said. "You're all talking about the men you miss—what it feels like to be alone right now. So, it should start out imperfect, which you've got down."

I glared at him. He ignored it.

"But we want it to become fluid and natural," he said. "You're all learning how to be on your own. And you like it."

"Of course I do," I said. "Men just get in the way."

Cal rolled his eyes. "Think about that old saying—that Ginger Rogers did everything that Fred Astaire did—"

"—but backward and in heels," I finished.

"Bingo," Cal said. "You're doing this backward and in heels."

"Easier said than done," I muttered.

"Okay." Cal stepped toward me, arms up.

I stepped back. "What are you doing?"

He lowered his hands. "I thought we'd try it together," he said. "Like with the walk, it might be easier to subtract than add, if you know what I mean."

I did, but that "this is a bad idea" feeling was stronger than ever. We'd done a good job of not really touching each other throughout this whole process.

Cal noticed my hesitation. "But if you're not comfortable—"

"No," I said. I was being ridiculous. "It's fine. It's work. We're professionals."

I straightened my spine and lifted my arms. Cal stepped right into the space between us, one hand on my hip, the other linking fingers with me. It was unnerving how intimate it felt to have his palm flush against mine. I put my hand on his shoulder.

"One, two, three," Cal counted off.

There wasn't anything like dancing with a partner who was in complete control. Who knew how to move.

And Cal knew how to move.

It was effortless. Our bodies were in complete, silent synchronicity. I could read his next movements by the gentle pressure of his hand in mine or the push of his palm against my hip.

Today had been hard. It was work, and even though it was work that I enjoyed—for the most part—it could still be wearying. And with Cal, I felt like I was on edge. Like I was waiting for the other shoe to drop. Waiting for everything to implode. Again.

Right now, though, I just followed his lead.

I'd been so focused for hours—worried about my characterizations, my choices, my performance—that it was nice to not worry. To not stress. To not think about anything except Cal leading me around the rehearsal room.

I'd always loved dancing. Loved knowing what my body could do, how it could move. Loved challenging myself and working harder to get better, stronger.

It wasn't until we slowed that I realized I didn't even know how long we'd been dancing. I'd lost myself completely in the moment, forgetting why we were here in the first place. And as we came to a stop, I had to take a step back after noticing exactly how close we'd been to each other. My cheek had practically been pressed against his, his hand moving from my hip to my lower back.

We stood there, arms still lifted, fingers still linked.

The room was spinning, but we weren't.

Cal let go of me, but he did it slowly, his touch all but burning through my clothes as he dragged his hand from mine, as he peeled his fingers away from the curve of my spine. He brushed the side of my ribs before he withdrew completely, and I shivered.

He noticed, and opened his mouth to say something, but I wasn't about to let him.

"I think I've got it," I said.

I made sure to keep my voice flat. Professional.

"Right," he said, doing the same.

An ocean of space opened between us.

"Good," I said.

CHAPTER 9

Perhaps it was a holdover from all those years spent surrounded by people twenty-four seven, but in my advancing age, I'd grown to appreciate doing things by myself. One of my favorite things to do was get lunch and then go to a midday show—movie or theatre—or a museum.

Harriet thought I was nuts—the thought of eating alone in a restaurant was downright terrifying to her—but I savored the freedom of those days. I could order whatever I wanted, stay as long as I chose, and see whatever I wanted to see.

I'd been looking forward to a day off. It was exhausting to memorize lyrics and choreography all summer while pretending that Cal and I were just totally fine. That there was no complicated, messy history between us. That I wasn't whipping between resenting him and wanting him. There were days when I couldn't help bristling at his directing, though I did my best to hide it. It wasn't the actual quality of his direction, which was fine. Okay, more than fine. He was a great director.

I just hated being directed by him. Hated being told what to do.

Maybe that was part of getting older as well. Back in my Katee Rose days, I'd been eager—sometimes overeager—to please. I would have literally bent over backward if I thought it meant everyone around me would be happy and satisfied.

Now? I didn't really care.

I wasn't mean or cruel or thoughtless. I just didn't put everyone else's needs before my own anymore.

For the past decade or so the only performing I'd done had been for myself. Singing in the shower. Dancing for my students. Acting like I was a totally normal member of society, not a washed-up pop star with a "reputation."

I had an audience again, and I wasn't used to it.

Then there was all that pesky unresolved history with Cal. It made it impossible to trust him, and it was hard to take direction from someone I didn't trust. Even if he was right most of the time.

I pushed Cal from my thoughts as I headed into the Museum of Natural History. I intended for this day to be a break—a reset—before we moved into the final week of workshop rehearsals.

I'd already had a long, leisurely lunch at my favorite hidden Italian place right on the edge of the park, and planned on spending the rest of my afternoon wandering through some of my favorite exhibits.

I was standing under the blue whale when something small and dressed like a dinosaur crashed into my legs.

"Rawr," it said.

"Rawr," I said back.

The kid was probably around five, but that was only a guess. I liked kids, but had no desire for my own, and I couldn't really gauge their ages once they were mobile.

"Sammy!" a frantic voice called. "Sammy, where are you?"

"Mommy!" Sammy (presumably) said.

"Over here," I said, waving a hand above my head.

A dark-haired woman came rushing over, followed by a tall man that I unfortunately recognized. A man that, as far as I knew, didn't have a young child.

"You've got to be kidding me," I said under my breath.

"Sammy!" The woman dropped to her knees in front of the dinosaur. "What did I tell you about wandering off?"

"Uh," Sammy said, face scrunched in thought.

"That it makes your mother worry," Cal said.

I told myself I didn't care, but I still found myself checking his ring finger to see if I'd missed a wedding band. I hadn't.

"That's putting it mildly," Sammy's mother said. "It makes me start screaming your name in crowded spaces and then everyone looks at me like I'm a bad parent who just lost her child."

"Sorry, Mommy," Sammy said.

She sighed and gave him a hug. "Thank you," she said, hoisting Sammy in her arms as she stood. Her eyes narrowed. "Wait. Do I know you?"

I gave her a polite smile. "Hi," I said, before tilting my head to address Cal behind her. The smile I gave him was forty percent less polite. *Doesn't he know this is my day off?* "Hey."

Sammy's mother looked between us. "Do *you* know each other?"

"Whitney, this is Kathleen," Cal said. "Kathleen, this is Whitney."

We shook hands, with realization coming to Whitney's eyes halfway through.

"Holy shit," she said. "You're Katee Rose."

"Kathleen Rosenberg," Cal and I said at the same time.

"Sorry," Whitney said. "It's just . . . wow. I was a really, *really* big fan of yours. Still am."

I wasn't that surprised—she looked close to my age, so it would have been more unexpected if she *hadn't* known who I was. And I appreciated the quick amendment to her comment. I still had an ego, and it had a tendency to bruise easily.

Whitney's gaze bounced between me and Cal again, and I could see her remembering everything that had been implied about the two of us back in those days. Implied, never confirmed, but that didn't really matter. It was all true.

And if they were friends—or more—she probably knew that.

"Oh my god," Whitney said. "You. Her."

Cal just stood there, his expression patient and placid.

"Just say it, Whitney," he said.

Instead, she slapped him on the arm.

"Don't be an asshole," she said.

"Asshole!" Sammy echoed.

"Shhhh," Whitney said.

Cal didn't seem ruffled by any of it.

"I'm sorry for him," Whitney said. "Both the kid and Cal."

"I like you," I said to Whitney.

"Why am I not surprised?" Cal asked. He seemed to be

speaking rhetorically. "Of course you two would become immediate friends."

"Did we?" Whitney asked.

"Since it seems to annoy Cal, then yes," I said.

Whitney beamed. "This is the best day of my life. I can't wait to tell my husband."

"He won't care," Cal said.

"He will," Whitney insisted to him, and then to me. "He will."

"If you were a Katee Rose fan, does that mean you were a CrushZone fan too?" I asked.

Whitney laughed. It was a deep belly laugh. A "wow, that is really very funny" laugh.

"Not exactly," she said.

"Whitney is responsible for CrushZone," Cal said.

"That's giving me too much credit," Whitney said. "I just dared *him* to audition. I'm not responsible for . . . the others."

My eyes widened. I'd always wondered exactly how Cal had gone from college graduate to boy band superstar. Everyone knew that he'd been plucked from a cattle call lineup; I just never bothered to ask how he'd gotten in that lineup in the first place.

"You did not dare me," Cal said.

Whitney scoffed. "Uh-huh," she said.

"Did you go to college together?" I asked.

"Sure did," Whitney said. "Want to hear some embarrassing stories about him?"

"Always," I said.

"Mommy." Sammy squirmed. "Mommy, can we go see the sparkle rocks?"

"The Hall of Gems," Whitney interpreted.

"Ah," I said. "That's one of my favorites."

"I can take him," Cal said, "if you want to regale Kathleen with tales of our college years."

"I can multitask," Whitney said. "Unless you've got something better to do than walk around looking at rocks with the three of us."

I thought about it for a moment.

"Actually, that sounds like a perfect way to spend my afternoon."

* * *

"And this one is my favorite rock," Sammy said.

"More favorite than your other favorites?" I asked.

There had been at least a dozen.

"Uh-huh," Sammy said.

"Cool," I said.

"Want to go look at some meteorites, Sammy?" Cal asked. "Let your mommy and Kathleen get a chance to gossip about Uncle Cal?"

"It's not gossip if it's the truth," Whitney said as Cal slung her kid up onto his shoulders.

"Have fun, you two," he said.

Both Whitney and I watched him walk away. I might have stared at his butt while he did, but even my general annoyance and distrust of him didn't erase the fact that he had a really, really nice ass.

"Sammy loves him," Whitney said.

"Bet he saves cats out of trees," I said, only slightly under my breath.

She laughed. "I think he's afraid of heights, but yeah, he probably would."

"You don't need to tell me what a great guy Cal is," I said.

Whitney raised her eyebrows. "I don't?"

"All I care about is making the show good," I said.

"Then you two are in agreement," Whitney said. "But I wasn't going to tell you what a great guy Cal is."

This time I was the one raising my eyebrows.

"Okay." She lifted her hands. "Maybe I was going to try to grease the wheel a little, but he's a grown man."

"Mm-hmm," I said.

I'd unfortunately noticed. It made all this even more complicated and confusing. My brain and my body were not in agreement over how to handle Cal. My brain wanted to keep him at arm's length. My body . . .

Well. It wanted to handle him. Carnally.

My body was an idiot.

"It must be hard," Whitney said.

"Excuse me?"

"Working together," she amended. "After everything that happened."

I admired her nerve. I couldn't remember the last time someone had been so direct about the whole thing. Even Harriet and I tended to give it the side-eye.

"I'm impressed that you're doing the show, honestly."

"It's a good show," I said.

"Sure," she said. "But there must be others."

Wow. We were just putting it all out there, weren't we?

"Nope," I said.

"Really?"

"Really."

I'd tried. A few times. Always as Kathleen Rosenberg. Either they didn't recognize me—and I didn't get the part—or they did and the whole process changed. The expectations changed.

There had been a few opportunities that I'd considered, until it became clear that they were hoping for Katee to show up on the first day.

I didn't know how to tell people she wasn't real. And if she was, she was long gone now. I didn't think I could be Katee Rose if I tried. And I really, really didn't want to.

"Huh." Whitney leaned back. "People really don't forgive, do they?"

"When you cheat on your beloved boy band boyfriend? No," I said. "They really don't."

"You were a kid," she said.

It was a generous explanation for why things had happened the way they had. And patently false. We'd both been adults. Not fully grown but old enough to know better.

"I'm pretty sure the term is Heart Smasher," I said.

That's what Ryan's first solo album had been called. One last foray into music before transitioning completely to acting.

"I thought it was dumb then, and I think it's dumb now," Whitney said. "And Mason was always the better singer."

"No argument here," I said.

If Mason hadn't been so distracted by other things, he would have been the breakout star, not Ryan. But I was pretty sure Mason didn't care anymore.

"Sorry to interrupt," Cal said.

He had Sammy draped over one shoulder. Snoring.

"I think we might be all museumed out," he said.

"Oh boy," Whitney said, taking her kid out of Cal's arms. "Guess I better take this little dino home."

"Want me to get you a cab?" Cal asked.

Whitney waved him off. "Like I haven't taken a sleeping child on the subway before." She snorted. "What kind of New Yorker do you think I am?"

"I'm not even going to dare to answer that," Cal said.

"Smart man," Whitney said before turning to me. "Nice meeting you, Kathleen."

"You too," I said.

"I'm sure we'll see each other around," Whitney said.

She exchanged an awkward hug and cheek kiss with Cal, all around a still-sleeping Sammy.

"Be nice," she said.

"Me?" Cal asked. "I'm always nice."

We stood there as Whitney and Sammy walked away.

"So," Cal said.

His hands were in his pockets.

"Sammy's not my kid," he said.

"I didn't think that for a moment," I said. It was basically the truth.

Cal gave me a look. I shrugged.

"Too cute to be your kid," I said.

"Ha," he said. "I think the CrushZone fan club might disagree with you."

"It still exists?"

Cal thought about it for a moment. "You know, I haven't checked recently."

"Maybe Whitney has," I said.

"If she has, it's purely for the purpose of embarrassing me."

"Good," I said.

"My ego isn't *that* robust," Cal said.

"Please," I said. "That kid looked at you like you were the best thing since *Hamilton*."

"That's because I'm just the fun uncle type," he said. "Much easier than being a parent."

"It is a much shorter time commitment," I said.

"Suits me perfectly," he said.

Well. That was something we had in common. It wasn't the only thing—we used to have *a lot* in common—but it was kind of a nice reminder.

Then I remembered exactly why it didn't matter what we had in common.

"Do you think we can make it to the exit without bickering?" Cal asked.

I hated how he made it sound like we were two little kids who were fighting in the backseat. Or like I was the child, and he was the adult.

"I'm sure I can," I said, probably not helping my case.

"Okay," he said.

"Wait," I said.

We were standing in front of the T-Rex.

"Yes?"

"I'm not ready to leave," I said.

"Oh," he said.

"You can go," I said.

He looked up at the dinosaur and down the hall toward the other exhibits.

"I don't think I'm ready to leave either," he said.

"Oh," I said.

Guests walked around us, the two of us very much in the way.

"I don't suppose you'd want to—"

"We can just ignore each other," I said at the same time Cal was gesturing back toward the rest of the museum.

"Okay," he said.

Had he been about to ask if I wanted to spend the rest of the day with him? We'd only just declared a truce of sorts—taking a leisurely walk through the Natural History Museum seemed a little too advanced for where we were at.

"I'm sorry," I said. "Were you—"

"Nope," he said. "Let's just ignore each other."

I gave him a searching look.

He shrugged, stuck his hands in his pockets, and turned away.

"See you around, Rosenberg," he said over his shoulder.

"You can bet on it," I said.

CHAPTER 10

I would have made a fortune if I had.

Because no matter where I went in the museum, Cal was there. Every exhibit, every hallway, even the goddamn planetarium show.

"This is ridiculous," he said, standing at the end of the aisle, looking at me.

"It's not my fault that you keep following me," I said.

"Ha," he said and sat right next to me.

I raised my eyebrows.

"I'm not moving," he said. "I'm exhausted. I've been chasing a pop star around the museum all day."

"Ha," I said.

The silence wasn't awkward, but it wasn't *not* awkward either. The armrest between us remained conspicuously untouched, while we both leaned away from each other as if sharing the same general space might cause us to burst into flames.

The lights went down in the planetarium, and I leaned back in my seat to look upward at the rounded ceiling, now illuminated with the swirls of galaxies and endless stars. In another life, this could pass for a very romantic date. Stargazing without the cold and discomfort of being under the actual sky. After all, no one had ever accused me of being the outdoorsy type.

As a low, deep voice intoned about the big bang and the cosmic calendar, I found my attention wandering to the man sitting to my right.

I remembered another night, the two of us, side by side in a dark theater, watching exciting and brilliant images flash across the screen. We hadn't been as nervous about touching back then. But it had all been so innocent. As far as we'd known.

So much time had passed.

I couldn't help looking over at Cal, his face mostly in darkness, but just enough light to trace his profile, which annoyingly remained as appealing as ever.

Where had he been all these years? Sure, I'd filled in some of the blanks from articles and interviews and announcements, but the truth was that I really didn't know what had brought him here, to this moment.

I barely paid attention to the show, my mind going over all the miscellaneous tidbits I knew about Cal, trying to put together a picture of who he was now. But the truth was, I was missing too many pieces to assemble anything.

The lights came up and we both sat there, waiting for everyone else to leave.

"I'm going to look at those big dioramas," I said. "The ones with elephants and stuff."

Cal's shoulders sagged slightly.

"What?" I asked.

"That's where I was going to go," he said, somewhat sheepishly.

Of course.

"It's fine," he said. "I'll go look at the dinosaurs again."

We'd already run into each other there right before passing each other in the Hall of Birds.

"Don't be silly," I said. "Surely we can look at stuffed animals together without attempting to throttle each other."

We'd slow danced together, after all.

He lifted an eyebrow. "Can we?"

"I promise to try," I said.

He raised his pinky and wiggled it at me. I rolled my eyes, but hooked my pinky to his anyway. I ignored all the shimmering, shaky sensations that came from just that brief contact. Weird how it somehow felt even more intimate than dancing together. We both blew on our thumbs and released the other.

We walked toward the Hall of African Mammals.

"So," I said.

"So," he said.

"You were *dared* to audition for CrushZone?"

He chuckled. "Whitney likes to take credit for my fifteen minutes of fame, but it didn't take that much convincing."

"You always did love the spotlight," I said.

Cal snorted. "Yeah. Exactly." He put his hands in his pockets. "It was more like, why not?"

"Why not what?"

"Why not audition," he said.

"Did Whitney dare you to direct a Broadway show too?" I asked. "Another 'why not' situation?"

The question was a little too pointed to be taken as anything but an accusation.

Cal was quiet for a moment.

"Someone once told me I'd be good at directing," he said.

My face grew warm with shame.

"I worked really hard to get to this point," he said. "I took any and all jobs that I thought would give me the kind of experience I needed. Music videos, live shows, whatever I could get."

"Do you still dance?" I asked. "For fun?"

Cal cast me a sideways glance.

"Sometimes," he said.

It wasn't fair how that single word—and its implications—sent electric thrills up and down my spine. Because it had always been a joy to watch Cal dance. He was someone who knew exactly what his body was capable of. Who knew how to move it.

"I mostly help other people," he said. "Take what they can do and try to put it in the best light. Make them look good."

"I saw the movie," I said without thinking.

But then again, who hadn't? It had been a big deal—the first American cast as James Bond—and Cal had choreographed the opening scene. A waltz that *everyone* had been talking about.

For good reason, I could grudgingly admit to myself. The dance *had* been sexy as fuck.

Cal looked a little too pleased with himself. "Oh, you did, did you?"

I scrunched up my face at him. "I was bored."

"Mm-hmm," he said.

Cal didn't need to know that I'd seen it more than once. Bad enough that I'd confessed to seeing it at all.

"My big break," he said, but it wasn't prideful. If anything, it was a little bashful.

It annoyed me.

"Yeah," I said. "Lucky you."

Because, of course, Cal had gotten that break. That chance. He'd managed to escape the scandal without too many scars and had continued on doing the kinds of things that others dreamed about.

The air between us changed. What had been casual and somewhat cordial now became tense and fraught. Because it was impossible to talk about the past without talking about *The Past*. Or around it, as we were doing now.

Cal's jaw was tight.

"Look—" he said, as if he was gearing up to say something more. As if he wanted to really get into it.

"I've seen enough," I said, interrupting him before he could.

Because as annoyed as I was now, I had a feeling it would be a thousand times worse if I had to stand there and listen to Cal try to justify why he'd let me take all the heat back then. Why he'd felt emboldened to walk away without a second glance, to continue working with Ryan, to pretend like he was removed from it all.

I didn't want to hear him say "You have to understand" or "Things were complicated" or "I had my sisters to think about." Even if all of it was true, it didn't matter.

"I'm going to go," I said.

"Okay," he said.

It was better this way. We'd gotten too close to the fire. Pretending like we could chat about the good old times as if we were just friends catching up. We weren't. There was too much history. Too much anger.

And I had to stay away from that—from those memories—if I wanted to survive the workshop.

"Thanks for . . ." Cal trailed off.

I wasn't sure I wanted to know what he'd planned on saying.

"Yeah," I said, and headed toward the exit.

THEN

CHAPTER 11

"No one gets my costume," I shouted over the music.

"What?" Ryan shouted back.

"My costume! No one understands what it is!"

He paused his dancing and looked at me. Frowned.

"What *are* you dressed as?" he shouted.

I sighed, but of course he didn't hear it. I didn't even hear it.

It was time for a dance break anyway. I was sweating up a storm and incredibly thirsty. I just found it hard to stop when the DJ kept playing such good music.

I gestured that I was going to leave the dance floor and get something to drink. Ryan followed me. It was a little quieter over by the bar, thankfully.

We were at some enormous, beautiful apartment in the seventh arrondissement, with gilded wallpaper and chandeliers and gorgeous winding staircases. I thought about the brownstone in Brooklyn that I'd just bought, how I was going to need to fill it with a bed and a couch and plates and silverware and all the kinds of things that homes usually had.

I'd been on the road or living out of hotels for years now. My financial planner had said that buying property was a good investment, and he was urging me to buy another place, or possibly two.

"Always good to have a house in Los Angeles," he said. "And then, somewhere fun. Or secluded. There are ranches in Montana that you can get for a good price."

But what was I going to do with a ranch in Montana?

I could pay off my parents' mortgage, buy my sister a place of her own, but I knew that even offering would leave me feeling disappointed. My relationship with my family could best be described as "respectfully indifferent." The less we spoke—and saw each other—the better we all got along.

Harriet was standing with some of the other CrushZone guys. They'd been given costumes by their management—all five of them were dressed as old-school horror movie monsters. Ryan was Frankenstein, Cal was a mummy, Wyatt was a werewolf, Mason was Dracula, and LC was the Phantom of the Opera.

"Where's Cal?"

Wyatt jerked a thumb toward the other side of the room.

"Being smarter than all of us," he said.

Cal had his hand up against the wall, leaning and grinning down at a gorgeous Parisian girl dressed all in black.

"Is that one of the waitresses?" Harriet asked.

The jealousy I felt was very inappropriate. Why should I care if Cal was flirting? He was single. He had the right.

"I'm bored," Mason said. "I'm getting out of here."

"Me too," LC said.

"Want to share a cab?"

"Sure."

They didn't invite anyone else, but I could tell that Wyatt and Ryan had no intention of leaving. Ryan, for one, was waiting for a chance to talk to a big movie exec who had attended with his extremely young girlfriend. She was dressed as a cat. He wasn't wearing a costume.

"He's getting champagne." Ryan grabbed my arm.

He'd spent most of our time on the dance floor trying to position me so I'd "accidentally" bump into one of them. Luckily my balance was way too good for that to work.

"Now's your chance, dude," Wyatt said.

"Yeah?" Ryan asked.

"Sure," Wyatt said.

Ryan squared his shoulders and headed toward the exec, his awkward gait working well with his Frankenstein costume.

Wyatt also wandered off, but I didn't ask where he was going. I'd found that the fewer questions you asked Wyatt, the better off you'd be. No doubt he was trying to find his own Parisian waitress to help him pass the time.

"Are you having fun?" I asked Harriet.

"Totally," she said. "You?"

"So much," I said.

I looked at her. She looked at me.

We both burst out laughing.

"I miss the way we used to spend Halloween," she said.

Back when I was on *Show N Tell*, I'd had a tiny apartment in Washington Heights, but I was rarely there. If I wasn't recording the show, I was at Harriet's in Harlem with my de facto New York family.

"Our musical movie marathons?" I asked. "The nerdiest way to spend Halloween?"

We'd spent every Halloween together until I became Katee Rose and started touring all the time.

"The *best* way to spend Halloween," she said. "Staying up all night, stopping only to answer the door for trick-or-treaters."

"It was fun," I said. "But this is fun too."

"Yeah," she said.

But it was clear that she wasn't having as good a time as I was.

I felt bad—I wanted her to enjoy herself, but I also knew that no matter what I did, Harriet would probably always feel like an interloper in my world.

Not that my world was great one hundred percent of the time. I didn't love getting chased by paparazzi while trying to buy tampons or being unable to eat a full meal without the tabloids suggesting that I was pregnant or just getting fat.

But there was something intoxicating about fame. About the power it gave you.

Like at this party. I belonged, without having to do anything. I just walked into a room, and everyone wanted to talk to me.

It was weird, and the truth was, I was more comfortable onstage than off, but I liked the attention. I liked being known.

"We should have chosen different costumes," I said.

I'd thought I was being so clever. A black fedora, men's black coat, black tights, and black heels. I'd looked in the mirror and seen Judy in *Summer Stock*.

"Everyone thinks it's some sort of *Risky Business* reference," I said.

"Yeah," Harriet said. "Try hearing that there's no such thing as a Black Dorothy."

I looked at her. "Has no one seen *The Wiz*?"

"Apparently not," she said.

"Well, I think you look great," I said.

"Likewise," she said.

We stood there, on the outskirts of the party. Ryan had managed to corner the film exec and seemed to be doing a great job charming him. There was laughter and backslapping and handshaking.

Somehow Wyatt had ended up behind the bar and was lining up shots for guests. How he managed to get all these glamorous Parisians in their glittery, sparkling masquerade-like costumes to throw back tequila shots, I'd never know. Such was the mystery and power of Wyatt.

I looked around for Cal and his waitress, but they had disappeared from their cozy corner. That jealous feeling returned, gnawing at my stomach. Or maybe that was just hunger. I hadn't eaten much today. There had been a few too many images of me lately where I looked bloated. It was just easier to skip a meal or two, especially when I knew I was at risk of getting photographed.

"Do you want to go back to the hotel and watch some TV in French?" Harriet asked.

I was torn. On the one hand, I could tell Harriet was kind of bored, but on the other, I knew that this was a rare opportunity. For both of us. How many times in a life did one get to attend a fancy Halloween party at an expensive Parisian apartment while on a worldwide tour? And I wanted to share all the perks and benefits of my job with my best friend.

"You guys aren't leaving, are you?"

Cal had appeared out of nowhere. He was alone.

"We were thinking about it," Harriet said. "No one gets our costumes."

"Judy Garland and Dorothy," Cal said. "Thematic. Nice." Harriet shrugged.

"How about another kind of party?" Cal asked.

"What kind?" Harriet asked.

"The kind you'd like," he said. "I promise."

"Where's your friend?" I asked, unable to keep the jealousy at bay.

Cal gave me and Harriet an eyebrow wiggle. "At the other party," he said.

Suddenly *this* party seemed good enough.

"I don't know," I said. "We can't just leave Ryan."

We all looked over toward the other side of the room where Ryan had been. He was gone.

"I think he left with that movie exec," Cal said.

I wasn't really surprised, and I couldn't blame Ryan. I knew he had big plans—plans that went beyond CrushZone— and he was always looking for opportunity. Sometimes I felt like I should do the same, but the truth was it was exhausting enough being Katee Rose. At least Ryan had the other guys; they didn't all have to be *on* all the time. There was just one of me.

Plus, no one ever seemed to comment on Ryan's weight or Cal's hair or Wyatt's cold sores.

"Come on," Cal said. "Elizabeth said it would be a good time. I promise you'll love it."

I really didn't want to go and hang out at another party

with Cal and his paramour, but I glanced over at Harriet, and she was already nodding eagerly. Even though I knew she'd be fine if I told her that I wanted to stay here or go back to the hotel, I could tell that she'd prefer to see more of Paris.

"Fine," I said. "Let's go."

* * *

The annoying thing about Cal was that he was usually right.

"This. Is. Awesome," Harriet said.

Elizabeth, the waitress, had finished her shift, ushered us into a cab, and taken us to a movie theater in a far less fancy part of the city.

"You know the show?" she asked.

"*Rocky Horror*?" Harriet asked. "Uh, yeah. We know it."

"Très bien," Elizabeth said. "Then you know what to expect."

I didn't. Because even though I knew the show—what musical theatre kid didn't—I'd only seen the movie at home. And it turned out that watching it live in a theater with an audience was a completely different experience.

Harriet gave me the rundown. Not only were there going to be actors onstage dressed up as the characters, but there was a whole call-and-response thing—with props! Plus the entire thing was in French.

Not a single person seemed to recognize me. The theater was crowded, and Elizabeth had disappeared after getting us situated. I didn't realize that she'd given Cal a bag of props until he passed me and Harriet some pieces of toast.

"I'm not hungry," I said.

A lie. I was starving.

"It's for the show," Harriet said. "You throw it at the screen."

"What? Why?"

Cal shrugged. "It's just part of the fun. When Frank-N-Furter says 'toast,' you throw bread. But I guess in French it would be *pain,* maybe?"

"Where did you learn all this?" I asked.

"NYU would do *Rocky Horror* every Halloween," he said. "It was run by all the theatre kids who didn't want to do Shakespeare and Ibsen."

"Fordham did it too," Harriet said. "It's a lot more fun live. And a lot raunchier."

I felt a twinge of envy. I didn't regret not going to college, but there were times—when Cal or Harriet would mention things they'd done or memories they shared—when I felt left out. Not just from their conversation but from life. From all the things young adults were expected to do.

Because even though they hadn't gone to the same college, there were times when their experiences seemed so parallel that it was hard to believe it wasn't universal. Or supposed to be universal.

What kind of person would I have been if I'd gone to college? If I'd gone to *Rocky Horror* every Halloween with my friends? If I'd been that kind of theatre kid?

But there was no point in wondering. That hadn't been my life.

Instead of morning classes, I'd had early call times. Instead of spring break, I went on tour. Instead of school dances, I went to award shows.

I didn't regret it. This is what I wanted. What I'd always wanted.

We were in Paris for fuck's sake. *Paris.*

The best hotels. The best food. The most exclusive experiences.

I was the reason we were here watching *Rocky Horror* in the first place. I was the reason we were watching Tim Curry on-screen—and a look-alike onstage—strut around while a room of people screamed at the screen in French. I didn't realize until she came out onstage in an enormous red wig and a completely different waitress outfit that Cal's date was in the show as well.

And experiencing it live was absolutely the best way to see it.

The audience was raucous and vocal. Despite being given the heads-up about audience participation, I didn't expect the extremely explicit callbacks that were constantly being shouted at the screen. Thankfully, both Cal and Harriet would shout them out in English, so I at least understood what was going on, but also, I didn't.

"What's the deal with all the blow job jokes?" I asked. "And calling Brad an asshole and Janet a slut?"

Cal glanced over at me. "It's part of the show," he said.

"But why?"

Cal thought about it for a moment.

"That's above my pay grade," he said. "It's just the way it is."

I supposed that was the "cult" part of "cult classic." But though I didn't understand the origin of or meaning behind most of the jokes, it didn't matter. I was still having a blast, and participating whenever I could.

"This is awesome," I said.

"I thought you'd like it," Cal said.

"Did you ever perform?"

Cal's expression was one of adorable embarrassment.

"Oh my god, you did!" I gave him a gentle punch in the arm. "Who were you? Frank-N-Furter? Brad? Meat Loaf?"

He said something, but I couldn't hear over the audience's chant of "Say it! Say it! Say it!" or rather, "Dis-le! Dis-le! Dis-le!" as Tim Curry spent three years saying the word "anticipation."

"What?"

"I might have been Rocky," Cal said.

I turned my entire body toward him.

"Excuse me?"

He was looking at the floor. Very much not looking at me.

"You were Rocky?" I asked.

He nodded.

"In the . . . ?"

He nodded again.

"And nothing else?"

One more nod.

"Wow," I said.

Because now all I could think about was Cal onstage, wearing a tiny, shiny gold Speedo.

"That's . . . well . . . good for you," I said.

When I was really thinking: *Do you have any pictures?*

His costume had been unraveling—literally—throughout the evening. Now, it was mostly around his shoulders and his waist, his face free. Someone had given him the appearance of sunken eyes by smearing dark eyeliner beneath them, his face paler than usual with the help of powder.

He was really cute, especially when he was embarrassed. As if he could tell I was imagining him in his Rocky costume.

"It's not a big deal," he said.

"Oh sure," I said. "Not a big deal at all."

"Shut up," he said.

I stuck my tongue out at him. He did the same to me.

I was about to say something else, but the screen—or rather, the faux redhead in front of the screen—grabbed his attention, and he gave my leg a squeeze before turning back to the show.

The warmth of his hand and that smile of his stayed with me through the rest of the evening, even after he and Elizabeth dropped Harriet and me off at the hotel before disappearing into the night to have their own fun.

NOW

CHAPTER 12

I hated this stupid number. It had too many kicks, too many turns, too many fancy fucking steps.

And that wasn't the worst of it.

If the workshop went well, and we moved to out-of-town tryouts, we'd be doing all that damned choreography on a moving conveyor belt. Because Cal was a sadist.

At least I wasn't the only one struggling with it.

"Jesus fucking Christ," Melissa said.

We were both bent over, hands on our knees, wheezing like a pair of broken bagpipes.

"Is he insane?" she asked.

"Yes," I said.

We'd been working on the number all day and had yet to get through it without a mistake.

"I mean, I'd been warned that he had high standards but *whew*," Melissa said.

"He's a monster," I said.

"Yeah," Melissa said, but the look she gave him wasn't one you'd give a monster. There was no loathing, just admiration. "It's going to be great, though."

"If we get it," I said.

"You'll get it," Cal said.

I hadn't noticed him come up behind us.

"Shall we go over it again?" he asked. "Slower this time?"

"Yes, please," Melissa said.

"We're fine," I said.

"It's okay to ask for help, Kathleen," Cal said.

"I'll be sure to keep that in mind," I said. "When I need help."

I was being stubborn and ridiculous, but I couldn't bear the thought of Cal pitying me. Of him thinking I needed special treatment. Because the truth was, I *knew* I could do this number. It was complicated and it was exhausting but it wasn't impossible. I'd done far more intricate choreography as Katee Rose, and I'd done it under less encouraging circumstances.

"Let's take a break, then," Cal said.

"Fine," I said.

I went to get some water from my bag. He followed me.

"Remember the 'Give It to Me' video?" he asked.

He'd lowered his voice, leaning up against the mirrored wall but not looking at me. Instead he watched the rest of the cast and team take a break—stretch, get water, check their phones.

"Are you fucking kidding me?" I asked.

"Give It to Me" had been my biggest hit, and the music video had won countless awards and played almost nonstop for weeks. *Everyone* had seen it.

I'd like to think it was because of the complicated choreography, but I knew it was really because I'd been doing all of it underneath a waterfall in a white dress. I'd practiced that number for days, intent on making it perfect, only to spend the day soaking wet and shivering while the director ordered the camera operator to get enough close-ups of my tits and ass.

That's what people remembered about that video. All the wet jiggling my body had done.

"That choreography was twice as hard as this," Cal said. "And you get to do it in dry clothes."

"I'd rather re-create 'Give It to Me' naked in the middle of Times Square than do this number one more time," I said.

The look Cal gave me indicated that he was imagining it. I told myself the shiver I got was unrelated.

"You still remember it?" Cal asked.

"Yes."

Maybe.

"Do you have a problem with my choreography, Kathleen?"

"No," I said.

Yes.

"How about this," he said. "If we can't get it right after tonight, we'll give that old number a shot."

"Over my dead body," I said.

"That's my girl," he said.

I glared at him.

"What are you trying to prove, Cal?"

He raised an eyebrow.

"You're not Bob Fosse or Jerome Robbins," I said. "You don't need to kill your actors to make yourself feel like a real director."

It was a low blow, but I was tired and sore and extremely, extremely annoyed.

"Funny," he said. "Because I was just going to say that you don't need to act like a fucking diva to feel like a real actor."

A throat cleared.

Cal and I turned to find Harriet standing in front of us.

"Yes?" Cal asked.

"Oh, I'm sorry," Harriet said. "Am I interrupting something?"

"Actually—"

"Because what it looks like to the rest of the room is the two of you standing here and bickering like a pair of very bitter squirrels."

I took a quick glance around the space, and the way that everyone's eyes—which had been focused on us—darted away indicated that Harriet was right. Everyone was watching us fight.

"We were just discussing choreography," Cal said.

Harriet crossed her arms.

"We *are*," I said.

"Which is apparently too difficult for our leading lady," Cal said.

"Because Cal here thinks he's Michael fucking Kidd," I said.

"Maybe you should be grateful I'm not making you do this with axes," he said.

"Maybe *you* should be grateful that I don't have a sharp object in my hand right now."

"Jesus," Harriet said.

We looked at her.

"Are you kidding me?" she asked. "Grow. The. Fuck. Up. Both of you."

There was nothing like being chastised by your best friend. Especially when she was right. It was a bad look to be fighting with the director in front of the cast. It made me seem like a diva and made Cal look like he couldn't control me. Which he couldn't, but the illusion was important to the power dynamics of this whole situation.

"This whole combative thing isn't as cute as you think it is," Harriet said. "It's embarrassing and unprofessional."

Both Cal and I hung our heads.

"Sorry," I said.

"Sorry," Cal said.

"Don't be sorry," Harriet said. "Be adults."

She stalked off. I realized, looking back at Cal, that we had moved progressively closer and closer to each other. If I turned to face him, our noses would be practically touching.

I took several steps back.

"Okay!" Cal clapped his hands, addressing the whole room. "We're going to go again. From the top."

He looked back at me.

"Ready?" he asked.

No apologies. No concessions. Fine. He wanted to work? I could work.

I gave him the biggest Katee Rose smile I could muster.

"Ready," I said.

CHAPTER 13

I still wasn't getting it. I knew the steps, but I couldn't make my body do them fast enough. Every time I tried, I seemed to miss a step. I knew it looked sloppy and unprofessional, and I was trying my best, but it just wasn't working.

It was especially embarrassing because today was the day that the producers had decided to come in to watch a rehearsal. I kept fucking up the number and now had to face the unsmiling, gray-tufted Statler and Waldorf, who I could practically see recasting my role in their heads.

"Let's take five and reset," Cal said, and headed straight toward me.

I liked being special in most situations, but not this one. I didn't want him to think I needed hand-holding. Especially since I did.

"How's it going?" he asked.

I narrowed my eyes at him.

"Just peachy," I said.

He hummed and nodded.

I waited. Adjusted my weight.

"Cal?"

"Hmmm?"

"Spit it out," I said. "Whatever you're trying to say, just say it."

He offered the floor a crooked smile. One dimple.

I stood there, hands on my hips, waiting for him to tell me the truth. That I was fucking up and it was his job to tell me that it wasn't acceptable. That I needed to get my shit together.

"I know you're doing your best," Cal said.

I stared at him.

"I've been thinking about what you said yesterday, and you're right," he said. "The number is too complicated."

Shock wasn't even the right word.

"I've worked on an alternative," he said. "Take out that last turn and the kick-ball-change in the middle. That should give everyone enough time to hit their marks."

Not everyone. Me.

"I know it's not ideal, changing something at the last minute, but I know you all can handle it."

He turned his whole body to face me.

"What do you think?" he asked.

It took a moment for me to compose my thoughts.

"I think it's bullshit," I said.

Cal blinked. "Excuse me?"

"It's not the number," I said. "It's not the steps. It's me. I'm not getting them. I'm screwing up."

His eyebrows were halfway up his forehead.

"You should be telling me to get my shit together and be prepared to rehearse the number until my feet bleed," I said.

He was quiet for a moment.

"I'm not going to do that," he said, voice low. "I'm not Ms. Spiegel or Diana. I'm not going to threaten you."

"Maybe you should," I said. "Because this whole Mr. Nice Director thing? It's not getting results."

He crossed his arms.

"How about this," he said. "You don't tell me how to direct and I'll let you continue to embarrass yourself with a sequence that is clearly out of your range."

I gritted my teeth.

"I don't want your pity choreography," I said.

Cal sighed.

"Jesus, Kathleen," he said. "I'm not doing this out of pity."

I wanted to believe him.

"I can do the number," I said. "As is."

"You can't," he said.

"I can," I said.

"There's not enough time," he said.

"One more try," I said. "If I can't get it then I'll give up."

Cal pinched the bridge of his nose between his fingers. "It's not giving up," he said. "I'm trying to help you."

I narrowed my eyes at him.

"That's the problem," I said. "I don't want your help. I don't want special treatment."

Cal looked at me like I was crazy. Maybe I was.

"It's not special treatment," he said.

"Really?" I asked. "Are you changing the choreography for anyone else?"

He was silent.

"I can do it," I said. "One more try."

Cal pointed a finger at me. "One more try," he said. "If it doesn't work, then maybe you could trust me? Let me direct for once?"

I snorted. "Please," I said. "We all know you're the boss."

"Sometimes I wonder," he said.

He glanced across the room and seemed to catch the attention of Statler. Or Waldorf. I could barely tell the producers apart and just thought of them as interchangeable. Like the real Muppets.

Cal sighed.

"One minute," he said. "And then we're going from the top."

"I'll be ready," I said.

The moment he walked away, and my indignation faded, I realized what an absolute idiot I was being. What was I trying to prove? I wasn't in my twenties anymore. I wasn't the workhorse I'd prided myself on being during my first decades. Why couldn't I let Cal give me a break? Why couldn't I accept that I needed help?

All very good questions for a therapist. I made a mental note to schedule an appointment.

The break ended and I shoved my water bottle back into my bag. Closing my eyes for a brief moment, I shook out my hands, trying to focus. I went over the choreography in my head once more, my feet tapping out a quick and dirty version of it.

I knew I could do it. I knew I could.

We took our places. Smiled. The music started.

And I missed my cue.

It was like my feet had disconnected from my brain. Not only did I *not* get the problem steps right, but I fucked up a bunch more. I tried to keep my gaze away from the mirror, but it was impossible to ignore the half-lame giraffe floundering in the middle.

Thankfully, every time I glanced over at the producers, they were both looking down at their phones.

It ended and I wanted to cry.

I'd never felt this way before. If anything, I was the perfectionist, the one who got things done. I'd performed with the flu, with a sore throat, with a sprained ankle, with back pain and knee pain. I'd performed after red-eye flights, after days on the road, after nights where I didn't sleep.

That was my superpower—put me onstage and I flourished.

Not anymore, it seemed.

I'd lost the magic. Lost the part of myself that made me special. That made me worthwhile.

Cal came over, but I just stared at the floor. I couldn't look him in the eye.

"You win," I said, head down.

"It's not a competition," he said. "We're on the same team."

"Ha," I said.

"Kathleen—"

"It's fine." I pushed my hair back and smiled, focusing on his left ear so I wouldn't have to see my own disappointment reflected back at me from Cal's eyes. "Just give me a moment and then we can do the new choreography."

I didn't wait for him to respond. I went to the bathroom, cried a single tear, splashed water on my face, and came back ready to work.

CHAPTER 14

I made it through the rest of rehearsal without a mistake. The whole thing was a blur, as I had long detached from my body and was floating above myself, buoyant with shame and embarrassment.

All I wanted was to go home, soak my muscles, and collapse onto the couch so Fish could stand on my stomach and look down at me with well-won superiority. It was late. I was exhausted and disappointed.

Thankfully, Cal was still chatting with the producers, so I was able to get out of there with nothing more than a half-wave and no eye contact. I didn't want to talk to anyone, but most especially not Cal. It was bad enough that he had been right, I didn't need to discuss it.

With my bag slung over my shoulder, I headed toward the elevator, already mentally running through my trip back, how many blocks, how many subway stops. Tonight it felt like I lived in the Bronx. Like I'd never get home.

I leaned up against the wall of the elevator. Usually, I'd take the stairs, but I wasn't just physically exhausted, I was mentally drained as well. I desperately needed a good cry, but I also wasn't in the mood for the soggy aftermath, swollen eyes, and sore throat.

The elevator doors dinged and opened.

"Fuck," I said.

Rachel was standing there.

Does the elevator go straight to hell?

"Hello to you," she said.

I stepped out of the elevator, expecting her to get in and leave. Instead, she just stood there and let the door close.

"How are you?" she asked.

It sounded like an innocent question, but I knew better.

"Living my best life," I said.

It probably would have been more convincing if my voice hadn't cracked halfway through.

Rachel's smile was smug.

"I hope you're enjoying your time on the production," she said.

There was an ominous tone to her words. I didn't say anything. Clearly there was something she wanted to tell me, and I wasn't going to get in her way.

"Though I am hearing you're having some trouble with some of the numbers," she said, looking at her nails.

I didn't know where she'd gotten that information, but I could guess.

"I've actually seen the choreography," Rachel said. "It's not that hard. I could help you if you wanted."

"No. Thanks," I said through gritted teeth.

She shrugged. "Suppose it doesn't really matter," she said.

"It's just a workshop. And so much can change between now and out-of-town tryouts."

I crossed my arms.

"And well, Broadway is a whole different story," Rachel said. "But I guess you wouldn't really know about that, would you?"

"Remind me," I said. "How many Broadway shows have *you* starred in?"

Her cheeks went fuchsia. There was no shame in being in the chorus, or being a featured performer—both things that I knew Rachel had done. But I also knew she was aiming for my soft underbelly. It seemed only fair that I do the same.

Strangely, though, it didn't make me feel better.

Was that growth? Or was I just *that* tired?

"There's a first time for everything," Rachel said.

I was done with this dumb cat and mouse game.

"What are you doing here, Rachel?"

New York was a small town, but it wasn't that small. She was clearly here for a reason. Just like at the audition.

"Oh, just picking up my sweetie for dinner," she said. "He's the one who keeps me updated on the show . . . and the cast."

I didn't like surprises and this one was a fucking doozy.

"Well, isn't that nice," I said.

Fucking Cal.

It was one thing to be dating Rachel—no doubt he'd kept it a secret because Harriet would have been just as disappointed—but it was quite another to be sharing details of the production with her.

I could only imagine their pillow talk.

"He keeps telling me to keep my dance shoes ready." Rachel paused and gave me a faux thoughtful look. "It's funny. How karma works."

I sucked in a breath through my nose.

"Seriously?" I asked.

She shrugged. "I didn't think I'd have to wait this long, but c'est la vie."

"You're still blaming me for what happened at camp? When we were kids?"

"Oh, come now," Rachel said. "Just admit it was you."

"I would," I said. "If that was true."

Rachel tsked. "Sad," she said. "All this denial."

"You broke the rules on your own," I said.

"What goes around comes around," Rachel said.

I was finished talking to her. "I'm going to leave now."

"Always a pleasure," she said. "Toodles."

It was a little cool outside, but it wasn't the weather that was giving me chills. I walked to the train station, my brain buzzing, sorting through all this new information.

"We're on the same team," Cal had said.

Like fucking hell we were.

I felt foolish. I should have known better. No doubt, now that I'd acquiesced to the less complicated steps, Cal had proof—real tangible examples—of how I was falling short. He could bring Rachel in—have her nail the choreography—and just like that, I'd be out, and she'd be in.

She'd get her misplaced sense of revenge and Cal would get to destroy my career. Again.

Well.

Fuck that.

Fuck Cal's behind-the-scenes machinations. Fuck his "I'm not like other directors" schtick. Fuck our truce.

I stewed and simmered. Through dinner. Through my

bath. I got in bed, took an edible, and watched Jinkx Monsoon YouTube clips in hopes that they would calm me down.

They didn't.

If anything, the combination of the weed and the bottle of wine I then opened made me angrier.

Cal never intended for me to go with the show to Broadway. He had made me jump through the humiliating hoops of auditioning—which he tried to sabotage by throwing an unrehearsed song request at me—and was now undermining me with this whole choreography bullshit.

He wanted to push me out and replace me with Rachel James.

In the back of my head, I could hear the voice of reason. That Harriet would never let him do such a thing. That Rachel was a liar out for revenge. That I was just having a bad day and I needed to sleep it off and start over again.

Unfortunately, that last glass of wine had all but drowned out my voice of reason. All I had left was the voice of anger and vengeance. She was very loud. And very persistent.

I didn't even know what time it was when I picked up the phone and dialed his number.

"Kathleen?" Cal sounded like he'd been asleep. "It's two in the morning."

"Oh, I'm sorry," I said. "Did I wake you and Rachel up?"

The thought of her sleeping next to him . . . her arms around him . . . his around her . . .

"What are you talking about?"

"It doesn't matter," I said. "Look. I'm going to make your fucking night, okay?"

"Kathleen—"

"I'm out."

There was a long silence.

"Excuse me?" he sounded wide-awake now.

Good.

I was feeling a bit hazy, but it didn't matter. I'd set this train in motion. Time to send it off a cliff.

"I said I'm out."

"You're joking," he said.

"Nope," I said. "And you're welcome, okay? I know what you've been doing. I know your plan. I'm going to make it easy for you. I'm out. I'm done. I'm so fucking done. You can have the show you want, the cast you want, all of it. I'll get out of your way because the truth is, I'd rather teach kids with no rhythm and two left feet how to dance than spend another day being criticized by you."

I sounded crazy. I knew I did. I also didn't care. I didn't care about anything but hurting Cal.

"I'm going to hang up," Cal said. "You've clearly gone insane and I'm going to do both of us a favor and pretend this conversation didn't happen."

"I'm DONE!" I shouted at him. "I'm not going to Rhode Island. I'm not going to Broadway. Wake Rachel and tell her she wins. She fucking wins."

"You're nuts," Cal said. "And drunk or high or something."

"That's beside the point," I said.

He groaned. "Good night, Kathleen."

"Fuck you, Cal," I said, but he had already hung up.

CHAPTER 15

I woke up to a pounding headache. And someone pounding on the door.

I didn't need to look through the peephole to know who it was.

"You better be sick, Kathleen," Cal said from the other side. "You'd better have food poisoning or a stomach flu and be throwing up and delirious because that's the only acceptable reason for calling me in the middle of the night and telling me that you quit."

Do it, I told myself. *Tell him you ate a bad sandwich. Tell him you don't even remember last night. Tell him what he wants to hear.*

And I would have. Except, through the door, I heard him say, "I knew it. I fucking knew this was a mistake."

I yanked the door open.

Cal gave me a long, searching look.

"Not delirious," he said. "Not sick."

"Not talking to you," I said.

But before I could slam the door, he'd slapped his palm against it and pushed it all the way open, letting himself in.

"I'm not doing the show," I said, taking out a metaphorical shovel and digging myself even deeper into the self-destructive hole I'd already begun.

"The fuck you aren't," he said. "You signed a contract."

"Get out," I said.

"You can't do this, Kathleen," he said. Slowly. Evenly. Like he was speaking to a child.

"I quit," I said, slamming the door because I had to slam something, even though he was still on the wrong side of it. "You can't make me do anything."

He sighed. Long and slow.

"Actually, I can," he said. "Did you read the contract before you signed it?"

My face—and anger—flared hot.

"Of course I read the contract," I said. "I'm not a fucking idiot."

"Then you'll know that you can't just quit," he said.

"What are you going to do?" I taunted. "Toss me over your shoulder and drag me back to the rehearsal space?"

"Don't. Tempt. Me," he said.

It shouldn't have been hot. We were fighting. I was furious at him. For making me do this. For Rachel James. For making me think I was good enough.

And yet.

His fucking cologne. It was good. Very good.

I put my hands on his chest and pushed him back. He let me.

"What happened?" he asked, softening his voice. "What's going on?"

I hated the pity I heard. That careful, cautious "poor lost little girl" tone. I'd heard it so much as Katee Rose, especially in those last few months when no one could understand why I wouldn't just do what I was told. Why I couldn't.

But they were the same people who'd thought if I apologized—if I begged Ryan to take me back—if I laid myself at the mercy of the press, that things would be fine. Instead, I was sacrificed at the altar of public opinion and left for dead by the same people who said they'd protect me. Who said that everything would be okay.

Who said that they loved me.

"I ran into an old friend of yours," I said.

Cal's expression went from sympathetic to cautious. Then realization.

"I swear to God . . ." he said.

I could see Cal grit his teeth, the muscle in his jaw tensing.

"Oh no," I said. "You don't get to be the aggrieved one here."

"This is ridiculous," he said. "You can't think—"

"You lied to me, Cal," I said.

He looked up. "I did not."

"You said I was the only one you considered for the role," I said.

"And that is the truth."

"But she said—"

"I don't care what she said!" Cal said. "I don't care. She's jealous and defensive and an *actor*. You, on the other hand—"

"Not an actor, I suppose."

He let out a groan. "You're a fucking diva, that's for sure."

I growled at him.

"Don't even start," he said, pointing a finger at me. "You are being unprofessional, and you know it. You can't just quit a workshop like this. Do you have no concern for your fellow castmates, or me for that matter?"

"I'm so sorry, Mr. Director," I said.

"And what about Harriet?" he asked. "Did you think about her at all?"

I hadn't. But even my shame wasn't enough to calm me down.

"This is beneath you," he said.

"I heard that's where you like your leading ladies," I said. "Beneath you."

I couldn't help myself.

"Are you kidding me?" His voice was low. Dangerous.

I drew myself up to my highest height.

"Am I wrong?"

He stared at me, and I could tell that he was counting to ten in his mind. He was trying to calm down, but I didn't want that. I wanted a fight. A no-holds-barred, bare-knuckle, knock-down, drag-out fight.

Because we had one coming.

"She was certainly talking about you like she knew," I said.

"No," Cal said.

"No, you didn't sleep with her?"

"No, we're not doing this," he said.

Not a denial, but I hadn't really expected one.

He tried to leave, but I would not be rebuffed.

"Love this move of yours," I said. "Classic Cal. Walk away when things get hard. When they get complicated."

He stopped, shoulders tensed up to his ears.

"You really want to get into it, Kathleen?" he asked.

"I really do," I said.

"Fine," he said, looming over me, voice low. "You are acting like a spoiled little brat. You're rude, you're disrespectful and scared out of your goddamn mind."

"I'm not scared," I said.

But he was right. He was completely right.

"This is our chance," he said. "This is what I've—what *we've*—wanted to do since we were kids. Broadway. *Broadway.* And I want to do it with you. Because I think you're fucking great in this role. I think you're talented and smart and good. Just really good." He looked at me. "But you can't pull shit like this," he said. "Call me in the middle of the night. Threaten to quit."

Even his compliments couldn't cut through my anger—couldn't diffuse my impulse to be contrary to the point of destruction.

"Who said it was a threat?"

"For fuck's sake, Kathleen," he exploded. "This isn't some fucking game!"

His anger surprised me—knocked me back—because Cal was not someone who lost his temper. I'd watched him in rehearsal, watched him cope with the daily frustrations of dealing with actors. Nothing ever seemed to faze him.

Nothing except me.

I was gratified to see some of that calm peeling away. Because as good and powerful as my own anger felt, there was something to be said for bringing someone as measured as Cal down to my messy, fucked-up level. Again.

"I know it's not a game," I said.

"Then why are you acting this way?" he asked. "I know this isn't you."

"You don't know me, Cal," I said.

He ran his hand through his hair and let out a groan of frustration.

"You know," he said. "I wish I didn't."

Slapping me would have been just as effective.

"You need to grow the fuck up," he said. "You're part of a team now and you need to act like it. This isn't just about you. About *your* dreams. There are other people to think about."

That was a low blow.

"Fuck. You. Cal."

"Is this about what happened?" he asked. "Between us? Because I have to tell you, I got over it. I've been over it. You should do the same."

He reached behind me for the door, but I stopped him.

"*You're* over it?" I asked. "You can't be referring to what I think you're referring to."

He better fucking not be.

"You know what I'm talking about," he said. "Don't play dumb."

I sucked in a breath.

"Why don't you explain it to me." I moved closer to him. "Because I'm certain you're not talking about what happened all those years ago. I'm certain you're not telling *me* to get over it. Don't forget, you wanted it. You practically begged for it, *Cal State*."

The old nickname got him. He leaned down, his eyes narrowed, his nostrils flaring.

"I'm certain *I* wasn't the one begging," he said.

Desire whooshed through me—hot, intense, raw. And I knew he felt it. I could feel the electricity in the air, the way it felt before a storm. Every hair on my body lifted like I was weightless.

I licked my lips and Cal watched.

"I am not having this conversation with you," he said.

I wasn't scared. Even with his temper flaring, he was still Cal. And I knew exactly how to handle him. Or how to set him off.

"You can show up ready to work or just don't show up at all," he said.

"I thought you said I couldn't quit."

He got close, crowding me up against the door. His eyes kept dropping down to my mouth, his chest heaving with each breath he took. I felt my heart hammering in my throat.

"You can't," he said. "But I can sure as fuck fire you."

We were practically nose to nose. The smell of his cologne—of him—was overwhelming. Intoxicating. I wanted to fall into it. Wanted to lose myself in the scent of him. In him.

"You wouldn't dare," I said.

"Try me," he said.

I didn't know who moved first, but with my hand curled around the back of his neck, and his arm around my waist, our lips found each other's like a planned collision.

CHAPTER 16

It had been a long time since I'd kissed Calvin Kirby.

All those years ago, it had been a mess. Hands, mouths, tongues. Neither of us had really learned how to use all those body parts to our best abilities and the end result had been . . . well, it had been what it was.

But this?

This was something completely different. Something completely new.

It was *everything*.

I opened to him completely, my mouth, my arms. I drew him in as if I could swallow him whole, the touch of our tongues, the heat of our breath. Each kiss was the length of a heartbeat, we parted only to meet again.

His hands were in my hair, cradling my face, and that was Cal, that gentleness beneath all else. I hadn't appreciated it when I was young, hadn't known how rare it was.

But now I knew the beauty of tenderness and what it felt like in concert with my own wild need.

I dug my nails into his shoulders, dragged them down his chest before cupping his ass and pulling him to me.

My back hit the door, Cal pinning me there, but I needed him closer. I needed more. More. *More.*

His mouth found my throat and I found myself thanking whatever lovers he'd had between then and now, because this? This wasn't a boy unsure of himself. Fumbling and awkward and too ready. Too eager.

This was a man.

This was Cal and he knew what he wanted.

Me.

I forced his mouth back to mine, needing to taste him, needing to kiss him until he understood. Until he knew.

But before I could, he was already stepping back. Already pulling away.

I pressed my hands flat against the door as he stood in front of me. He was looking down at the floor, his shoulders rising and falling with each heavy breath, hands on his hips.

The silence between us seemed to stretch out into decades.

"Fuck," Cal said, a hand going back through his hair and then forward again, giving him a majestic, slightly ridiculous plume. "What the fuck was that?"

"I have no idea," I said, having exactly all the ideas. "I despise you."

"The feeling is mutual," he said.

We were both terrible liars.

"We can't do this," he said.

"*You* kissed *me,*" I said.

I wasn't even sure if that was correct, but we *had* been equal partners in what had just happened. This wasn't *my* fault.

Not this time.

"Fuck," he said. "I *know*."

He was making a real mess of his hair and part of me wanted to still his hand, but I wasn't sure what he'd do if I touched him right now. Probably kiss me again.

I raised my arm, and he took a step back.

"*No*," he said.

I glared at him, trying not to be hurt.

It very nearly worked.

"I'm sorry," he said.

"Please stop," I said. "This is awkward enough, okay?"

"I'm sorry."

"Cal!"

I could tell he wanted to say it again, but I fixed him with a stare strong enough that he shut his mouth and gave me a sheepish smile.

"Right," Cal said. "Okay. Well, I'm going to go."

"Okay," I said.

I stepped back so he could get to the door, making sure to keep plenty of distance between us. I had a feeling if I so much as brushed his arm with my elbow, we'd be naked and on the floor before either of us could think any better of it.

He opened the door and stopped. "Rehearsal," he said. "Ten o'clock."

"I'll be there," I said.

He gave me half of a smile. "Good," he said.

His fingers tapped on the door, hesitating. I thought once more about smoothing his hair down, not letting him go out into the world looking like he'd been manhandled, but I let it be.

"Ten o'clock," I said.

He nodded.

"Go," I said.

Another nod, and this time he stepped out onto my front stoop.

"Kathleen?"

"Hmm?"

"It was always your part," he said. "Always."

✧ CONFRONTATION ✧

I didn't get a solo. I didn't even get a duet.

"I'm sorry," Harriet said. "Competition was pretty tough this year."

I kept staring at the cast list, as if my name might suddenly appear up at the top, instead of down at the bottom where the rest of us were lumped into the chorus.

It was hard not to feel like all of my plans were falling apart. If I didn't have a solo or a duet, there was no way I'd be able to attract the attention of the scouts at the showcase. And if I didn't get their attention, that would be it. There was no way I'd get my parents to send me back here next summer. They already thought this experiment was a waste of time and money.

I swallowed back my feelings of unfairness.

Life was unfair, but showbiz even more so.

That's why someone like Rachel James, mean-spirited

and golden-voiced, not only got the end of show solo but also got to duet with Cal Kirby, baritone of my dreams.

We would have sounded so good together.

At least I was in the chorus with Harriet.

We walked back to our bunk, arms linked together.

I could tell that Harriet wasn't as disappointed.

"At least we'll have time to do other things," she said. "Rachel's going to be stuck inside rehearsing every day."

"Yeah," I said, even though that was what I wanted to do.

We turned the corner and all but ran into Rachel and the older girls. They were sitting on the front steps of their bunk, passing around a water bottle.

"Oh look," Rachel said. "It's the chorus."

Her laughter was a sloppy, sputtering cackle.

I felt Harriet's arm tense.

"How many summers have you been coming here?" Rachel came down toward us. Or toward Harriet. She barely acknowledged me. "Have you ever gotten a solo?"

Harriet didn't say anything, her head down.

"It's getting kind of pathetic," Rachel said. "Don't you think?"

Her friends laughed as Rachel took a long swig from her water bottle. She was close enough that I could tell that it wasn't water. She reeked of vodka, and she was swaying on her feet.

She was sixteen.

"If I were you," Rachel said, "I'd quit while I was ahead. Although—" She snickered. "You've never been ahead, have you?"

She lifted the water bottle like she was about to pour it on Harriet's head.

"Stop!" I said, and threw my hand out.

It made contact with Rachel's arm and the water bottle went flying, spraying vodka over all of us.

It went deadly quiet.

Rachel looked at us and then at the bottle, now lying in the dirt, its contents trickling out in a sad little stream. I could smell the alcohol on my skin, in my hair.

"What. The. Fuck," Rachel said.

"I can't believe you did that," one of her friends said.

"It's not like I was actually going to do it," Rachel said. Her smile was cruel. "I wouldn't waste it on someone like Harriet."

"Fuck you," I said.

I'd never said those words out loud. It felt good. Powerful.

Rachel narrowed her eyes and got real close to my face. My eyes watered at the smell.

"You're just like the others," she said. "Jealous."

She wasn't wrong, but I didn't respond.

"Come on, Kathleen." Harriet pulled at my arm. "Let's go."

"Yeah, Kathleen," Rachel mocked. "Run away."

I didn't want to, but I also didn't know what else to do. At least I'd ruined her night, just the way she'd ruined mine and Harriet's. Unless she planned on fishing that bottle out of the dirt, her drinking was over for the evening.

Harriet managed to drag me away, though I couldn't help looking back at Rachel and her friends—all of them laughing like hyenas—and wishing that she'd get what she deserved.

NOW

CHAPTER 17

There was only one place in New York that was perfect for celebrating a successful workshop showing. A tiny downstairs bar, with a low wooden ceiling, decorated with fairy lights, and a piano against one wall.

"How does it feel?" I asked Harriet, handing her a vodka cranberry with a straw.

She was looking around Marie's Crisis.

"Feels like coming home," she said.

"All hail the conquering hero," I said.

We tapped our plastic cups together.

Before I was truly famous, in between seasons of *Show N Tell,* Harriet and I would bring our fake IDs to the piano bar, our Friday nights spent singing show tunes along with the other patrons. During and after college, Harriet sat behind the ivories for the late-night shifts, taking requests and honing her playing skills.

"You should go back there," I said. "For old times' sake."

Harriet shook her head. "I'm celebrating tonight," she said. "Not working."

I couldn't put my finger on it, but something had been off between the two of us. On the surface we seemed fine, our usual best-friend-ness firmly in place. But at moments like this, just the two of us together, I could feel that we were out of sync.

It was subtle, but still disorienting.

We'd both been so busy over the past few weeks, and it seemed like the only thing we had to talk about was the show.

"You guys were great," Harriet said. "Everyone was talking about that number at the end of the first act."

The one with the retooled choreography.

"I'm just glad we got through it without any mistakes," I said.

Harriet nodded.

My stomach got this weird little cramp at her reaction. It was fine—nothing wrong at first glance—but we had been friends for over two decades. We'd just finished the first workshop of her first musical. We were going to leave for out-of-town tryouts in a week. It seemed very possible that our lives were going to change.

And Harriet could barely look me in the eye.

"It's going to be weird," I said. "Not going to the rehearsal studio anymore."

She wasn't paying attention, instead she was waving at Cal, who had just arrived.

"Congrats," he said. "Great showing."

"Thanks," I said.

I wanted to savor the praise, but I was distracted by Harriet's coldness. It also didn't help that everything had been extremely awkward and uncomfortable between me and Cal since the kiss.

A kiss I certainly wasn't constantly replaying over and over in my head.

The three of us just stood there. It was even more uncomfortable than the first lunch, where I'd alternated between wanting to cry and wanting to throw my drink in Cal's face.

"How does the money feel?" I asked.

Cal tilted his head.

"The producers," I clarified.

"Ah," he said. "They're pleased. Very pleased."

"With everything?" I asked.

Cal gave me a look. "With everything," he said.

"They didn't ask for changes?" I asked.

Harriet was now paying attention.

"Changes?" she asked.

Cal shook his head. "No changes," he said. "I *am* still the director."

"What are you talking about?" Harriet asked. "Did I miss something?"

"No," Cal and I said at the same time.

It was clear that Harriet didn't believe us. I took a sip of my vodka cranberry.

"I'm going to get a drink," Harriet said.

She still had the one I'd given her, but I didn't stop her as she walked away.

"What are you doing?" Cal asked.

"Me?"

He sighed. "Harriet's already stressed about the show," he said. "And now you've just gone and made it seem like we've been having secret conversations about it behind her back."

"She's stressed about the show?"

That was news to me. And my surprise was clearly unexpected to Cal as well.

"I thought you guys were thick as thieves," he said.

"We are," I said.

"Well, don't stress her out, okay?" Cal said.

I bristled. It was *my* job to make sure that Harriet was all right, not Cal's.

It also cemented my fears that something was going on with Harriet that she wasn't telling me about. As far as I'd known, she was extremely pleased with the progress of the show. What was worrying her?

The piano player started up a round of "Wouldn't It Be Loverly?," and soon the entire bar was singing along. It was hard to hear anything, or be heard, so I had to lean closer to Cal.

"What about me?" I asked.

Mmm. His cologne.

"What about you?"

"Aren't you worried about stressing me out?"

Cal lifted his eyebrows. "Not especially," he said.

We were standing very close. My chin was practically on his shoulder, my mouth inches from his ear.

Cal turned toward me, and I had to step back.

"You come alive onstage," he said. "I've never seen anything like it."

My heart was pounding, and I was certain I could hear it over the music.

"This show is going to make you a star," he said. "If you let it."

I couldn't remember the last time someone had had such confidence in me.

"But the choreography . . ."

I couldn't help myself. What was the point of being an artist if you weren't your worst critic as well?

"It doesn't matter," Cal said. "It's one song. One or two steps. The show is great. You're great. No one is going to care if you do three turns or two. They are going to come to see you, and you're going to blow them away."

My throat felt dry.

"Well," I said. "Thank you."

He gave me a look.

"What?"

"Nothing," he said. "I just can't remember the last time you accepted a compliment from me."

I scowled at him. "Don't push your luck."

"There's the Kathleen I know," he said. "See you in Rhode Island."

I saluted. "Yes, Mr. Director."

CHAPTER 18

"This is the best fucking birthday ever!" LC shouted as Wyatt took a bow.

He'd just rocked the room with a rendition of Queen's "Somebody to Love," delighting all of us by hitting each high note with aplomb.

"Shots!" Ryan lifted his glass and downed it.

The rest of us did the same. The tequila burned but I didn't care. Somehow Cal had found a private room in a karaoke club in Ireland where we could party and play without the watchful eyes of fans or paparazzi.

It was absolute heaven.

"Who's next?" LC held up the enormous book of songs.

I'd already done a few numbers in the Katee Rose register—singing from the back of my throat and way up in my nose—but I was ready to let loose. To sing the way I always wanted to sing.

I grabbed the book from LC and flipped through it until I found the perfect choice.

"My turn!" I punched in the number and waited for the room to react.

"Oh shiiiiiiiit," Wyatt said when the song title came up on the screen.

"Ah man," Ryan groaned. "A musical?"

He thought they were lame and cheesy. He refused to go see them with me. I always laughed when he complained, like it was all this big joke that we were in on together, but the truth was that it hurt when he said things like that. When he diminished the things that I loved.

And sure, *Cats* was strange—the kind of show that people who hated Broadway shows always pointed to as proof that we theatre kids were absolute freaks—but what they missed was the purity of it all. There was something about singing a song like "Memory" that just allowed you to feel everything you needed to feel.

Musicals were just so *big*. Big and bold and fun and yes, a little nuts too.

And I loved it.

Plus this song was special. If I hadn't gotten the chance to close out the showcase that summer at Curtain Call, who knew where I'd be right now? If it wasn't for this song, I probably wouldn't have gotten the chance to audition for *Show N Tell* and I probably wouldn't have met Ryan.

If anything, he should be fucking grateful for *Cats*.

The song started and I closed my eyes and sang my lungs out.

I hit every note.

I killed it.

When I finished the room was silent.

I opened my eyes, ready to accept the cheers and applause that every other performance had gotten. Instead, I found looks of complete and utter shock on almost everyone's faces.

The only one who didn't look surprised was Cal.

Everyone else was looking at me like I'd unzipped my skin and a lizard person had stepped out.

"Wow," LC finally said. "You have a *great* voice."

"A really good voice," Mason said.

They hadn't known.

I looked over at Ryan. He blinked.

He hadn't known either.

It was like being punched in the heart.

I knew that people talked about how bad Katee Rose's voice was. All tight and nasally, a little bit whiny. But that was how my team wanted me to sing. Marilyn Monroe—if she was a pop star with Auto-Tune.

My fans didn't care, but it stung anytime I read some review that commented on my sound. It had become second nature by now—to sing like that—but that didn't mean it was the only way I could sing. It also didn't mean that it was easy. It didn't mean that everyone could do it.

And I had been able to ignore the critiques, for the most part, because I knew that it wasn't true.

I'd thought Ryan had known as well. After all, he had always claimed he was the reason I'd gotten the *Show N Tell* gig. Because he'd seen my audition. Or so he said.

But he looked more shocked than anyone.

I stumbled as I got off the stage. My feet felt numb. My hands. My lips.

"Do another one!" Wyatt said.

I managed an exaggerated bow with a hand flourish, but it was mostly to hide how I wasn't smiling.

"Another one!" Wyatt repeated, and quickly got the others to follow him in a chant. "Another one! Another one! Another one!"

But I didn't want to do another one. I wanted to leave.

Instead, I played coy and excused myself, making some vague noise about a bathroom or needing air or whatever. It didn't really matter because everyone was already focused on finding their next karaoke pick.

I left just as Mason started crooning "Glory of Love."

The club was a maze, but I found a door. Mercifully it opened onto an alley, and I let it close behind me, filling my lungs with the fresh night air.

I closed my eyes, but all I could see was Ryan's stunned expression.

He knew I could sing. Didn't he?

I placed my palms against the brick wall behind me. It was cold. I wasn't. I was still warm from the small room and the embarrassment.

I didn't know why *I* was embarrassed. But the feeling was there, along with shame and disappointment. Was I *that* different as Katee Rose? Was it that shocking that I could actually carry a tune?

The door opened.

"They're drunk," Cal said.

He joined me against the wall.

"They still didn't think I could sing," I said.

"They're idiots," he said.

I shook my head. "No," I said. "They're not."

"Jury's out on Wyatt."

"Fair," I said. "But the rest of them?" I let out a breath. "They all thought I was a talentless hack. Famous for my tits and how well I can shake them."

"Stop," Cal said.

"It's true," I said. "Even Ryan was surprised."

Cal didn't say anything.

"Ryan isn't an idiot," I said.

Still nothing.

"I thought he knew," I said.

"Ryan knows about himself," Cal said. "There's no room for anything else."

I looked over at him. I knew that Cal and Ryan didn't really get along, but I didn't realize there was such animosity between them. The bitterness in Cal's voice surprised me.

"He's my boyfriend," I said needlessly.

"Yeah," Cal said.

Bitter. Bitter. Bitter.

I didn't mind. I actually liked it.

Which I knew made me a bad person.

But Cal was right. Ryan cared about Ryan, and ever since CrushZone had started, I'd noticed that he'd been focused more and more on getting himself as much of the spotlight as possible. Everything else was secondary.

Even me.

"It's strange, isn't it?" he asked.

"What?"

Cal gestured to the general space around us.

"This," he said.

I didn't understand.

"You. Me," he said.

My breath caught.

"Katee Rose. CrushZone," he continued.

I didn't know what I'd been hoping for him to say.

"It's strange, right?" he asked.

"I guess," I said. I still didn't get it.

"It's just"—he frowned—"this whole thing. It's all a bunch of pretend."

I didn't like how that sounded. As if I was being deceitful. Lying.

Even though, in a way, I supposed I was.

"We're the all-American teens that everyone is supposed to aspire to," he said. "We're not even teenagers."

"We're not role models," I said.

I was so fucking tired of everyone assuming that.

"I know," Cal said. "And we shouldn't be. Because it's all made-up." He turned toward me. "I mean, we have a song called 'Prom King.'"

"You could have been Prom King," I said.

Cal gave me a look. "My point is that Ryan didn't even go to high school, let alone prom. None of the guys did. And yet, we're all out there, every night, singing songs like we're just regular guys with regular lives."

"That's what I do too," I pointed out, feeling a little hurt and a lot judged.

"It's not the same," Cal said.

"No?"

He thought about it for a moment.

"No," he said. "Because you're real."

"Katee Rose is *literally* invented," I said.

"But *you* aren't," he said.

"No one sees *me* when I'm onstage," I said. "They see a dumb blonde with big boobs that jiggle when she dances. Who can't sing."

"So make them see you," Cal said.

As if it were that easy.

"What about Harriet's songs?" he asked. "Wasn't she writing, like, a whole bunch of songs for you?"

Harriet was back in New York living a "real life," though she'd promised to join up with us again for my birthday. The songs she'd written were on a CD at the bottom of my suitcase.

I tapped my nails against the brick.

"They don't want to hear them," I said.

I'd tried to play them for Diana, but she was always too busy to listen. It took a while for me to get it, but I finally understood that "too busy" meant "not interested."

Even Ryan was too busy.

"Are they good?" Cal asked.

"Yes," I said. "And I sound great singing them."

"Then make them listen," Cal said.

"How?"

He shrugged. "They need you, don't they?"

Did they? Ever since I'd gotten signed—before that even, back when I was basically Ryan's backup dancer—I'd believed that I needed them. That I had to do everything they told me to do or I'd never get what I wanted.

But now I had it and I wasn't sure if I wanted it anymore.

"You have more power than you think," Cal said.

I laughed. "Do I?" I asked. "I mean, they made me change my name. Said Rosenberg wasn't *universal* enough."

Cal didn't respond.

"They wanted me to change my nose too," I said.

"What? When?"

"When I got cast on *Show N Tell*," I said. "And before the first album."

I was gratified by the disgusted look on Cal's face. I decided not to tell him that Diana brought it up before every other album and tour as well.

"Just a minor adjustment."

"They'll just shave a bit off of the bridge."

"We'll tell everyone you had a deviated septum."

Weird how there wasn't any time in the schedule for a limited Broadway run, but apparently there was plenty of time for major surgery and recovery.

"I'm glad you stood up to them," Cal said.

I wanted to cry. Because the truth was that I hadn't resisted because I disagreed with my management. I'd refused to have it done because I was terrified of needles and blood, and everything associated with something like that.

It wasn't bravery. It was cowardice.

And I still thought about doing it. Every time I saw an article that pointed out how much prettier I'd be if I fixed it or whenever a blogger drew unnecessary arrows pointing to it, I thought about going to my management and saying, "Okay, let's do it."

I knew it would help my career.

"They want me to do a Christmas album," I said.

Cal waited for me to continue.

"I shouldn't be surprised," I said. "I mean, I perform at some Christmas concert or show every year. And I did plenty of Christmas specials on *Show N Tell*. Of course, they'd want me to record a Christmas album."

"Do you want to record a Christmas album?" Cal asked.

"No," I said. "Yes. Maybe."

I leaned my head back against the wall.

"I mean, there's just something weird about it," I said. "It's not enough that I had to get rid of my last name—now

I have to do an entire album about a holiday I don't even celebrate?"

"What did you tell them?" Cal asked.

"That I'd think about it," I said. "They were not pleased."

I was always accommodating. This and the nose job were the only things I'd ever really pushed back on.

"They kept saying that it wasn't really a Christmas album—that it was a winter album, but they showed me the list of songs they wanted me to record and they're all about Christmas. They want me to sing 'O Holy Night,' which is *literally* about the birth of Jesus."

"Wasn't that song written by an atheist?" Cal asked.

"How did you know that?"

We exchanged a look.

"Harriet," we both said.

"Apparently the composer was Jewish," I said.

"It's like Harriet's here with us right now," Cal said.

"She'd probably say something about how *most* Christmas songs were written by Jews anyway and I'm part of a long cultural tradition."

I glanced over to find Cal staring at me.

"That was extremely specific," he said.

"I already spoke to her," I said. "Earlier today."

"Ah," Cal said.

We stood there.

"Okay," Cal said. "Use it as leverage."

I tilted my head.

"Tell them that you'll do the Christmas album if they let you do Harriet's songs first," Cal said.

Fuck.

That was genius.

I felt a twinge of disappointment. In myself.

I could still remember how much confidence and bravery I'd had when I was younger. How sure I was that I was going to make it. And now that I had—now that I had, in a sense, gotten everything I'd wanted—I'd become scared and timid. Afraid to lose it all.

But did I even have what I wanted? What I really wanted?

I loved my fans. I loved performing.

Did I love being Katee Rose?

Why hadn't I fought harder to keep Kathleen Rosenberg alive?

I was ashamed.

"What about you?" I asked, needing to deflect, needing to talk about something else.

"What about me?" Cal asked.

"What do you want out of this whole thing?"

Cal looked up at the sky. It was brilliant with stars.

"Ryan wants to be a famous actor," I said. "Wyatt wants to go solo. LC and Mason are always whispering about something—what about you?"

"I don't know," Cal said. "I guess I haven't thought that far ahead."

I couldn't really chide him, because I hadn't either. And now that we were, it was terrifying. This life was intense and overwhelming and stressful, but it was the only life I knew. Maybe that's where some of the shame was coming from. The realization that I wasn't even sure I knew how to be anyone but Katee anymore.

"I just wanted something to do after college," he said. "And they promised I'd make enough that I could help my family out."

I'd never met Cal's family, but I knew that he was smack

dab in the middle of four girls. It was the reason he'd gotten into dance in the first place—it was just easier to take all five of them to the same activity—and then Cal became the best of the bunch.

"And have you?" I asked.

He nodded. "Took care of college loans for the older ones, put together a fund for the younger ones. Paid off my parents' mortgage."

"So generous," I said.

"I *did* spend some of it on myself," he said. "I'm not *that* altruistic."

I wasn't sure I believed that.

"You like performing," I said.

"Sure," he said. "But I don't think I want to do it forever."

"Really?"

I couldn't imagine doing anything else. Not truly.

"It's fun now," Cal said. "The money is amazing. I get to see the whole world. And I like the guys." He paused. "I like *most* of the guys."

"But?"

He shrugged. "I don't know," he said. "I don't need the spotlight, like you do."

It sounded like an insult, which apparently showed on my face, because Cal immediately backtracked.

"What I mean is that you're happy in the spotlight," he said. "You shine."

"So do you," I said.

Because it was true—he was an incredible performer. I loved watching him dance. He was definitely the best out of all the guys. It was hard to look at anyone else when they were onstage.

"But it invigorates you," he said. "I can see it on your face

when you get offstage—you're . . . you're . . . you're like a
big glowing ball of energy."

I didn't know what to say to that.

"You belong up there," Cal said. "You belong where everyone can see you. And hear you."

"I've seen you helping the other guys with choreography," I said. "You're really good at it."

He shrugged. "I like being helpful."

"It's more than that," I said. "You know what looks right
and you know how to tweak things so they don't make mistakes."

"It's not a big deal," he said.

"You're doing someone else's job," I said. "Without
credit. Without pay."

Cal snorted. "No one is going to pay me to choreograph
the band I'm in. And Ryan would lose his mind."

"Maybe," I said.

Definitely.

We stood in silence. I could hear the bar on the other side
of the brick wall, but it felt far away. Like another world.
Another life.

"If any of our fans knew we were having this conversation they'd laugh at us," I said. "We're the biggest pop stars
in the world and we're complaining."

"We're not complaining," Cal said. "We're commiserating."

"Okay, Cal State," I said.

His expression darkened.

"Sorry," I said.

"It's okay," he said. "It's just that . . ."

"What?"

"I fucking hate that nickname," he said.

I was surprised at his anger. Cal was never angry. He was always so even-keeled. I envied it. Sometimes.

But anger could feel good.

"I'm sorry," I said.

"It's not your fault," he said.

It's Ryan's was the unspoken part.

"You can tell him to stop," I said.

Cal snorted. "Yeah. Right."

He had a point. If he said something, Ryan would probably just double down and do it more. He was mature like that.

"He's jealous," I said. "Of you."

"He's the star," Cal said.

"Yeah, but you're smarter than him and he knows it."

"Because I went to college?" Cal asked. "It's not that big of a deal."

"Maybe not," I said. "But it matters to Ryan. It makes him feel small."

Sometimes it made me feel small too.

"That's his problem, not mine," Cal said.

"I'll tell him that."

Cal laughed, and looked at me.

"What about you?" he asked.

"What about me?"

"Are you jealous?"

I thought about lying.

"A little," I said.

Cal pressed his lips together and gave a tight little nod.

"I just wonder sometimes," I said. "What it would have been like. To go to high school. College."

"I can tell you," Cal said. "It's pretty boring."

I smiled. "I wonder what that's like too."

"What?"

"Boring," I said. "Because this life?" I gestured around myself. "It's not boring."

Cal shifted, arms crossed.

"I don't know," he said. "Tour buses can get pretty boring. You can only listen to Wyatt singing 'Ninety-Nine Bottles of Beer on the Wall' so many times."

"Has he ever gotten to one?"

Cal shook his head. "He always gets lost around the seventies."

We both laughed at that.

"He's a nice guy," Cal said. "They all are."

"Not Ryan," I said.

I was only half joking.

Cal didn't answer.

We stood there in silence, and I wished I had something to do with my hands.

"He should have known," Cal finally said.

"What?"

"That you could sing," Cal said.

"Oh."

"And you should make them listen to Harriet's songs," he said.

"Yeah?"

"Yeah."

I turned to face him. "Okay," I said. "I'll make you a deal."

He gave me a suspicious look. Smart of him.

"I'll play the songs for my team if you ask yours to let you direct the next music video."

Cal's laugh was a burst of surprise.

"They'd never allow that," he said.

"Okay," I conceded. "Then you get to choreograph it. Or a new number for the next tour."

He regarded me.

"You're serious," he said.

"Were you serious about Harriet's songs?"

"I was," he said.

"Then I am too," I said. "Come on. Pinky promise?"

I extended a pinky. Cal looked at it. Looked at me.

"Pinky promise," he said.

We hooked our fingers together and blew on our thumbs the way we'd done back at camp.

"Should we go back in?" Cal asked.

"Sure," I said. "I think I owe them another song from a musical."

"You definitely do," he said.

Ryan would hate it, but I didn't care.

Cal held open the door for me.

"And just for the record," he said, "I like your nose. A lot."

NOW

CHAPTER 19

"Stop scowling at me," I said. "You can have dinner when we get there."

The only response I got was a very disappointed *mew.*

"I know," I said. "I'm terrible. I'm forcing you to spend a few months in a beautiful furnished apartment in Rhode Island while I live out one of my lifelong dreams. I should have just left you in Brooklyn to fend for yourself."

"*Meow.*"

I'd wanted this for so long but now I was starting to have second thoughts. And they were coming at rapid intervals, keeping me up at night, burrowing into the muscles at the base of my neck, keeping a tight grip on my lower back.

What if I was too late to pursue a dream like this? What if I'd missed my chance?

After my career had gone up in flames, after Diana—who had always discouraged me from doing theatre—had dumped me, I tried to get in the door on my own. But my brand was so damaged that no one wanted to touch me. The one or two offers that had been floated my way had felt more like cash grabs from producers hoping I'd draw attention—and ticket sales—from people who wanted to see me fail.

At least I'd been in shape back then.

Not just physically but emotionally. The scandal had leveled me in a lot of ways, but I'd been well calloused from years in the public eye—accustomed to the abuse that came with fame.

I was softer now.

Maybe too soft.

"I thought you and Harriet were going to ride together."

I looked up, not entirely surprised to see Cal standing in the aisle. Because of course.

He hesitated, and I could tell he wasn't sure if he wanted to just keep walking and find another seat or . . .

"Sit down," I said. "We can handle a train ride just the two of us."

He sat. The cat yowled.

"Oh," he said, peering into her carrier. "You really do have a cat."

"I really do have a cat," I said, thinking that it would be a weird thing to lie about, but I couldn't really blame Cal for believing I was somewhat unhinged.

We still hadn't talked about the kiss, but we also hadn't really talked about the phone call I'd made to him at two in the morning. How completely bonkers and unprofessional it had been.

And we also hadn't talked about Rachel. How—*if*—they were involved.

"What's their name?" Cal asked.

He was still looking at my cat.

"Fish," I said.

He raised an eyebrow. "You named your cat Fish?"

"Her given name is Gefilte Fish," I said.

"Ah. That makes more sense."

Cal settled into his seat, his long legs stretched out away from mine. It didn't matter. I was still painfully aware of his presence. And his cologne—that damned orange grove— seemed to fill up the space, making it feel even smaller and more intimate.

The train jolted a bit and began to move.

"No Harriet?" Cal asked.

"She wanted to take an earlier train," I said.

I'd been hurt but hadn't pushed.

I suspected it had something to do with the fact that it was my name in all the headlines about the show, with Harriet listed at the very end, more like a side note. Now that we'd moved past the workshop stage and were at a point where we needed to sell tickets, the show was becoming synonymous with what was being called my "comeback."

Of course, there were also plenty of articles that mentioned Cal, and took the time to give readers a quick recap of our "relationship." I'd seen plenty of think pieces about our reunion, how it was some sort of weird karma or payback. It was unclear who was paying back who, but I'd long learned that when it came to the gossip sites, facts weren't always the most important detail.

All that mattered was that we were working together and the last time that had happened, scandal had occurred. No doubt, everyone was hoping for a repeat.

Unfortunately, it seemed to be the one thing everyone wanted to talk about when it came to the show. There were no details about the production, except that I was playing a blond, buxom "Katee Rose–esque" character. Articles seemed to vary wildly in their predictions of the quality of my performance, which made it clear that reviews were likely to be just as mixed.

I just hoped my past didn't poison the well too much.

I wanted this to be Harriet's moment.

She'd never cared about things like fame or attention before, but it still wasn't fair. Then again, that was showbiz. There was nothing fair about this industry.

It wouldn't be forever. Once previews started, once people starting hearing about the show and the music and the songs, the attention would shift to Harriet. And away from me and Cal and a scandal that had happened a thousand years ago.

Or maybe Harriet knew about the kiss.

Except I knew she didn't because Cal wouldn't say anything, and I certainly hadn't.

He'd taken a book out and was sitting there reading. I looked out the window, watching the golden and plum leaves flash by. It was getting colder, and everything smelled bright and brand-new. For me, it wasn't spring that signaled a new start but the fall. It was the season of coziness, of comfort. Bears had it figured out—this was the time to rest, to rejuvenate.

The thought of finding a nice, warm cave and spending the next few months there was very, very tempting.

I loved the way everything turned from lush to barren, the air and the ground becoming crunchier. I felt at home in the fall, wrapped up in sweaters and scarves—much easier to hide when you were all bundled up. And the paparazzi had been less likely to stake out my house during the cold months so those were the times I had the most privacy after permanently locating to New York.

Fish let out a plaintive meow, which caused Cal to look up from his book.

"She's fine," I said. "Just annoyed."

"Has she ever been on a train before?"

I shook my head. "Unless she was taking little adventures before I got her. Since then, she's been strictly at home."

"It will be nice to have her with you in Rhode Island," Cal said.

"I've been meaning to ask you about that," I said.

He raised an eyebrow.

"Rhode Island? Really?"

"What do you have against Little Rhody?"

This time I was the one raising an eyebrow.

"It's a great theatre," Cal said. "They don't get a lot of tryouts. It's cheaper than some of the usual places, it gives the town a boost, and the theatre as well. It will generate a lot of excitement for the show, and I always enjoy forcing New York theatre writers to leave the island. Win-win-win."

"And it's just a coincidence that this is the exact same theatre where Camp Curtain Call does its summer show-case?"

Cal shrugged.

"Oh please," I said. "Again. With *feeling*."

That's what our old instructor, Ms. Spiegel, had said after almost every rehearsal.

"She was the worst," Cal said.

"What are you talking about?" I asked. "She was great."

"She was a terror," he said.

"She was discerning."

"Critical."

"Honest."

"Abusive."

I looked at him. "You think Ms. Spiegel was abusive?"

He did a double take. "You think she wasn't? She thwacked you in the back of the legs with a stick."

"I wasn't hitting the note," I said.

Cal didn't say anything for a long time.

"What?" I finally demanded.

"Nothing," he said. "This just . . . this explains a lot."

I didn't like the way he said that. Like he'd figured out something about me that I still hadn't worked out.

"She made me a great performer," I said. "I wouldn't have had the career I had without her."

"I don't believe that," Cal said. "Talent always rises to the top."

"Oh please," I said. "You're a grown man. You know that's not true."

"It is for me," he said. "With my projects. My shows."

"You're adorably naïve," I said.

"Thank you," he said.

He didn't seem very bothered by it. Then again, very little seemed to bother him. It was annoying.

"For the record," Cal said, "I've had a relationship with this theatre for many years. It started with Camp Curtain Call, but they've always been supportive of me, and I wanted to return the favor. It felt like the right place for the show."

"Full circle," I said.

"Something like that," he said.

Fish meowed, and Cal leaned forward to give her a little scratch through the carrier door.

"No pets?" I asked.

He shook his head.

"I travel too much," he said. "Wouldn't be fair."

I nodded. That had been the case for me too. Being able to stay in one place for an extended period of time was something I'd learned to value. The ability to put down roots. To make a home for yourself.

I realized I didn't know where Cal called home anymore.

His family was from Texas, his college years spent in New York. CrushZone went all over the world, but I assumed that when things ended, he'd wound up in Los Angeles.

"If we go to Broadway, you'll be able to stay in New York," I said.

"Sure," he said.

I thought about Rachel. Bet she was thrilled that he'd be staying put for a while.

It was a little strange that he hadn't said anything about her—that after the kiss, she hadn't come up as a reason why it was a bad idea. It remained a bad idea, but there were moments when I kept forgetting why.

Like now. And the moment in Marie's Crisis.

"You come alive onstage," he'd said.

It was time to change the subject.

"How are ticket sales?" I asked.

"Good," Cal said. "But you shouldn't worry about that."

"I shouldn't worry about the success of the show I'm starring in?"

Cal sighed.

"I don't want to fight with you," he said.

I lifted my hands. Truce.

"People are buying tickets," he said. "We'll have a full house. On most days."

The train continued on. It was clear that Cal was much more comfortable with silence than I was, so I stopped trying to engage him. Tried to embrace the quiet. It wasn't that hard, I found. I didn't have a book, but I did have my phone and I was long due for some retail therapy. At some point we left New York, but I couldn't tell when. It was all fall leaves and gray skies until Rhode Island. By the time we arrived, I'd ordered a pair of new boots, overpriced moisturizer, some toys for Fish, and a cute beret that I was certain I'd never wear, but also knew I needed in my life.

Cal, ever the gentleman, pulled my suitcase off the top rack for me, and waited patiently as I gathered my things. We got off the train together without exchanging a word—not counting Fish's meows, which were increasing in volume with every jostle and perceived slight.

"Share a cab?" Cal asked.

Even though we'd just spent several hours next to each other on the train, the cab ride was much, much more intimate. Fish and her carrier were on my lap and somehow my thigh was wedged up against Cal's.

It was a nice thigh. Very strong.

I wondered if he was thinking the same thing about mine.

Once a dancer, always a dancer.

I was dropped off first. I'd chosen a place walking distance to the theatre as a reminder of what I was doing here. I had to focus. Had to get it right.

Cal helped heave my suitcase onto the sidewalk. I was pretty sure I'd brought or shipped more things for Fish—litter box, toys, bed—than I had for myself. Because what did I need? I was going to be at the theatre all day every day. I wasn't going out, I wasn't exploring, I was working.

"I've got it from here," I said, fairly certain he would—

without really thinking—offer to help bring my things inside.

Not a good idea.

"Yeah, sure," he said. "See you at the theatre tomorrow."

The cab waited, no doubt on Cal's request, until I had finished fumbling with the keys and managed to unlock the door. With it propped open against my hip, I gave a little wave.

The cab didn't move. It didn't leave until everything was inside and I had closed the door behind me. I watched from the front window as it finally pulled away.

I reminded myself that it was just polite for Cal to wait until I was inside. That it wasn't some sign of his exceptional goodness or his being deserving of praise. That it was, in actuality, a very basic thing that all humans should do for each other to show they care about one another's safety.

Cal was just a man.

And I wasn't going to risk my career—again—to fuck around with him. Again. There were sayings about making the same mistake twice. Mainly that people who did it were idiots.

Besides, Cal wasn't *that* hot.

It felt stupid trying to lie to myself.

Cal *was* that hot, but it wasn't like I hadn't worked with attractive men before. I'd shot music videos with half-naked men, both of us covered with water, and managed not to get all bent out of shape about it. I'd even made out with some of these men on camera and been able to keep it professional after.

A lot of them had been gay, but still.

I just had to stop thinking about the kiss. About his hands. About the way he smelled.

Other men could kiss. Other men had great hands. Other men showered. Cal wasn't special. He wasn't exceptional.

He wasn't worth the pain. Any pain.

I could control myself. I was a grown-ass woman with self-control. Wasn't I?

Wasn't I?

CHAPTER 20

"How does it feel?" Harriet asked.

She wasn't looking at me—she was staring out at the empty seats instead.

"Weird," I said. "You?"

"Very weird," she said.

It smelled the same. A mixture of floor polish and stale air and dust. It was a beautiful theatre, but it also felt like a time machine. This was where I'd stood, all those years ago, singing for my future.

What would I say to my fourteen-year-old self if I could? That we'd take a few detours, but eventually—*eventually*—we'd end up right where we belonged. Which was right where we started.

Full circles and all that.

Is that how Cal felt too? Like he was fulfilling the dream he'd had back then?

I looked over at Harriet, wondering if we all shared this same sense of coming home.

But she kept avoiding my eye.

All those vows I'd made to myself about checking in on Harriet had been quickly forgotten. Instead, I'd been focused on myself. On Cal. On whatever the fuck it was that was going on between us.

I was equally—if not more—responsible for this distance. I'd promised to be a better friend and I had done absolutely nothing to fix a problem that was only getting worse.

"It feels tiny," I said.

Nothing like resorting to small talk with your best friend of over twenty years as the two of you inch closer to your lifelong dream together.

"Yes," Harriet said. "But we are also bigger."

In my memory the stage, the audience, the entire place, had seemed enormous. Backstage had seemed like a maze of thousands of potential paths with endless dressing rooms and hallways full of supplies.

Now it felt normal-sized, maybe even a little cramped, as Harriet and I headed backstage and into the belly of the theatre, down a long hallway where I found my name on a door.

I stopped a few feet into my dressing room.

"Oh," I said.

"This is nice," Harriet said, coming in behind me.

Not seeing that I'd stopped, she bumped up against me.

"Let's go look at the rest of the theatre," I said.

But she was already inside.

"Oh," Harriet said.

Sitting on the vanity were Red Vines and a bowl of Swedish Fish. The top of the licorice tub had been left slightly askew.

We both stood there for a moment.

"Well," Harriet said, "he always did have a good memory."

I didn't say anything. I didn't know what to say.

"It's just a nice gesture," I said. "I bet there's something for everyone in their dressing room. I bet there's something for you . . . somewhere. . . ."

Harriet gave me a look.

"It doesn't mean anything," I said.

The look didn't improve.

"What's going on here?" Cal asked. "Did someone shove a pony in there or something?"

He had appeared in the hallway, his head leaning into the dressing room.

"We were just admiring the amenities," I said.

I waved a hand toward the vanity.

"Ah," Cal said. "Well. Whatever my leading lady wants . . ."

Harriet coughed.

"Thank you," I said. "It's very thoughtful."

"You're welcome," he said.

We all just stood there for a moment. To give myself something to do, I reached over and took a Swedish Fish.

"It's perfect," I said. And it was.

He *did* have a good memory.

"I manhandled each fish just to be sure," he said.

I paused with it halfway to my mouth.

"Don't worry," he said. "I don't have cooties."

We stared at each other. I ate the Swedish Fish. Then he left.

"Shit," Harriet said once he was gone.

"Shh," I said.

I knew exactly what was going through her head.

"Kathleen"—her look was frantic—"you can't sleep with him."

Fucking Cal. What had he been thinking?

"Harriet!" I pulled the dressing room door closed. "Can you not say that in a place known for thin walls and gossipy ears?"

News never traveled faster than backstage.

"I'm sorry," she said. "But you can't. You know that, right?"

At least she was talking to me again. It wasn't the kind of conversation I wanted to have, but it wasn't small talk, and she wasn't avoiding my eyes. If anything, she was staring too intently at me.

If I didn't know any better, I would have sworn she could see exactly what I was thinking, which unfortunately was a play-by-play of *the* kiss.

I tried to play it casual.

"He gave me candy," I said, "not a saucy note with his underwear tucked into it."

Harriet wrinkled her nose at the thought.

"Not just candy," she said.

"You're overreacting," I said.

"Oh really?" she asked. "Didn't you hear him? This wasn't something he had his assistant do—*he* put this together."

"He touched all of my food," I said. "That's gross."

"Your obsession with stale candy is what's gross," Harriet said. "What Cal did was thoughtful."

"He's a thoughtful guy," I said.

That, at least, was true. And it gave Harriet pause.

"And," I said, "he knows I'm a diva who needs to be coddled."

Still, Harriet's expression was one of concern. And I had a pretty good idea what she was thinking. I just couldn't bear to hear her say it out loud.

"Please, Kathleen," Harriet said. "We've both worked too hard—"

Fuck.

"I'm. Not. Going. To. Sleep. With. Him," I said.

Harriet didn't look convinced, and I really didn't have any right to feel indignant, but I did. Even though she had good reason to be concerned, I still hated that she was. That she didn't trust me.

Then again, hadn't I just been worrying about trusting myself?

"I know how important this show is," I said. "Cal does too. Neither of us would do anything to jeopardize that."

"Not intentionally, no," Harriet said.

I'd always suspected that she judged me for what happened all those years ago with Cal. That even though she'd stood by me and supported me, she still thought less of me because of it. I couldn't blame her, but it did sting. A lot.

"Nothing is going to happen," I said. "It's just candy."

But it wasn't just candy. That was the problem. It was history and intimacy and care.

Harriet nodded but kept chewing at her lip. I hadn't convinced her at all. Suddenly, I couldn't stand to be with her in this small space. I would have paid anything to go back to stilted small talk than face Harriet's judgment right now.

"I think I'd like a moment," I said. "Alone."

"Sure," Harriet said.

She didn't meet my eye, and I felt the chasm between us widening. The distrust growing. That had always been my one constant—Harriet and her belief in me. In us. But now I saw that even that was shaky. Even that could break.

* * *

I dropped down into the seat behind Cal. Everyone else was getting ready for our first run-through in the new space. But this needed to be dealt with. Now.

"What are you doing?" I demanded.

He didn't look up from his script.

"My job. Directing this show," he said. "Speaking of, aren't you supposed to be backstage, waiting for your cue?"

"The candy, Cal," I said. "What the fuck?"

"You have an interesting way of saying thank you," he said.

"Harriet thinks we're sleeping together," I said. "Or will be doing so imminently."

He immediately put his script down and turned toward me.

"What is wrong with you?" he hissed. "Keep your voice down."

I threw up my hands in frustration.

"Oh, *now* you care about discretion."

I could see a vein in his temple ticking.

"Candy in your dressing room is not the same as shouting in a theatre with amazing acoustics."

"I was *not* shouting," I said. "Don't make this into a thing where I'm being hysterical and you're being normal."

Cal didn't say anything, but his expression indicated that was exactly what he was thinking.

"We *despise* each other," I said.

"We do not," he said.

His gaze dropped down to my mouth. My knees got all trembly. I wanted to slap him.

"Well, *I* despise you," I said.

"No, you don't," Cal said. "I think you might actually like me."

"Don't be ridiculous," I said.

Even after the kiss, we'd still managed to keep our distance from each other during rehearsals, speaking to each other only when necessary and exchanging as few words as possible. I'd held my tongue. A lot.

He shrugged. "Things change."

"Because you kissed me," I said.

"I think *you* kissed *me*," he said.

I was going to climb across the seats and strangle him. He was not taking this seriously.

"It doesn't matter," I said through gritted teeth. It absolutely did matter—he was wrong, but I didn't have time to deal with that now. "You're treating me differently because of it."

"Kathleen," Cal said, "we were being unprofessional. The *kiss* was unprofessional."

"I know," I said.

I didn't appreciate his tone. I didn't need to be spoken to like I was a naughty child. If anything, he had behaved just as inappropriately—maybe even more so.

"I was hoping to start over," he said. "Treat these performances like a reset."

As if it were that easy. As if it just took some fucking candy to make everything okay.

"All you accomplished is making Harriet suspicious."

"You didn't tell her about the kiss?" he asked.

"No! Of course not. I didn't tell anyone." I looked at him. "Did you?"

"No," he said. "But you and Harriet are . . . close."

"She's my best friend," I said. "And if you recall, the one person who stood with me after everything happened."

I could see Cal clench his jaw. He clearly didn't like being reminded of that. No doubt it was counter to his "good guy" self-image. I didn't much care at the moment.

"Exactly," Cal said. "I figured you told her everything."

"Well, I don't," I said. "And I'm glad I didn't because the candy on its own was enough to make her freak out that I—that we—are going to put the show in jeopardy."

God. Saying it out loud made it hurt even more.

"That's not going to happen," Cal said. "It was one kiss. It's not going to happen again."

He sounded confident, but he was still staring at my mouth.

"No candy," I said. "No special treatment."

"I was just trying to be nice," he said.

"Well stop it," I said. "You're not nice."

"I am," he insisted.

"Not to me," I countered.

He thought about it.

"Fine," he said. "No candy."

I could only hope it would be as easy as that.

CHAPTER 21

"A re you sure this is how you want to spend your birthday?" Harriet asked.

"For the last time," I said, "yes. This is exactly what I want to be doing tonight."

Harriet shrugged and climbed onto the bed, where I'd set up a truly disgusting amount of candy and popcorn.

We were in Edinburgh, and it was wonderfully cold out, and Harriet had come all the way from New York, and I had the night off, and I had very specific plans for how I wanted to spend it. Which mostly involved eating a lot and not leaving the super luxe hotel suite I'd been given.

"Guessing none of the guys are coming?" Harriet asked.

"I invited them all," I said. "LC said he might stop by."

I had been trying to get Harriet and LC to spend some time together. The more I got to know him, the more I was convinced that he'd be a great match for Harriet. He was cute and smart—loved history as well—and besides Cal, he was the only one of the guys who didn't roll his eyes and pretend to gag every time I talked about musical theatre.

"Kathleen"—Harriet shook her head—"I don't need a boyfriend. Especially one that's on tour year-round."

I knew she had a point, but I also secretly hoped that if she started dating LC then she'd put her New York plans on hold and travel with us for the rest of the tour. I missed her. A lot.

Things were just easier when she was here.

When she was around, Ryan didn't complain about me spending time with Cal. When it was the three of us, things were easy. Fun. And things weren't that awkward when Ryan wanted to join—we could transition fairly easily into a quartet.

But with Harriet back in New York, Ryan had begun to express annoyance at how often I hung out with Cal. It became an either-or situation. I could hang out with Ryan, or I could hang out with Cal—not both of them at the same time.

There was a knock at the door.

"Maybe that's LC," I said.

Harriet was reclined on the giant hotel bed, reading *Cosmo*. I was on the cover.

It wasn't LC at the door. It was Cal.

"Movie night still happening?" he asked.

"You know we're just watching a bunch of musicals, right?"

"That was the promise," he said.

Ryan had refused. "I'm not going to watch a bunch of people singing for hours," he'd said. "But maybe we can do something special, just the two of us, for your birthday."

He hadn't made any alternative suggestions, though, and

I figured he'd probably get me a cupcake or something the next day. He wasn't the best at remembering things like that.

"Yay!" Harriet said when she saw Cal.

"What are we watching first?"

I looked over to where Cal was in the process of twisting the lid back on to a tub of licorice.

"Hey, hey, hey!" I said. "What are you doing?"

He stepped back, hands raised. "I was just trying to keep it from getting stale."

I tsked, holding the bucket to my chest. "Poor Cal," I said. "Did no one teach you that Red Vines are best when they're a little stale?"

"Um, no," he said. "My family tends to prefer things fresh."

I twisted open the lid and held the tub out toward him.

"Try it," I said. "Change your life."

Cal pulled a red tube from the middle of the batch and ate it.

"Well," he said. "I guess you're right."

"Yes!" I pumped my fist in the air. "I mean, of course I am."

"He's lying," Harriet said.

"He is not," I said.

I looked at Cal, but he was eyeing the rest of the candy setup.

"What are these?" he asked.

"Swedish Fish," I said.

"Those are Kathleen's favorite," Harriet said.

"They are," I said. "But they have to be firm, not squishy."

"She touches all of them," Harriet said.

Cal withdrew his hand from reaching for a brightly hued gummy fish.

"Oh, come on," I said. "It's not like I have cooties."

I plucked one from the top of the bowl and handed it to him.

"They're good."

"As good as slightly stale Red Vines?" he asked, and I knew that Harriet was right—he had been humoring me.

"Believe it or not," I said, "they're better."

"That reminds me." Cal reached into his pocket. "I brought you a birthday present. One that might make the candy taste even more incredible."

He pulled out a joint.

"Oh shit," Harriet said, putting her magazine down and bouncing off the bed. "You are a genius."

He grinned at the compliment. "Should we get this party started? What movie are we watching first?"

I expected him to groan and beg off when he learned that the plan was to watch some extremely nostalgic, nerdy shit. I wanted to start with *Newsies,* then move on to *Grease 2,* and end with *Into the Woods.* I really couldn't blame Ryan for not wanting to spend his evening watching all three.

But Cal didn't even blink. Instead, he lit the joint, pulled a chair over to the side of the bed, and settled in for the evening.

It didn't take long for the weed to take over.

And Cal was right—it *did* make the candy taste unbelievably good. It was like eating candy for the first time. I couldn't get enough.

I had also been avoiding the stuff for most of the tour, since it usually made me break out, but tonight, I didn't care. If I woke up tomorrow with a face full of zits, it would be totally worth it.

"What is it about men in suspenders and rolled-up sleeves that's so hot?" I asked.

"I think it's just Christian Bale," Harriet said.

I shook my head. "No way." I pointed at the screen. "They're all hot." I shifted, looking over at Cal. My head felt very heavy. "*You* guys should do a *Newsies*-inspired number. Your fans would lose. Their. Minds."

The truth was that CrushZone didn't really need any help in that area. Their popularity had skyrocketed, and it seemed like more and more of their fans were coming to the shows, splitting the audience close to fifty-fifty.

It seemed likely that by the end of the tour, I might be opening for *them*. I was both thrilled for Ryan and Cal and the guys, and worried for myself. The industry was fickle, and fame was fleeting. Or so everyone had told me. It was hard to believe it when you were being mobbed whenever you went out and performing to packed stadiums, but I could sense that things were shifting.

I just wasn't sure what to do about it. I had ideas. I had plans. But no clue how they would turn out.

"Maybe when you ask to choreograph the next video, you can throw in some *Newsies*-inspired pelvic thrusts," I said.

Cal snorted. "You bet," he said. "How's your end of that bargain going?"

I grinned at him. "Actually . . ."

Rolling off the bed, I went over to my dresser and pulled out a flat wrapped box with Harriet's name on it.

"What?" Harriet turned it over in her hands. "It's *your* birthday. Why am I getting a gift?"

I could tell she didn't really mind.

"It's a gift for both of us," I said. "Open it! Open it!"

I could hardly stay still while she tore the wrapping paper off, bouncing on my knees on the extra-soft hotel bed.

"It's a CD," she said, and turned it over. Her eyes widened. "Hey. This is the demo we recorded of my songs."

It wasn't professional by any account—Harriet, me, and a piano—but it had been enough to use as leverage.

"That's my next album," I said. "Well, the next-next album."

Harriet stared. "You're kidding."

"You did it?" Cal asked.

I felt jubilant and all-powerful. And extremely high. It was incredible.

"I told them that I'd do the Christmas album if this was the follow-up," I said.

"Yes!" Cal pumped his fist in the air.

"You knew about this?" Harriet was still turning the CD case over in her hands as if it might reveal more information.

"It was his idea," I said.

"Oh my god," Harriet said. "Oh my god."

She hugged the CD against her chest, eyes gleaming.

I was *so* happy.

"Let's listen to it," Cal said.

"Yes!" Harriet said, leaping off the bed. "Where's the CD player?"

All of a sudden I felt self-conscious.

"We don't have to do that," I said.

"Uh, yeah we do," Cal said. "You owe me."

"I owe you?" I asked. "What about your end of the deal?"

"What are you guys talking about?" Harriet asked.

She'd found the CD player.

"Just a promise we made to each other," I said. "That I'd push to do the kind of album I wanted if Cal asked to choreograph the next CrushZone music video."

"Or performance," he said.

"And?" I asked him.

He looked down at the floor.

"Cal!" I slapped his arm. "You promised. We pinky-swore! It's like you can't trust anyone these days."

"Except," Cal said, "you're looking at the choreographer for the 'Shore Leave' single video."

I shrieked. "Are you joking?"

"I take pinky promises *very* seriously," he said, doing a poor job keeping the smile off his face.

I leapt off the bed and into his arms, nearly landing both of us on the floor. I hugged him tight.

"I'm so proud of you," I said.

"I'm proud of you too," he said, his chin against the top of my head.

His arms were wrapped around me, and they felt so good. So strong.

"I can't believe it!" Harriet said.

She was still focused on the CD player, fiddling with the volume until my voice—small and fresh, accompanied only by her piano—grew to fill the room.

We sat there and listened. Unlike when I'd played it for Diana and watched her face intently, hoping to read her answer in her expression before she gave it, this time I closed my eyes and pretended that I wasn't listening to myself.

The songs were good, and I sounded good.

I just didn't sound like Katee Rose.

We'd recorded them in a rehearsal space with so-so acoustics, but the music overcame the less-than-overwhelming quality of the recording. My voice was front and center, and I handled each song with confidence and skill. It sounded beautiful. Rich and layered and steady.

"Wow," Cal said, once we'd listened to the whole album. "That's incredible."

Harriet beamed, before doing a slight double take at me and Cal.

That's when I realized we were still sitting with our arms wrapped around each other, my body all but curled up in his lap. It was weird how not weird it felt. How normal it was to be held like that. By Cal.

I didn't want to, but I untangled myself and stood.

"You think people will like it?" I asked.

"I think people will love it," he said.

He stood awkwardly, tugging at his jeans. I had a pretty good idea what he was adjusting. I'd felt it against my thigh.

"Excuse me," he said.

Harriet grabbed my arm the second he left the room.

"Oh my god," she said.

"It's good, right?" I asked.

"I'm talking about you and Cal!"

I shushed her. "He can probably hear you."

She didn't seem to care, her hands tight on my arms.

"What are you going to do?" she asked.

"About what?"

She gaped at me. "About the fact that Cal is totally in love with you."

The world seemed to slow to a halt, everything suddenly in slow motion.

"What?" I asked, but in my brain it sounded more like "Ww-hhh-aaaaaaaa-t?"

Harriet gave me a look that was both pitying and ecstatic. "Oh, come on," she said. "You know he's been in love with you forever, right? Like, since summer camp."

I shook my head. "No way," I said. "That's not . . . true. . . ."

But I couldn't really deny it. I'd never told Harriet what happened between Cal and me on the roof that last night of camp, and I wasn't sure why. She was my best friend, I told her everything, especially back then. But for whatever reason, I'd kept it a secret.

"He's not in love with me," I said.

Harriet gave me a look.

"Besides, I'm with Ryan," I said, though it had been hours since I'd even thought about him.

"Oh yeah," Harriet said. "Ryan."

I slapped her arm. I knew she wasn't a fan, but he *was* my boyfriend.

Sure, he didn't want to spend my birthday with me because he couldn't stand watching the kind of movies I liked the best. Okay, yeah, he'd been distracted lately and unable to make much time for me in other ways. And he *had* abandoned me at the Halloween party to go suck up to that film exec who hadn't even offered him a chance to audition, but that was just how Ryan was. He was focused. He was driven. I admired that.

"Have you played him the CD?" Harriet asked.

"I was waiting to tell you first," I said, but it was a lousy excuse.

I hadn't even mentioned the album to Ryan, let alone expressed that I wanted to do things differently. As far as he knew, I loved being Katee Rose and was prepared to be her—to sing like her, perform like her—for the rest of my life.

"I'm going to tell him," I said.

But Harriet didn't look convinced.

"Cal is a good guy," she said, her expression becoming serious.

"I know," I said.

"Don't hurt him," she said.

I put my hand to my chest as if *she'd* hurt *me*.

"I would never do that," I said.

"Not intentionally," she said. "But I don't think you realize the power you have. Especially over him."

Except I did.

I knew that Cal looked at me when he thought I wouldn't notice. I knew he spent more time with me than was really acceptable. I knew he hadn't dated anyone for months now.

It was fun being admired. It felt nice. Especially being admired by someone like Cal.

"I'll be careful," I said.

"Careful about what?" Cal asked.

He'd practically snuck up on us.

"Nothing," both Harriet and I said.

I had no idea how long he'd been standing there—the weed seemed to make everything fuzzy and loopy, including space and time.

"Let's watch another movie!" I said. "*Grease 2*?"

Cal went back to his chair and Harriet and I piled onto the bed. The joint was relit and we passed it around as the opening number started.

"One of the rare instances where a sequel is better than the original," I said.

Cal coughed. "Are you joking?" he asked. "You can't be saying that this movie is better than *Grease*."

"Oh, but I am," I said. "It's way better."

"No way," he said. "Travolta. Olivia. Stockard Channing! Who can beat that?"

"The music is better," I said. "'Cool Rider'? 'Score Tonight'? 'Reproduction'?"

"I'm concerned you've lost your mind," Cal said. "Harriet?"

"Sorry," she said. "I agree with Kathleen. And now that we're talking about sequels, I think we can all agree that *Sister Act 2* is better than the first."

Cal threw up his hands. "You've both lost it. I don't know if I can sit here and listen to this blasphemy."

It felt good. The three of us arguing over movies and musicals. The perfect birthday.

But I couldn't get Harriet's warning out of my head. The last thing I wanted to do was hurt anyone. Cal was my friend.

I just needed to stop sneaking looks at him and spending so much time alone with him. Whatever I felt was probably just an ego boost—having a guy like Cal admire me—and Harriet was right, I had to be careful.

How hard could it be?

NOW

CHAPTER 22

"How's the fit?"

I stretched my arms out and up, testing the shoulders of my costume.

"Good," I said to Morgan, the wardrobe mistress. "It's a little loose back here, but the rest of it is perfect." Which was a feat in itself considering my breasts usually needed special treatment to fit into most clothes.

But they'd had my measurements, and the dress hugged but didn't constrict my curves.

"And the wig?" she asked, making notes on her clipboard.

"Itches like hell," I said.

"That's how you know it's working," she said.

We exchanged smiles.

"You look great," she said.

"It's a beautiful costume," I said.

It was for Peggy's final number. Except for the opening

and finale, the cast spent most of the show in blue uniform coveralls, our hair pulled back in that iconic Rosie the Riveter bandanna. This was a va-va-voom moment for my character—where her sexuality was on display and everyone's fears around it bubbled to the surface.

Peggy was dangerous and wild, and she scared the other women with what she was willing to do in order to get what she wanted. Until they realized exactly what she did want. Because Peggy wasn't the husband-stealing man-eater that she was suspected to be. She was a Jewish woman pretending not to be Jewish, going out every night with different men in order to secure money to get her family out of Nazi-occupied Europe.

She was mercenary and relentless, all of that wrapped up in a faux fur coat and formfitting dress, with perfect blond curls and legs for days.

I could relate. Somewhat.

It had been a long time since I'd been blond—even if the bright white of the wig was closer to Marilyn, it still felt like looking at my younger self.

"Hello, Ms. Rose."

Apparently I wasn't the only one who thought so.

"What do you think?" Morgan asked Cal.

I did the requisite spin, the dress's skirt flaring out around me. I knew that combined with my dance shoes, it made my legs look incredible.

Sure enough, Cal got a good gander at them.

"Looks great," Cal said. "Fantastic work, Morgan."

She beamed with pride.

"Are they ready for me?" I asked.

"Yep," Cal said.

Not only was this the first fitting for our costumes, but it was the first opportunity to see them under the lights.

As I followed Cal to the stage, I noticed that he had dark circles under his eyes. A second glance revealed that overall he looked pretty damned exhausted.

"You okay?" I asked.

He glanced over at me.

"I'm fine," he said.

We'd been painfully polite to each other since arriving in Rhode Island. Lots of "good mornings" and "how are you doing?" and "isn't that nice?" and "hope you have a lovely evening." The most banal of small talk was also the safest. It kept us from wringing each other's necks. Or trying to bite them.

He did have an incredible neck. *Very* bitable.

"You look terrible," I said.

"Thank you," he said, rubbing his eyes. "I haven't been sleeping well. Glad to see it shows."

"Is something wrong?" I asked.

"No," he said, and then quickly amended himself. "Nothing that you need to worry about."

We were in the wings, but I grabbed him before he could walk onstage.

"What does that mean?" I asked.

He looked down at where my arm was grasping his. I released him.

"I shouldn't have said anything."

"Well, too late now," I said.

He sighed, looked around, and lowered his voice.

"Tickets sales have stalled," he said. "We sold out the first week, but the rest of the run . . ."

He waved a hand, the gesture revealing his frustration.

"Well, it's still early, isn't it?" I asked, but I could feel the sharp bite of panic at the base of my spine.

"It is," Cal said. "And everything will be fine. It's just . . ." He ran a hand through his hair. "I really shouldn't have said anything."

"I won't tell anyone," I said.

There were a million more questions I wanted to ask, but Cal was already onstage, so there was nothing to do but follow him.

"Okay," Cal said. "Peggy's number. Let's see how it looks."

He jumped off the stage and walked up the aisle to watch from the audience. The lights changed, going from neutral white to a soft yellowy glow. The song was supposed to happen early in the morning, when the other workers catch Peggy coming home from one of her "dates." They draw the expected assumptions and head inside, leaving her alone.

Cal wanted it to look like the sun was rising, which required lights changing at specific moments during the song. We walked through it, working out the timing of the lights. It was a slow process, starting and stopping, but I knew it would be worth it when it all came together.

"Okay," Cal said after the adjustments had been made. "Let's run through it one more time to see how it looks all together."

"I can just sing it," I countered.

It was a gorgeous song. I loved singing it. And part of me wanted to hear how it would sound in the theatre for the first time. With lights. In costume.

"I can play," Harriet said.

She had been sitting out in the audience with Taylor and

Mae, but headed down into the orchestra pit to sit at the piano.

Maybe this meant that whatever tension had sprung up between us was finally melting.

"If you're not worried about blowing out your voice," Cal said. "I'm sure no one is going to say no."

"Not even you?" I asked.

"Not even me," he said.

It didn't have the same bite as our previous "disagreements."

"Well, Mr. Director," I said. "Direct me."

✧ INTERMISSION ✧

The news spread through the camp like wildfire. There were no secrets among campers.

"Did you hear?" Harriet looked positively radiant with joy. "Rachel got kicked out!"

"What?" I looked around the cafeteria, still expecting to see her there in her usual corner with her popular girlfriends.

Instead, it was just them, and they all looked miserable and powerless without their leader. Although, they did keep shooting me death glares.

"How? Why?" I asked.

Harriet shrugged. "I mean, she was drinking and she's underage."

"Did you tell the counselors about the vodka?" I asked.

"No!" Harriet said. "Did you?"

"No," I said.

I'd thought about it, but I figured that Rachel would think it was Harriet and I hadn't wanted to get her in trouble.

"*Well, they found out and* fsst"—Harriet drew a sharp line with her thumb toward the door—"*she's gone.*"

"*Wow,*" I said. "*I guess dreams really do come true.*"

Harriet giggled, and I couldn't help but join in.

"*Kathleen Rosenberg.*" Ms. Spiegel, one of the instructors, suddenly appeared at the end of our table. "*Come with me.*"

Harriet and I exchanged wide-eyed looks. Had Ms. Spiegel overheard us? Was I about to get kicked out for not telling?

I followed her out of the cafeteria and toward the rehearsal rooms. I didn't want to get my hopes up, but I figured they'd take me to the main office if they were going to kick me out. Ms. Spiegel didn't say anything, so I remained quiet as well, managing to bite back an excited gasp as she pushed one of the doors open to reveal . . .

Cal. Kirby.

He was standing in the rehearsal room next to the piano. His hair was so floppy and shiny, the tops of his cheeks sunburned and freckled. His hands were spread across sheet music and they were very, very nice hands indeed.

"*I'm sure you've heard the unfortunate news,*" Ms. Spiegel said.

"*Huh?*"

"*About Rachel James.*"

"*Uh-huh,*" I said.

I was still staring at Cal. He'd looked up when we entered, but had gone back to examining the sheet music.

"*We've decided that you will be taking her place in the showcase,*" Ms. Spiegel said. "*A solo and a duet with Cal here.*"

It took a moment for her words to sink in.

"Ms. Rosenberg?" Ms. Spiegel asked when I didn't respond. "Do you want the songs or not?"

"Yes," I said. "Yes. Definitely."

"Good," she said. "You're behind, but if we add a few extra rehearsals, you should be fine."

"Okay," I said.

"I'll leave you two to get to know each other," Ms. Spiegel said. "Go over the song a couple of times and then I'll be back to direct you."

Cal had finally given me his attention, but his expression was unreadable. Was he glad that I was replacing Rachel? Was he annoyed that he'd have to rehearse more? Was he sleepy? Hungry? I couldn't tell.

"Hi," he said, as I came over to the piano. "I'm Cal."

"Kathleen," I said.

We shook hands. His skin was so warm. A little rough, but not too much. Like he picked up sticks and wood and stuff but still washed his hands when he was done. I liked it.

That's when I realized I didn't even know what duet Cal and Rachel had been cast to perform. I glanced down at the sheet music.

"Oh," I said. "I like this song."

It was "Easy Street" from Annie.

"Yeah," Cal said. "Me too. Have you seen the show?"

"Just the movie," I said. "You?"

He shrugged. "I saw a touring company do it. It was pretty cool."

"Yeah," I said, as if I knew.

"I remember your audition," he said. "You were really good."

"Thanks," I said. "You were kind of flat."

I couldn't believe I'd just said that. What was wrong with

me? Of course, I was correct—he had *been flat*—but what kind of asshole said that out loud?

"*I'm sorry,*" I said.

Cal was staring at me. Then he burst out laughing.

"It's okay," he said.

"I didn't mean it," I said.

"I was kind of flat," he said. "But I'm also one of five guys here, so it didn't really matter, I guess."

There were more than five guys at the camp, but the ratio was *way* off. And he was right—none of the guys had been quite as impressive as the girls, but Cal had been better than most. A few sour notes notwithstanding.

"I promise I'll do better at the showcase," he said.

"Good," I said, before realizing how rude that sounded. "I mean. I'm sure we'll both do better."

But Cal was shaking his head, thankfully still smiling.

"You don't hold back, do you?"

"This is really important to me," I said. "I need to impress the talent scouts."

Cal looked at me, and then nodded.

"Okay," he said. "I think we can do that."

NOW

I wrapped my coat tighter around myself as I stood on the front step of Harriet's rented Rhode Island apartment waiting for her to answer the door. In the reflection of the windows, I could see snow coming down. The sky had been gray all morning, crowded with clouds, but it hadn't started to get wintery until I was already halfway to Harriet's place.

If things hadn't been so awkward lately, I could have easily imagined us sharing an apartment during the out-of-town tryouts, or at least finding places in the same building or block. Instead, she was a good twenty-minute walk, which I'd discovered for the first time today since I hadn't yet been to her place.

The door swung open.

"Shit," she said. "It's really starting to snow, isn't it?"

She stepped aside so I could knock my boots off on the mat and peel off my jacket and hat. I shivered even though her house was warm, my hair slightly damp from the walk.

"I'm feeling like rehearsal is going to be canceled tomorrow," I said.

"Can't remember the last time I had a proper snow day," she said.

"Your place is nice," I said.

It was. Very Harriet. Either she'd brought a good portion of her records with her for the duration, or she'd found a short-term rental that had an impressive collection of its own. She had brought her own record player, though, which didn't surprise me in the least. She'd gotten her love of music from her dad and her love of history from her mom. Which is why the massive stacks of books on the floor weren't unexpected either.

"Researching the next project?" I asked.

She shrugged. "Maybe," she said. "Looking for inspiration, mostly."

Everything still felt so stilted between us, but now it wasn't completely one-sided. I'd be lying if I didn't admit that I'd been avoiding her a little as well. After the whole candy-in-the-dressing-room thing, I'd seen a version of myself in her eyes and I hadn't liked the reflection at all.

Whether that was on me or her remained to be seen.

But we were trying. At least, that's what tonight was an attempt at. Dinner and a movie, just the two of us. Like old times.

When I'd been in New York for *Show N Tell,* Harriet had been one of my only friends. Her family lived in Harlem, so after a long day of shooting, I'd come over and get a home-cooked meal and a pretend family life.

My own parents, who had never truly understood why I did what I did, were on the other side of the country in Northern California. They were also "extremely disappointed" in the choices I'd made, starting with wanting to go to Camp Curtain Call, followed by accepting the job on *Show N Tell* as a dancer, and then when I'd gotten emancipated at Diana's recommendation.

I wasn't on my own, but I kind of was.

Except for Harriet and her family.

"It smells incredible," I said, following the scent to the kitchen. "Gumbo?"

"Of course," Harriet said.

We'd eat bowl after bowl after bowl during the winter months. Smelling it was like being a teenager again. But without any of those pesky hormones causing trouble.

"Wine?" Harriet asked.

She'd already poured herself a glass and from the amount left in the bottle, I could tell that it was her second. I didn't mind. Harriet was a cozy, sleepy drunk.

"Sure," I said.

"I was thinking we could watch an old classic tonight," she said as she filled our bowls with stew packed with shrimp and okra. "*Strictly Ballroom?*"

"I haven't watched that in years," I said. "Sounds great."

Of course, she could have said that she wanted to watch YouTube videos of dogs falling off beds and I would have said yes. I wanted us to get over this fight or whatever this was, and I was prepared to acquiesce to just about anything.

But *Strictly Ballroom* was no hardship. It was a movie we'd watched multiple times together and it was nice that she'd chosen it for tonight. If she was feeling nostalgic, that was a good sign.

We took our bowls to the living room, and without saying a word to each other, both of us sat on the floor at the coffee table, our backs against the couch. It was how we'd always eaten during movie nights because Harriet's mom would have murdered us if we'd gotten any food on her sofa.

"No disrespect to *Moulin Rouge* or *Romeo + Juliet*," Harriet said, "but this is the best Baz Luhrmann film."

"One hundred percent agree," I said. "And the way Scott spins on his knees and then rises slowly in front of Fran during the last dance? So hot."

"It's not bad for a straight guy," Harriet agreed.

I was halfway through my second bowl of gumbo when the doorbell rang. Harriet had gone into the kitchen to open another bottle of wine, so I got up and went to the door.

"Are you expecting anyone?" I called to her and looked out the window.

Cal.

I opened the door.

"What are you doing here?" I asked.

He looked just as confused as I felt. He looked at his phone and then up at the number above the door and then at his phone again.

"I thought this was Harriet's place," he said.

"Shit," Harriet said from behind us. "I totally forgot."

"I can come back another time," Cal said.

It was then that I saw how hard the snow was coming down and that the shoulders of his coat were damp. His hair too. His ears and nose were red, and he was shivering slightly. It *was* freezing out.

"Get inside," I said.

"Yes, ma'am," he said.

I could have sworn his teeth chattered.

"Gumbo?" I asked.

"Is it warm?" he asked.

"It is indeed," I said. "Hot, even."

"Then pour it all over me," he said.

I tried not to imagine that. In reality it would probably be very weird and maybe sticky and not sexy. It would probably sting. But in my fantasy . . .

"I'm so sorry," Harriet said. "I totally forgot."

Her lips were wine red, her eyes just slightly unfocused. Another glass and she'd be telling us forgotten history tidbits with wild gesticulations before passing out. I knew her stages of drunkenness pretty well.

"It's okay," Cal said. "I can come back later."

"Not a chance," I said. "It is snowing way too hard for anyone to be leaving."

We all looked out the front window at the snow steadily coming down. There were at least two inches on the fence already.

"You called it," I said to Harriet. "Snow day."

We got Cal a bowl of gumbo, and he stripped off his wet socks and sweater, hanging them up in Harriet's bathroom. His jeans were wet too, but I wasn't about to suggest he take them off.

"What are you doing here?" I asked.

"We were supposed to work on alternates for the act two opener tonight," Harriet said. "But I totally forgot."

"Don't worry about it," Cal said. "I don't think there's anything wrong with the current act two opener."

"It's not strong enough," Harriet said. "It just kind of farts out at the end."

"Well, when you put it like that," Cal said. "What are you watching?"

But I knew that neither of us needed to answer that. If there was anything you could count on Cal knowing, it was movies with dance scenes in them.

"We're just about to get to the best part," I said.

"Where he spins on his knees?"

"Exactly," I said.

"Such a hard move," Cal said. "So cool."

"So cool," Harriet echoed.

She'd lain down on the couch behind me and Cal, her hand playing with my hair. It felt nice, that soft, dreamy touch as she started to fall asleep. I knew I'd have trouble getting her into bed, but it would be somewhat easier with Cal there.

We watched through the entire credits, and when the TV went silent, the only sounds in the room were Harriet's soft snores.

"Guess we better get her to her room," I said.

Cal was looking out the window again.

"How's it look?" I asked.

"Fine," he said. "I should be fine to walk back in this."

Except it wasn't fine. It was all white out there.

"Absolutely not," I said. "We're both staying here. Harriet would full-on kill us if either of us tried to walk home in this mess."

I could tell that Cal wanted to argue, but also knew he was smart enough to realize when he was beat.

"I can sleep in Harriet's bed with her," I said. "We've done it tons of times. You can take the couch."

He eyed the couch, which he would barely fit on, but again, didn't push his luck.

"I'll see if I can find some extra blankets or something," I said.

"I'll get Harriet to her room," Cal said, helping her to her wobbly feet.

Harriet mumbled something and put her arms around Cal's neck.

"I'll ask her," Cal said to her.

I gave him a look.

"She wants to make sure you don't hate her," he said.

My heart gave a little twist. I knew Harriet was drunk and she was probably referring to falling asleep during the movie, but still. It meant something.

"I could never," I said.

Cal nodded and half walked, half carried Harriet out of the living room. I put away the gumbo and washed the dishes, watching the snow from the kitchen window as I did. It was beautiful and peaceful. Quiet and untouched, like a brand-new world, or the making of one.

Harriet's house was warm and cozy, and though I wished I could snuggle up with Fish tonight, I knew she'd be fine in the heated apartment with my supersoft bed all to herself.

"I found some blankets," Cal said.

He had them piled in his arms.

"Great," I said, dishes done.

We stood there, in the snow globe of a kitchen, looking at each other. I wasn't tired at all.

"Do you need the bathroom or anything?" I asked.

Cal shook his head. "I'm good," he said. "I'll just . . ." He pointed his thumb toward the living room.

"Yep," I said. "And I'll just . . ." I gestured toward where he'd come from, where I assumed Harriet's room was.

She was sleeping on top of her covers, but I managed to roll her over to one side, pull the blankets back, roll her back over, and tuck her in. In the past, I might have helped her out of her jeans or sweater, but things weren't thawed enough for that intimacy. What we had was a tentative peace, and I wasn't going to risk that.

I stripped off a few of my own layers and climbed in next to her in my T-shirt and a pair of borrowed shorts from her drawer. We'd spent many nights like this over the years, not just as teens in her bedroom at home but on tour too. The hotel beds were always so big and overwhelming, and sometimes it was nice to have someone there with me, instead of being in those enormous suites all by myself.

It also helped that Harriet was a bit of a furnace when it came to body heat. It was like having a personal heater and it could be incredibly soothing in the winter.

Tonight, however, I couldn't sleep. I lay on my back and stared up at the ceiling, where the light from the outside streetlamps filtered through the curtains to create a soft, almost wavelike pattern. It was like being underwater. Quiet. Peaceful.

Even Harriet's snoring had its own calming rhythm.

My mind kept wandering to Cal in the next room. The couch was very small, but he'd also looked damned tired, so I hoped he'd fallen asleep.

I must have done the same because at some point, I woke up and was thirsty beyond belief. A glance at the clock told me it was well past four, but I knew I'd never get back to sleep unless I got something to drink.

The floor was cold as I padded to the kitchen. I found a glass and filled it at the sink, drinking the entire thing in one fast, greedy gulp.

I heard the couch shift and squeak as I put the glass in the sink.

"Kathleen?" Cal's head popped up, backlit by the snowy windows behind him. His hair was all over the place.

"Just getting water," I said. "Go back to sleep."

"Ha," he said. "*Back* to sleep."

His voice was hoarse, scratchy.

I knew I should just go back to Harriet's room, but instead I moved closer to the couch.

"Can't sleep?"

"Surprisingly, couches stopped being an acceptable sleeping arrangement many years ago," he said.

"You could have just said no," I said.

He shrugged.

I came around to the side of the couch. He hadn't even unfolded the blankets, but he had taken off his pants. He was sitting there in his boxer briefs and a T-shirt. Then again, I wasn't much more covered up and I wasn't wearing a bra. He didn't seem to be cold, but I definitely was, and wrapped my arms around myself both to stay warm and to keep my nipples from taking anyone's eyes out.

"The snow seems to have slowed down," Cal said.

He was right. It was still falling, but not at the same rate it had been a few hours ago.

"You're not thinking of sneaking out in the middle of the night, are you?" I asked.

I couldn't completely see his face in the half-light, but I was pretty sure there was a guilty expression there.

"No," he said.

A complete lie.

"Harriet's up early," I said. "And I'm assuming rehearsal is canceled for tomorrow. Today."

Cal looked at his watch. "Yeah," he said. "I'll send out a text in a few hours, but I'll probably go to the theatre anyways."

We were less than a week away from our first performance.

"No rest for the wicked, huh," I said.

It was a joke, but Cal frowned.

"There's a lot to do," he said.

"I know," I said. "And you're doing a good job."

Why I was stroking his ego right now, I didn't know. Something about it being nighttime and quiet and peaceful. Like we had stepped out of time—shifted to a different reality where we were friends.

He sighed and put his head in his hands. Just for a moment.

"Ticket sales still haven't picked up," he said. "They're not bad, but they're not great either. And if we want to go to Broadway, we need great."

I sat with that for a moment, knowing for certain that Cal had *not* wanted to tell me any of that.

"I've been trying to shake up some publicity to help our ticket sales," he said.

"That shouldn't be too hard," I said. "I've heard I'm a big draw."

I gave him spirit fingers and a smile. His own grin was half-hearted.

"You are," he said, but there was clearly something more.

"But . . ." I prompted.

He closed his eyes, squeezed them tight. He looked so tired.

"Everyone wants to interview you," he said. "But they all want to talk about . . ." he trailed off.

"Ah," I said.

"Yeah," he said. "They want a quote or two from me too."

"Wow," I said.

"Exactly," he said. "And I realize now that I should have asked you, but I assumed that you didn't want to talk about it—especially to the press—so I keep saying that the topic is off-limits and suddenly no one's available."

I didn't know what to say.

"I should have checked with you first, but it's not like I want to talk about it either," he said softly.

We both sat there, knowing that we'd have to find another way to get the word out about the show.

"I guess I could join social media?" I suggested.

"God no," he said. "Don't do that."

It was the only idea I had, but I was relieved he'd vetoed it. I really didn't want to get on social media.

But I also didn't want the show to stumble before it could make it to Broadway.

"Promise me something," I said after a moment of thoughtful silence.

"Sure."

"If it gets dire enough, tell me," I said.

He hesitated.

"Cal!"

"I promise," he said.

"Pinky promise?"

I held out my finger and waited for him to link his with mine.

"Promise," he said.

We blew on our thumbs. Just like we'd done at camp.

I tried not to notice how warm his hands were.

"Why do we do this to ourselves?" Cal asked.

I couldn't tell if the question was meant to be rhetorical.

"Do what?" I asked.

"This." He gestured around himself.

"That doesn't clarify anything," I said.

Cal heaved out a sigh and leaned back.

"Theatre, I guess," he said. "Performing. Art."

"Ah," I said. "Simple questions."

He smiled.

Those dimples.

I ignored them and thought about his question.

"Because it's fun," I said.

Cal didn't say anything for a long time.

"Fun." He said it so quietly that I very nearly missed it.

"Yeah," I said. "Fun."

But that was the truth. The reason we put ourselves through all this. Because at the end of the day, it was fun. It was joyful. It was an adrenaline rush. It was big and broad and bold.

"I shouldn't have told you," Cal said. "It's going to be fine. We'll figure it out. *I'll* figure it out."

"Where are your producers?" I asked. "Isn't this part of their job?"

"I can handle it," Cal said.

I could see him digging in his heels, getting all stubborn.

"Fine," I said.

But the wheels in my head were already turning. Already making plans.

THEN

CHAPTER 24

I hated my outfit. The skirt was way too short, considering I was going to be standing above everyone, and whatever they'd used to make the fluffy white part of my "sexy Santa" outfit made my skin feel like it was being jabbed by thousands of extremely tiny pins.

At least I'd convinced them to let me pick the song I was going to do at the holiday—read: Christmas—concert. Diana hadn't been pleased that I wanted to do "You're a Mean One, Mr. Grinch," but I was getting better and better at standing up for myself.

A pair of arms wrapped around my waist, and I leaned back into them.

"Did you gain some weight?" Ryan asked.

"Hey!" I slapped his hands away. "What the fuck?"

"Sorry, babe," he said, his palm remaining at my hip. "You just feel a little chunky here."

He wasn't the first to comment on it—Diana had already

expressed concern that I'd been plumping up—but it hurt more coming from Ryan.

"The costume's tight," I said.

"Totally," he said, and leaned in to give me a kiss.

I gave him my cheek, but if he noticed, he didn't say anything.

"This is so cool," he said, looking up at the float we'd be riding on.

The whole event started out with a parade, each act with its own float, with the exception of me and CrushZone. In addition to doing a Christmas medley, we'd been billed together over the past few months, and it seemed that people were used to seeing us together.

I got the sense that it was more than that, but I didn't ask. I didn't really want to know, which I knew was bad business, but I had my eyes on the album I was set to do with Harriet—the one that had just been announced.

"Is that what you guys are wearing?" I asked.

"Cool, right?" Ryan lifted his arms and turned to give me the full effect.

It was fine. White jeans, white shirt, white jacket, white hat. I'd definitely stand out among them, but I was also dressed in seventy-five percent less clothing, and it was fucking freezing.

"Yeah," I said.

I'd been avoiding Ryan lately. My birthday had been weeks ago, but I couldn't stop thinking about what Harriet had said. About Cal. About him being in love with me.

I wasn't sure what to do.

I knew Diana was thrilled that me and Ryan were together. It was good for both of our careers and there had been some whisperings—in the press, in the tabloids—that we were serious. *Marriage* serious. I hadn't said anything, but usually when stuff like that seeped out to the public, it was because someone had planted it there. Often for a reason.

Breaking up with him would cause problems. It would require multiple discussions—not just between me and Ryan but with our management teams, publicity, etc. There would have to be an announcement. *Everyone* would know about it.

It was just one more thing I didn't want to think about.

The Christmas concert was near the end of the tour. In a few weeks, I'd be able to go home, sleep in a bed that was my own, and then have two blissful months in the city while I worked on the next album. All of Harriet's songs.

I just had to get through it, all the way to our last show at Madison Square Garden. I wanted to savor these moments, but the truth was that I was so exhausted all I could do was focus on putting one step in front of the other.

"Okay." Diana, my manager, came over to us. "Katee, you're going to be over here."

I looked up. And up. And up.

There was a little crow's nest–type extension at the back of the float. I was sure it was secure, but it certainly didn't look that way. It looked like one of those metal display things that people use to prop up dolls.

"I'm going to be up there by myself?" I asked.

I wasn't afraid of heights, exactly, but I didn't love the idea of being half naked, suspended above a crowd in freezing cold weather. Alone.

"The guys will be right here," Diana said, seemingly oblivious to my concerns. She gestured to the front of the float, where there was level ground and a lot of space.

"I don't want to be up there alone," I said.

"Come on, babe," Ryan said. "You're going to look great."

The other guys had come over to look at the float. I avoided Cal's gaze, which felt mean, but I also didn't know what else to do. I knew I shouldn't be thinking about him at all, and it was much easier to avoid those thoughts when I didn't look at him that often. It wasn't my fault that the CrushZone team had done a really, really good job making all of the guys so damned appealing.

Not that I had thoughts about Wyatt. Or LC. Or even Mason.

It didn't matter. I just needed to keep my distance until I figured out what I was going to do. How I felt.

"You guys will be at the front of the float," Diana said. "And it's the last float so everyone will be excited and ready to see you."

I could tell that Ryan liked that.

"Do we all need to be there together?" Cal asked. "Can't we spread out a bit?"

"Uh"—Diana looked at her clipboard—"yeah. I think we want you all together."

But I could see the wheels turning in Cal's head.

"Katee," Diana said, "let's get you back in makeup. You're looking a little shiny. And we should cover up that zit more."

My hand flew to my face. It wasn't the first time I'd had my flaws pointed out to me in front of other people, but it never got easier or more fun.

By the time I got back, things had changed. The guys—per Cal's suggestion—were more spread out over the float. Wyatt was at the base of my sky-high platform, while LC and Mason were in the middle together. Ryan was up at the front by himself.

"Sorry," Cal said.

I hadn't noticed him come up behind me.

"About what?" I asked.

"I thought that Ryan would be the one in the crow's nest with you," he said.

We both looked at him, posing and preening on the unmoving float.

"I can switch with one of the other guys if you want," he said.

"Why would I want that?" I asked, even though I hadn't exactly been subtle about avoiding him these past few weeks.

Luckily Cal didn't even dignify that question with a response.

"It's fine," I said. "It's just for a half hour or something, right?"

"Right," he said.

"Okay," the stage manager called out. "Everyone to places."

I looked up at the stairs—if you could call them that; they looked more like slots dug out of faux snow—and felt very, very glad I wasn't going to have to be up there alone.

I gripped the railing and carefully, slowly, climbed up to the top of the float, balancing mostly on my toes since I didn't trust that my narrow heels would fit. I could feel Cal behind me, his warmth and strength giving me the support I needed to get to the platform.

"Jesus," he said when we reached the top.

It was higher than I had thought. Or maybe it just seemed higher because the space was so small and suspended so far out. Cal and I could barely fit up there together, our butts brushing up against each other as we both tried to face outward.

"This is ridiculous," I said.

"This is showbiz," he said.

We stood there silently, watching and listening to everyone else preparing.

"Are you guys okay up there?" Wyatt asked.

I peered over the railing and regretted it immediately.

"Yes," I said, though it came out more like a gasp.

"Don't *do* that," Cal said.

"Sorry," I said.

Is he afraid of heights?

I glanced over my shoulder, trying to get a look at him, but his face was turned away.

"I can't even see you guys," Wyatt said.

"Great," Cal said.

I couldn't see his face, but I could see one of his hands, which was gripping the railing for dear life. His knuckles were stark white.

"Hey," I said, putting my hand over his. "We're safe."

He jerked his hand away from mine.

"I'm fine," he said.

It hurt, for him to react that way.

"Fine," I said.

We stood there, both of us stiff with cold—and, I assumed, annoyance at the other—waiting for this whole thing to be over with. The worst part was we'd still have to perform after the parade. Once we'd thawed out.

Suddenly the float gave a lurch and I let out an involuntary shriek.

"Fuck!" Cal said, and I could feel his back tense up against mine. "You okay?" he asked.

"I think so," I said.

I couldn't help it, I leaned up against him. He was so warm and sturdy, and I was afraid of falling.

"Kathleen," he said.

His voice was low. Hoarse.

"Mm-hmm?"

"I heard you guys," he said.

I went completely still.

"I don't know what you're talking about," I said.

But I did. Of course I did.

Cal was silent. I was silent.

Then.

"Was Harriet right?" I asked.

The float lurched again and then began moving more steadily forward. But I barely noticed this time. My entire attention was focused on Cal and how he might answer. If he did at all.

"Yes," he finally said.

My heart started thumping in an entirely new rhythm. Like it had just learned a new song.

"Oh," I said.

"Yeah," he said.

I could hear music up ahead as we got closer to joining the parade. Pretty soon, we'd be in full view of everyone. I'd have to smile and wave and pretend that I wasn't worried about people looking up my skirt or freezing my ass off or processing the fact that Cal had just confessed that he was in love with me.

I reached over and put my hand on his.

"Kathleen," he said. "Don't."

I could hear the pain in his voice, but I didn't move my hand. Instead, I gave it a squeeze. He let out a breath.

"You have to break up with Ryan," he said.

"Okay," I said.

Cal's other hand came to lie on top of mine. I was safe. Protected.

"Okay," he said.

And the parade moved on.

NOW

We were days away from our first performance. Cal and I hadn't spoken about ticket sales since that quiet morning in Harriet's kitchen, but from the deep, tired lines in his face and the bags under his eyes, I could tell that things weren't improving.

But it was okay. Because I had an idea.

After rehearsal, as everyone was about to get ready to leave, I stood in the middle of the stage and made an announcement.

"Just wanted to say that I'm heading to Loudmouth tonight if anyone wants to join. Drinks on me!"

I heard excitement ripple through the theatre. I saw Cal standing in the audience, his arms crossed, one eyebrow raised.

"Isn't that a karaoke bar?" someone asked.

That eyebrow raised even higher as he caught my eye.

What are you doing? his expression asked.

"It certainly is," I said.

Why don't you come and see? I asked him with *my* eyebrow.

"I'll be there at six," I said. "It will be fun."

Harriet caught me on my way out.

"Karaoke?" she asked. "In public?"

But we weren't on tour anymore and I wasn't Katee Rose. Well, not exactly.

"Trust me," I said.

I could tell that she was confused, but I'd also never known Harriet to turn down a sing-along. Part of me wondered if she was aware of the problems with ticket sales. If Cal had told me, surely he'd told the writer-lyricist. Maybe it was part of the reason she'd been so distant. All of us keeping secrets from each other.

The place was packed when I arrived—practically all of the cast and crew had shown up early. It was a good sign, but I scanned the crowd, hoping there'd also be some locals, ideally with good cameras on their phones and a decent social media following.

It was possible that this was a terrible idea. It was also possible that it was utterly genius.

Karaoke started at six-thirty, so I ordered a drink and put myself on the list. There were a handful of names above mine, but I could tell that everyone from *Riveted!* had been waiting for me to sign up.

I kept watching the door, waiting for Cal to arrive. It wasn't until karaoke had already begun and he still wasn't there that I actually began to worry that he might not show up. His presence wasn't necessary for this to work, but I'd also never thought that he just *wouldn't* come.

"Next up is Kathleen Rosenberg," the host called.

The room—still mostly made up of the cast—cheered as I hit the stage.

"Hello, Rhode Island!" I said.

I got some hoots and hollers.

"Before I knock your socks off," I said, "I want to tell you all a little secret."

I could practically feel the room lean toward me.

"My real name *is* Kathleen Rosenberg," I said. "But it's possible that some of you might know me by another name." I held for a count of five. The perfect length for dramatic effect. "Does anyone remember Katee Rose?"

I could feel the vibration of excitement travel through the crowd, all those whispers of "OMG" or "I knew it" or "What is she doing here?" I had them in the palm of my hand.

"Well, in case you've forgotten about her, I'm here to jog your memories," I said. "Let's go!"

The music started and the crowd went crazy.

I couldn't remember the last time I'd performed one of my songs live. I'd spent so much time lip-syncing them that I wondered, for a brief, horrible moment, if I still had it.

Then, the door to the bar opened and Cal walked in.

My eyes locked on his and I began to sing.

"Kiss me, baby. Once. Twice. Kiss me again, honey. Doesn't it feel so nice?"

I watched as Cal's expression went from surprise to shock to what I assumed was understanding. He crossed his arms and shook his head, the smile on his face both encouraging and disbelieving.

I let myself really sing the song. I didn't do the Katee Rose version, everything coming up out of my nose. Instead, I put my whole voice, my whole throat behind it, and a silly song about making out became a heartfelt cry for love.

I finished, holding that last note way longer than I ever did on any of my records, and the room. Went. Nuts.

"Thank you!" I said, taking a bow. "If you like what you just heard, then you're going to want to see me and my amazing co-stars in *Riveted!* Tickets on sale now!"

I hopped off the stage, accepting compliments and high fives as I headed back to the bar where Cal was standing.

"Unbelievable," he said.

"I know," I said. "I'm incredibly talented."

He laughed and took a drink of his beer.

"Anyone get a video of it?" I asked.

"Just half the bar," he said.

"Excellent," I said. "Let's hope they included the part where I talked about the show."

He turned to face me. "You didn't have to do that," he said. "We—I—would have figured it out. The performances would start generating word of mouth, we'd sell the tickets. It was all taken care of."

I rolled my eyes. "Just say thank you."

I could tell that there were probably a whole bunch of other words he'd rather say, but in the end he just nodded.

"Thank you," he said.

"You're welcome," I said.

We sat at the bar while the rest of the cast got up and killed. I kept paying for drinks and even signed a few autographs for those in the bar who weren't involved with *Riveted!*

"Tell your friends about the show!" I told them.

It was shameless, but I didn't care. I wanted to sell tickets. I wanted to go to Broadway.

The truth was, if this didn't work out, I'd contact the press myself and give up the story—the real story—about what happened all those years ago.

But still. I was hoping it wouldn't come to that.

The performances were incredible. We got an amazing duet of "I'll Cover You" from *Rent,* while Taylor brought us all to tears with her hilarious version of "I Cain't Say No" from *Oklahoma!* I couldn't help myself and went up a few more times, doing "Joey" by Concrete Blonde and some Linda Ronstadt, while Harriet did a truly terrible rendition of "Hold On." Even the more reserved crew members, like Morgan in wardrobe, took a swing and surprised us with a sweetly sung "Hard Candy Christmas" from *The Best Little Whorehouse in Texas.*

The entire time, Cal stayed in the back, watching, applauding, but not moving from his seat.

As the night went on, the bar got more and more crowded. I signed up again to sing, willing, once more, to put myself on display for the benefit of the show.

But this time, I didn't plan on being alone.

I picked up the microphone.

"You're welcome," I said as the song started.

"Oh my god," Cal groaned.

"Oh my god!" everyone else cheered.

"Shore Leave" wasn't CrushZone's best-known song, but it was the one with the most iconic music video and the most memorable dance moves. Dance moves I still remembered. And I bet Cal did as well.

"Baby, baby, baby," I sang. "It's my last chance for love."

Cal had his head in his hands, but everyone else was on their feet cheering. I saw his shoulders shaking and when Harriet pulled him out of his chair, I could see that he was laughing, his face red. She dragged him toward the front of the room. Toward me.

"Don't leave me," the entire bar sang along, "like the waves from the shore. Come back, come back."

As the dance break approached, I went to the edge of the stage and reached outward.

"I could use a little help," I said. "Let's welcome up one of the founding members of CrushZone: Calvin Tyler Kirby!"

The room erupted in cheers, and I held my breath, wondering what Cal would do.

"You're a menace," he shouted up at me.

"Fun, remember?" I shouted back. "Come on, Kirby, show us your moves."

Shaking his head, Cal jogged up the steps, joining me just as the beat kicked up.

"Think you still got it?" I asked.

"Just watch," he said.

The dance was *so much* fun. It was all jumping and hip thrusts and chances for the guys to show off. Cal had been featured in the music video because he was the best dancer, and it had been one of the few times where he'd stolen the spotlight from Ryan.

It was one of my favorite CrushZone songs.

And Cal still knew every. Single. Move.

At this point, no one was paying attention to me. Everyone was watching Cal as he went through the routine like it was second nature. He was a gorgeous dancer. Confident and intense and so damned sexy.

I should have known he wouldn't have let those skills go rusty.

Watching him move took my breath away. I had stopped to watch like the rest of them.

"Come on, Rosenberg," Cal said. "Keep up."

I never could resist a challenge, meeting him step for step as everyone in the audience went nuts. We finished with a flourish and a huge cheer went up from the entire bar.

I was sweaty and out of breath, but I couldn't keep the smile off my face.

"Come see *Riveted!*" Cal shouted, and took my hand, pulling us both into a bow. "Thank you and good night!"

We shut the place down.

It wasn't until I saw Cal stumble on the step out of the bar that I realized he must have had more beer than I'd thought. He was definitely a little drunk.

But like Harriet, he was a friendly drunk.

"Come on," I said, putting myself under his arm, holding him up. "Let's get you to your apartment."

"I'm fine," he said, shaking me off.

"Mm-hmm," I said. "Just humor me, okay? Where's your place?"

He pointed and we began to walk.

It hadn't snowed since that night at Harriet's, but it was cold enough that the ground was still crunchy and frozen in places, and a bit dangerous. I kept a close eye on Cal, who seemed steady enough, though a bit pink-cheeked. It looked good on him. He was softer like this, a little less reserved.

And he'd had fun tonight. More fun than I was pretty sure he'd had in a while.

"I'm surprised you remembered," I said.

Cal tilted his head, a question.

"The choreography," I said.

"Ah," he said. "Muscle memory. Hell of a thing."

"Sure," I said.

But it was more than that with Cal. I imagined it was part of what made him a good choreographer. A good director.

My jacket was zipped up to my chin, but Cal's was open, revealing his sweater and a scarf hanging loosely from his neck. He looked cozy, and part of me imagined tucking myself in against his chest, listening to his heartbeat as he wrapped his coat around us.

"It's nice to know that our legacy lives on," I said.

We hadn't been the only ones who'd performed songs from our combined discography. Once the night had gotten going, we'd been serenaded by both the cast and Rhode Islanders—a veritable mixtape of our greatest hits.

And some of them had even come prepared with choreography.

"I was impressed with everyone else's moves," Cal said. "I thought we were old news, for sure."

"I think we're just on the cusp of going from ironic enjoyment to nostalgic," I said.

Which, honestly, didn't seem so bad anymore. There was something comforting about facing the past in this way. The time and distance had taken some of the sting off, but it had also felt safe in a way it hadn't in a long time.

Maybe it was because I was in control.

Yes, videos of tonight were most likely spreading across the internet, but that had been the point. Mostly.

It was using my notoriety for good. I hoped.

I would be really fucking disappointed if it didn't work. But even if that was the case, I didn't regret it.

"I remember the first time you guys did 'Shore Leave' live," I said. "People just about lost their minds."

What I didn't say was how pissed Ryan had been that Cal had overshadowed him. I'd had to listen to him bitch and moan about it for weeks.

"I'm a better dancer than him," Ryan had said. "I'm definitely a better singer."

One was true. The other . . . not so much.

I'd spent hours reassuring him that he was the star of the group. That he was the best. That no one was better. Not then, not ever.

It had been exhausting.

Ryan had been exhausting.

It wasn't an excuse.

But.

"Remember when Wyatt tore his pants onstage?" Cal asked.

I looked over at him. The streetlights were a soft yellow glow and they blurred him. He seemed more relaxed, less exhausted.

"You kept telling him his floor humping was too enthusiastic," I said. "Of course, your mistake was saying 'humping' and 'enthusiastic' in the same sentence."

"Did you hear he has five kids now?"

I tried to imagine horndog Wyatt as a dad. But maybe he'd changed. We'd all changed. Hopefully.

"We are ancient," I said.

"I think we've held up pretty well."

"What about Mason and LC?" I asked.

I hadn't kept in touch with any of them. I didn't much miss Ryan and Wyatt, but LC had been sweet and kind.

Mason, well, Mason had been mysterious, but nice. There were times I missed them.

"They're good," Cal said. "Out in Palm Springs."

"They own a motel, right?"

Cal nodded, and then his face split into an enormous grin.

"Remember when you tried to play matchmaker?" he asked.

I slapped him on the arm. "It was an honest mistake," I said. "It's not like any of them were out back then. Harriet certainly wasn't."

"Oh, come on." Cal gave me a disbelieving look. "Are you telling me you didn't know?"

Of course, now it seemed obvious. But then?

"Did I know that Mason and LC were schtupping each other between interviews about their perpetual singleness?" I asked. "No. I had no idea."

Cal laughed. "Schtupping?"

I tried to look affronted but couldn't help smiling.

"Okay, okay," I admitted. "In retrospect, LC and Harriet were not the perfect couple I imagined them to be."

In the end, I hadn't cared that my matchmaking didn't work out. I'd cared that my best friend didn't feel safe enough to tell me that she was gay. But things had been different then, and I'd been too wrapped up in my own straight-girl bullshit to pay close attention to anything else.

Was I making the same mistake now?

"You tried so hard," Cal said. "It was adorable."

I couldn't remember the last time someone had called me adorable. Or the last time I'd blushed.

"I was young, innocent, and hopeful," I said.

Cal snorted.

"Okay," I said. "I was young."

"We all were," he said. "God, we were so young."

"Stupid too," I said.

"About that," Cal said.

I sucked in a breath, worrying that this would topple our tentative peace and we'd be back to anger and resentment and bitterness.

But also, wondering what the hell he wanted to say about it. Did he regret what he'd said? Or what he hadn't said? In some ways, that had hurt the most. His silence after the fact.

Well, no. Public humiliation hurt the most.

Especially when I had to face it completely alone.

"I owe you an apology," Cal said.

I stopped abruptly. So abruptly that Cal had to backtrack a few steps after he noticed I wasn't following him.

"What?" he asked.

"Nothing," I said.

We kept walking. Until I stopped again.

"What?" he asked once more.

"I'm ready," I said.

"For?"

"That apology," I said.

I didn't tell him that in a way, I'd been waiting over a decade for it. I hadn't realized it before, but there it was. The need—the desire—to hear *him* admit that it wasn't all my fault.

"I'm sorry," Cal said. "I shouldn't have let it happen."

"Let what happen?" I asked. "The sex or everything else?"

"Both?" he said, and then he shook his head. "No. Everything else."

We continued walking. It was cold, but nice. I had my

hands in my pockets and the chill was tickling the apples of my cheeks and the tip of my nose.

"I was angry," Cal said. "Really angry."

"I know," I said. "I am sorry about that."

Because I was. Always had been.

He shook his head. "You don't owe me anything," he said.

I lifted an eyebrow. It was the last thing I'd expected him to say.

"For years I believed that we'd wounded each other equally," he said. "That my reaction measured up to yours, and that my hurt feelings meant it was all fair game. If you didn't want me, you didn't need me either. For anything."

"I didn't—"

He held up a hand. "I know," he said.

Did he? Did he know what I'd been about to say? Did I?

"I didn't know how bad it would get," he said. "I didn't think it would blow up that way. And once it did . . ." He let out a laugh that wasn't humorous at all. "Honestly, I don't think I took Ryan seriously enough. Couldn't even imagine that he'd weaponize the whole situation the way he did."

"He always did have hidden depths," I said.

Cal stopped, turned toward me.

"Kathleen," he said, "I am so sorry. For saying nothing. For doing nothing. For abandoning you."

My throat was tight.

It was a very good apology.

"And I'm sorry for what I said that day."

"Me too," I said.

We walked.

"Thank you," I said.

"You're welcome," he said.

I felt strange. Like something had shifted but I wasn't sure what. Or how it would feel tomorrow. Next week. Next month.

"This is me," Cal said.

I walked him to the door. All the way to the door.

The top step was small and crowded, but neither of us noticed it until we were smushed there together. Cal moved back and stumbled. Both of us reached for the other, his hand landing on my biceps, mine gripping his forearm. Steadying him brought us closer together, something we both realized at exactly the same moment. We were too close.

It would be so easy to lift my head. To lean forward, just a tiny bit. To tug him against me. To kiss the hell out of him.

We both dropped our hands immediately, separating. I all but fell off the step, arms flailing. He reached out, but I managed to right myself without his help. We were both breathing heavily. The tips of his ears were red. My chest felt hot.

"Okay," he said.

"Okay."

"See you tomorrow," he said.

"Uh-huh," I said.

He stood there for a moment, both of us hesitating.

"Kathleen," he said.

"Uh-huh?"

"Please go inside," he said.

"I can't," I said.

He sucked in a breath.

"I don't live here," I reminded him.

He looked back at *his* door. At the keys in *his* hand.

"Oh," he said. "Right."

He fumbled with the keys, while I tried to ignore the magnetic charge urging me to grab Cal by the collar of his shirt and shove him up against the door. It took him three tries to get the key in the lock. Hitchcock and his train speeding through a tunnel would never have accused us of subtlety.

The door opened. Cal stayed on the top step.

"Well," I said.

"Well," he said.

It would take one, two, three steps to get inside his apartment. Four or five to get the door closed. I didn't know where his bedroom was, but the entryway floor would probably be fine.

But then I remembered Harriet. Remembered the show. Remembered the complicated power dynamics at play. Remembered all the reasons we couldn't. We shouldn't.

An apology was nice, but it didn't erase the past.

"Good night," Cal said.

"Good night," I said.

He didn't move. I didn't move.

Three steps.

"Go inside, Cal," I said.

He looked at me.

"Yeah," he said.

I didn't wait to hear the lock turn before I left.

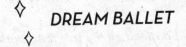

DREAM BALLET

Thwack!

"*Again!*" Ms. Spiegel ordered.

Thwack!

"*From the top.*"

Thwack!

"*And this time with* feeling!"

I caught Cal glaring at her, but he said nothing as we went back to one. The music started, the hot, jazzy rhythm that made you want to dance. Unfortunately, no matter what we did, it never seemed good enough for Ms. Spiegel. We barely got three lines in before she was hitting pause and smacking her baton on the table.

"No. No. No," she said.

Cal and I stood there, waiting for her to say more.

"I should just cut this number," she said.

"No!" I protested.

I still had the solo, which I had been working on with

another instructor, but the more I was in front of scouts during the showcase, the better chance I had to impress them. And there wasn't any dancing in "Memory," whereas "Easy Street" was about fifty-fifty.

Ms. Spiegel glared at me.

"Then get it right," she said.

We practiced for another hour and didn't seem to get any better.

"If I were you, I'd spend all my free time working on this number," Ms. Spiegel said before she left.

I looked over at Cal.

"What are we doing wrong?" I asked.

"Nothing," he said. "That's just her way."

"What?"

"She tells everyone they're terrible," he explained. "It's supposed to make us work harder or something, but it's stupid. We're fine. The number is fine."

"But fine isn't good enough," I said, my voice pitching upward. "I need to be amazing."

Cal looked at me. "You are amazing," he said. "You're great."

"Really?"

It was the first real praise I'd gotten from him—from anyone really—since I'd been given Rachel's parts. It was nice.

"It's one of my favorite numbers," I said. "I was always disappointed that my parents wouldn't let me do theatre when I was young enough to play an orphan or Annie, so I started memorizing the adult parts so I'd be ready."

Cal blinked at me.

"Wow," he said. "You're really determined."

"I need to go to Broadway," I said.

"What if you don't?" he asked.

"I will," I said. "I have to."

He gave me a long look. "Want to practice again?"

"Always," I said.

He laughed. "You never stop, do you?"

I shook my head. "One day, maybe, but now? No. I can't."

"Okay," he said. "Let's go from the top."

"But with feeling," *I said.*

He scowled and pressed play. I gave myself a little shake to warm up and then took my position. The choreography involved a lot of shoulders and fancy footwork, but Cal was good. He was great. There wasn't a combination he couldn't do, and he always seemed to make it look effortless.

It more than made up for his tendency to sing flat.

We were a good team—my voice could cover up any hiccups with his, and he was able to tweak the choreography to make it work better for me.

"Try this," he said, halfway through the number. "Left first, and then spin."

I gave it a try.

Cal watched, hand tucked under his elbow, chin resting in his palm. He looked like a real choreographer.

"I think that works," he said. "Besides, your left side is stronger than your right side."

"It is not!"

"Okay," he said.

I glared at him. He shrugged.

"It is, but I'm not going to argue with you," he said.

I had called *him flat. I supposed it was possible that my left side was stronger.*

"Won't Ms. Spiegel care that we've changed her choreography?" I asked.

"She's never noticed before," he said.

I raised my eyebrows at him. "Before?"

"It's not my first time working with the old bat," he said.

I was scandalized—Ms. Spiegel was a Camp Curtain Call icon—she was known for her discerning eye and her ability to turn raw talent into polished skill.

Cal caught my look.

"She's not that good of a choreographer," he said.

I couldn't believe what I was hearing.

"But . . . but . . . but . . . she was in A Chorus Line!"

She reminded us constantly. She'd played Cassie.

"She was in a touring company, and she started as an understudy," Cal said. "Not that there's anything wrong with that, but if she was such a talent, then why is she tormenting a bunch of kids instead of being on Broadway?"

I'd never thought about it like that. As far as I was concerned, the counselors at Camp Curtain Call were gods, and we were all lucky to work with them.

"It's not that easy to get on Broadway," I said.

Cal gave me a look. "And yet, you're confident you'll get there."

"Well, yeah," I said. "I have to."

"You keep saying that," he said. "Why?"

"Because," I said.

No one had ever asked me that before. Why did I want to be on Broadway? Why did I need to perform?

I just did.

"Okay," Cal said.

"I like being onstage," I said. "And I'm good at it."

"Okay," Cal said.

"And I should be on Broadway," I said.

"*Okay,*" *he said.*

"*I should!*"

"*Yeah,* okay," *he said.*

"*What about you?*" *I asked.*

"*I'm not going to Broadway,*" *he said.* "*My voice isn't strong enough.*"

Well. At least he knew that.

"*You could be a featured dancer,*" *I said.*

He laughed. "*And spend the rest of my life working with people like Ms. Spiegel? No thanks.*"

"*Then why are you even here?*" *I asked.*

He didn't say anything for a while.

"*Because I like it,*" *he said.* "*Performing. Being onstage. It's fun.*"

Fun.

"*My sisters and I would put on performances for my parents when I was younger,*" *Cal said.* "*Nothing big, but for Thanksgiving and stuff, we'd do a dance or a little skit or something and it was always really fun.*" *He shrugged.* "*I like dancing. It's kind of like a superpower, almost, being able to control your body like that—being able to make it do what you want.*"

I'd never thought about it that way, but he was right. Not just dancing, but singing too. All of it.

"*But it has to be fun,*" *he said.* "*Or else what's the point?*"

I didn't have a response to that. Instead, I just let his words marinate.

"*Want to try again?*" *he asked.* "*I have a few other ideas on how to make it better.*"

"*How much are you going to change?*"

Cal shrugged. "*As much as you let me.*"

"*And she really won't notice?*"

"*As long as we look like we know what we're doing, she doesn't really care.*"

I wasn't sure I believed him, considering she'd been yelling at us for days now about not getting the number right, but at our next rehearsal, when we showed her all the "practicing" we'd been doing, she let us do the entire thing all the way through. When it was done, she sat there looking at us, her expression as sour as usual.

"*Not bad,*" *she said.* "*But next time—with feeling.*"

NOW

CHAPTER 26

I walked into the expensive Midtown penthouse, and the first person I saw was Rachel.

The party was being thrown by one of the producers—either Statler or Waldorf—to celebrate the news that *Riveted!* was officially going to Broadway.

I supposed I should have felt somewhat smug given that after all her meddling and manipulating, Rachel hadn't managed to snag the role of Peggy from my clutches, but after eight shows a week, including two-a-days in Rhode Island, and a new late-night schedule, I was a little too tired to feel smug.

I was also fighting off the fear that had set in about the upcoming premiere on Broadway.

It had always—always—been the dream, but now that it was in my reach, I was starting to freak the fuck out.

And I couldn't stop thinking about Cal. About his apology. About what had happened then. About what was happening now. About us.

Of course, there wasn't an *us*.

I took a sip of wine and glared at Rachel over the rim of my glass.

"Hey, I know you!"

I turned to find Whitney standing there.

"Hi," I said.

Had Cal brought *two* plus-ones?

I'd brought no one.

I supposed, technically, Harriet and I had come together, but that didn't really count. We both were supposed to be there. Harriet especially. If this was anyone's night to celebrate, it was hers.

I'd tried to be a more present, supportive friend, but I was starting to worry I'd been too late. That Harriet was merely tolerating me, ready to move on to better and kinder companions.

"How's Sammy?" I asked Whitney.

"A delight as always," she said. "Started asking where babies come from."

"Fantastic," I said. "What do you say?"

"Let's just say we've had to listen to chants of 'penis' and 'vagina' for about a week now," she said. "Plus a lot of pointing at my and my husband's crotches during said chanting."

"Better than screaming 'hoo-ha' or 'ding-a-ling,' I suppose."

Whitney put a hand to her chest, horrified. "I'd never use the word 'ding-a-ling,'" she said. "One-eyed monster, maybe. Or, as one of my college professors once called it, 'the manly dangle.'"

"The. Manly. Dangle," I said.

"I know," Whitney said. "She was ahead of her time. And it was completely appropriate within the context of the conversation."

"Of course," I said.

"I'm excited to see the show," Whitney said. "I wanted to come see you guys in Rhode Island, but Cal told me to wait until Broadway."

I remembered how stressed he was about selling tickets out of town, and yet he was confident enough to tell his best friend to wait. He was an enigma in so many ways. Or he just had an excellent poker face. Poker existence.

"I heard you sold out," she said.

"We did," I said, feeling beyond proud.

The karaoke gambit had done its job and the internet hadn't just been buzzing about the show but about me and my "legacy." Apparently some people were beginning to re-examine what had happened all those years ago—the way I'd been treated by the press—and were starting to come to my defense.

In a lot of ways it didn't matter—the moment had long passed and there was nothing anyone could do to change that—but just like with Cal's apology, it meant *something* for the scandal to be put in context. For people to seem to understand what I'd gone through as Katee. The good and the bad.

"Cal's hiding on the balcony," Whitney said, even though I hadn't asked.

"Why?"

Whitney pointed to Rachel. "Apparently she gets very handsy around him."

I was confused.

"I'm the buffer," Whitney said. "Usually she backs off if I'm here, but if she's drunk enough, she's been known to corner Cal by the bathrooms."

"They're not dating?" I asked.

Whitney looked at me and burst out laughing. Then stopped when she realized I hadn't been joking.

"Oh. You're serious," she said.

I nodded.

"I don't know where you got that idea, but no, they are not dating," Whitney said. "But *they* are."

She nodded toward the other end of the room, where I saw Rachel interrupt Harriet and Statler/Waldorf's conversation to plant a kiss on the older man's cheek.

"Oh my god," I said.

"I mean, to each their own," Whitney said, raising her glass. "But yeah."

I let that information sink in.

Fucking Rachel. She really was devious. If it hadn't caused me such a headache, I might have even admired her tenacity.

Whitney was right. Cal *was* hiding on the balcony.

It was a beautiful one, with an incredible view of the city, but it was also freezing. I stood there, silently watching him for a moment, his elbows leaning on the railing, his entire form strong and solid and comforting as he looked out over Manhattan.

I stepped up behind him, lowering my voice to a barely passable imitation of Rachel's.

"Hey, baby," I murmured.

Cal jumped about five feet, and I couldn't help laughing. His head whipped around, and I could see his anxious expression morph into annoyance.

"Kathleen," he said. "I should have known."

"Whitney said you were out here," I said. "Playing keep-away from Rachel."

Cal let out a groan. "The woman is relentless," he said. "Whenever her boyfriend throws a dinner party it's like her hand is magnetized to my thigh."

I shouldn't have found it funny. It wasn't funny.

But even Cal was smiling a little.

"And you let me believe that you were sleeping with her!" I remembered. "What the hell?"

"I did not," Cal said. "I just didn't correct you when you made that assumption."

"Wow," I said. "That's some top-shelf mind fuckery right there."

"It wasn't your business," Cal said.

"Oh no?" I raised an eyebrow. "Rachel definitely tried to make it my business."

"And you took the bait."

"I—" I opened my mouth. Closed it. Opened it again. "Well. Fuck."

Cal turned toward me. "What does Rachel have against you anyways?" he asked.

I shrugged. "She thinks I got her kicked out of Camp Curtain Call. Because Harriet and I caught her drinking, she assumed that we told the counselors."

"Hmmm," Cal said.

There was something about that "hmmm" that had me giving him a closer look.

"What?" I demanded. "I *didn't* tell anyone. Neither did Harriet."

"I believe you," he said.

"Yeah, well, Rachel doesn't," I said. "And apparently she's still stuck on getting revenge."

"Hmmm," he said again.

"Okay, that is annoying," I said. "What are you not telling me?"

Cal gave me a sideways glance. "I know you didn't get her kicked out of camp, because I did."

I stared at him.

"Excuse me?"

"I told the counselors she was drinking," he said. "But they totally knew. I mean, she would come to rehearsal practically reeking of vodka. Ms. Spiegel was purposefully looking the other way."

My eyes were wide. "Seriously?"

"Yep," Cal said. "I threatened to tell my parents and they finally did something about it."

"Holy shit," I said. "This entire time Rachel has blamed *me* for getting kicked out, it's really been because of you—the person she keeps trying to play hide the sausage with?"

Cal winced. "Hide the sausage?"

"Sorry," I said. "You know what I mean."

"Unfortunately," he said.

"Statler or Waldorf don't mind?" I asked. "That she's after you?"

"Who?" The look Cal gave me was one of incredulous amusement. "Did you just call our producers Muppets?"

I shrugged. "If the Muppet fits . . ."

Cal laughed. "Oh my god," he said. "Now I'll never be able to think of them as anything else." He shook his head. "You've ruined me, Rosenberg."

"You're welcome," I said.

I put my elbows on the railing next to Cal's. The silence between us was comfortable. Calm.

"Can I ask you something?"

"Sure."

"Why 'Memory'?" I asked. "At the audition. Why the last-minute request, and why that song?"

"Ah." Cal glanced back at the party. "Well, I'm sure you've surmised that Rachel has been doing everything in her power to get a part in this show."

"It *was* a real threat," I said, feeling somewhat vindicated.

Cal shrugged. "I didn't take it too seriously. Especially her going after *your* role," he said. "But there were . . . murmurings of finding something for her."

"So instead of giving me a heads-up, you just surprised me?"

"First of all," Cal said, "you weren't exactly trusting me at that point."

"I wonder why," I muttered.

He ignored me. "And second of all, the last thing I wanted to do was look like I was giving you preferential treatment. I wanted you to get that role without any help from me."

"Oh," I said.

"And I knew you'd probably still know that song, which happens to be one of"—he cleared his throat—"the Muppet's favorite songs."

"Oh," I said again.

"I'm sorry," Cal said. "It seemed like a good idea at the time. I probably should have just been more straightforward."

"No," I said. "I get it."

And I did. We'd come far these past several months, moving from taut, spiky animosity to reluctant cooperation to . . . whatever this was. Friendship?

I glanced over at him. At his profile in the moonlight.

Was friendship really what I wanted from Cal?

"Jeez," Harriet said. "It's freezing out here."

Cal and I turned to find her standing in the doorway, an overly friendly smile on her face. It was undercut by the way her eyes kept darting between us, clearly looking for something. I stepped sideways, putting more space between me and Cal.

"We were hiding," I said.

"*We?*" Cal asked.

"It's not like I want to hang out with Rachel either," I said.

"Well," Harriet said, "everyone is looking for you two. Cal, you're supposed to give a speech or something?"

He patted his jacket pocket. "Are they ready for me?"

"Yep," Harriet said.

"All right." He extended an elbow to me, and then one to Harriet. "Let's go back inside."

CHAPTER 27

kept trying to break up with Ryan. I *did,* but he made it difficult.

It was almost as if he knew, because he'd suddenly started behaving like a really good boyfriend. Of course, it was mostly in front of the press—talking in interviews about how much he loved me, making sure to take my hand whenever the paparazzi were around, even throwing in a kiss or two until I told him to stop, and most annoyingly, he had begun dedicating songs to me during our concerts.

"It's because I love you," he'd say when I asked him to stop doing that as well.

It was all very dramatic and ridiculous and super annoying.

And I could tell that Cal hated it.

"I love you too," I would tell Ryan, because that wasn't exactly a lie. I didn't want to be with him anymore, but it also didn't erase all the feelings I had for him. We'd been together for a while. He was my first boyfriend. My first . . . everything. Almost.

"I just want to keep our private life more private, okay?"

He didn't seem to understand.

"Everyone knows we're together," he said. "And it's good for both of us."

Then again, when he said stuff like that, it made it a little easier to imagine breaking up with him. Sometimes I wondered how much of our relationship was based on mutual affection and how much was based on it being good for Ryan's career.

We were on the last leg of the tour. Everyone was exhausted. LC and Mason were sick with the same flu, which had been circulating through the crew for the last few weeks. Wyatt had sprained his foot jumping out the window of his hotel room. It had been on the first floor, so he hadn't been too injured, but the guys still had to retool their act to make it possible for him to perform with them.

I could see the light at the end of the tunnel, and I promised myself that once this tour was done, once I was back in the studio recording, once I was back home in New York, then I'd break up with Ryan, and Cal and I could be together.

The future felt too far away and too close at the same time.

Now it was Cal who was avoiding me. I couldn't really blame him, but I didn't like it. The road was already a lonely place, and it just seemed like it kept getting lonelier.

It couldn't be that hard to break up with someone.

I just had to tell Ryan. . . .

Tell him what? That I wanted to be with Cal?

It was the truth, and I knew Ryan well enough to realize

that if I just said I wanted to break up, he'd want to know why. He'd ask and ask and ask and ask until I just got so sick of hearing him whine that I'd tell him.

I didn't want to hurt him. I didn't want to hurt anyone.

But I was pretty sure that was inevitable.

I had gone to the hotel's restaurant to order LC and Mason some soup, to be delivered to their rooms—it was late and the restaurant was almost closed, but I'd learned a long time ago that if you were famous, you could get almost anything you wanted. It also helped to be polite and generous with twenty-dollar bills. And autographs.

Weird the power my messy scrawl had.

I walked back to the elevators, not ready to go back to my empty room but having nowhere else to go.

When the doors opened, Cal was standing there.

Because of course.

"Hey," he said.

"Hey," I said, getting into the elevator.

He wouldn't look at me, and I checked to see if my floor was pressed, which it was because we were on the same floor. The top one.

He smelled like chlorine and his hair was wet. No doubt he'd been swimming downstairs in the indoor pool.

We rode the first few floors in silence, but the tension vibrated in the air around us.

Finally, I turned to him.

"I'm sorry," I said.

"Yeah," he said. "Me too."

The elevator arrived at our floor, and he got out. I went with him.

"What do you mean by that?" I asked, following him to his door.

Cal turned and looked at me. He seemed tired. Worn.

"Look," he said, "I get it. You and Ryan. It's . . . it is what it is."

"No," I said. "I just need more time."

Cal shook his head. "No, you don't."

"Yes, I do," I insisted, realizing that I sounded like a little kid arguing about eating her vegetables or something like that.

He pushed his door open.

"I don't want to fight about this," he said.

"Neither do I," I said.

"Go to your room, Kathleen," he said and then closed the door in my face.

I stood there for a moment, my mouth hanging open, unable to believe what had just happened. He. Had. Shut. The. Door. Before I was done talking.

That *bastard*.

Curling my hand into a fist, I began banging on the door. All of a sudden it was yanked open, and I basically fell into Cal's room.

"What the hell are you doing?" he asked. "Do you want everyone on this floor—including Ryan—to hear you?"

"You were being rude!"

Cal threw his hands up in exasperation and walked back into his room. I knew it was a bad idea, but I followed him, letting the door close behind us.

I watched as he rummaged through the minibar, coming up with a handful of tiny booze bottles. He opened one and took a long drink.

"Give me that," I said.

He handed another bottle over to me. Vodka. Yuck. I drank it anyway.

"Can you go now?" Cal asked once I was done.

My throat felt warm. My face felt warm.

"You aren't being fair," I told him.

"Fair?" He sounded incredulous. "Are you fucking kidding me? Fair?"

No. He wasn't incredulous. He was mad. Really mad.

I'd never seen Cal mad before.

He came toward me, a tower of anger. But I wasn't afraid of him.

"You want to talk about fair?" he asked. "You think it's fair that I have to stand onstage every fucking night and listen to your absolute idiot of a boyfriend dedicate *our* songs to you? It makes me feel like a goddamn fool. Because you're never leaving him. And I'm the asshole for thinking you would. For pouring my heart out for what? To feed your ego? To make you feel better about yourself in between fights with Ryan?" His nostrils were flaring. "You don't get to talk to me about fair, *Katee*."

I stared at him. I couldn't remember the last time I'd heard him say that much all at once. It didn't help that all of it was painful and mostly true, but the worst part was him calling me Katee.

I'd always been Kathleen to Cal. Always been myself.

But now?

"You don't understand," I said, but it was a weak response.

"I understand," Cal said. "I think *you're* the one who's confused."

"I'm not!"

Cal came right up to me. Loomed over me. I was pretty sure I could feel his heartbeat thumping in the space between us.

"Really?" he asked. "Then what do you want? Who do you want?"

I looked up at him and knew that this was it. This was the moment. The decision.

I didn't hesitate.

"You," I said. "I want you."

His mouth was on mine, his hands cupping my face as he kissed me. Or I kissed him, my fingers digging into his shoulders, pulling him closer, closer, closer. Still, it wasn't enough. He pushed me up against the door, his lips moving down to my throat, and I cried out with how good it felt. How electric and hot and dangerous and perfect.

I started on his shirt, while he started on mine, stopping only to keep kissing each other. I didn't care how long it took. Didn't care if we kissed forever, removing a single article of clothing with every passing hour.

As long as I was in his arms. As long as he kept touching me. As long as he kissed me and kissed me and kissed me.

All that mattered was me and Cal.

NOW

CHAPTER 28

It wasn't immediately clear what had happened. One minute I was standing in the wings talking with the wardrobe mistress, the next, the entire place was in a panicked uproar as the sound of someone crying out in pain echoed through the theatre.

I rushed out onto the stage to find my understudy crumpled on the floor at the base of the conveyor belt set piece, which was still going.

"Shut it off!" I shouted, but everyone was focused on Jennifer.

The poor girl was facedown on the stage, her arm and leg bent at a crazy angle. I could hear her moaning, the sound only slightly muffled by the wig she was wearing.

I slapped the big red button for the conveyor belt, the one we used onstage to turn it on and off, and the thing came to a stop. I ran back to Jennifer, kneeling next to her. I didn't know what to do, but I was pretty sure I wasn't supposed to touch or move her.

"Out of my way!"

I looked toward the audience just in time to see Cal vaulting up onto the stage with the speed and agility of a man ten years younger. I couldn't remember the last time I'd seen him—or anyone, really—move that fast. He dropped to his knees in front of Jennifer.

"Call an ambulance!" he roared. "Now! Goddammit, now!"

He glanced over at me, and I swore he did a double take.

"Kathleen," he said. Confused. Relieved.

There was a crowd of us all gathered around Jennifer, but in that moment, it felt like it was just me and Cal.

"I don't know what happened," I said.

He looked at me. Closed his eyes for a brief moment, and then opened them.

Focused his attention on Jennifer.

"You're going to be okay," he said to her, his voice soft and soothing. Steady. "It's going to be all right."

His hands were shaking.

Jennifer let out a groan, followed by a low keening cry of pain. It seemed like several things were broken, but pain was a good thing. Wasn't it? I didn't know.

I just knew I was digging my fingernails into my arms so hard that I was pretty sure there would be bruises. *That* pain was good.

"Who's calling the ambulance?" Cal barked.

"I'm on it," came Mae's voice from the audience. "They'll be here in five."

"Did you hear that?" Cal said to Jennifer. "They're almost here. You're going to be fine."

He looked up and noticed the worried cast and crew gathered.

"Step back, guys," Cal ordered. "Everything is going to be okay. We just need some space."

Everyone moved away, but I didn't. I stayed put.

Cal kept shouting out orders. Completely in control. Totally in charge.

It was comforting.

"Someone head out front to wait for the ambulance," Cal said. "Make sure that they can get back here without any issues."

When they did, they were immediately led to the stage. They cleared all of us away from the scene, and I went back to the wings where I could watch but be out of the way. The atmosphere was tense and somber as Jennifer was lifted onto the gurney. The paramedics were calm and kind, but it was clear that we were going to need to find another understudy before the show opened.

Cal followed Jennifer out of the theatre, stopping only to talk to Mae.

After they were gone, Mae came back in.

"Everyone." Her voice wasn't quite as steady as Cal's, but it was clear. "There's nothing else we can do tonight. We will update you when we have more information, but until then, it's best that you all head home."

"Do you know what happened?" Taylor asked me.

I shook my head, feeling numb.

"I think she tripped," Nikki said. "Just a stupid, unfortunate accident."

We all stood there silently, the conveyor belt sitting in the middle of the stage like a giant looming warning.

"It's a hard number," Nikki said.

"Yeah," I said.

There wasn't much more for either of us to say. Nikki gave me a half-hearted wave and when I did the same, I realized I was holding Jennifer's wig. My wig.

The theatre was quiet—everyone else had gone—so I brushed off the dust the best I could as I headed backstage. Carefully, gingerly, I put the wig on its stand. Even though I knew it would have to be cleaned and reset, I did what I could to make it look right. Then I went to my dressing room. I meant to get my bag and leave, but I didn't. I just stayed.

I wasn't sure how long I stood there. Moments. Days.

"Kathleen."

I spun and found Cal standing in the doorway.

"You look terrible," I said.

He stepped inside and shut the door.

"She broke her elbow," Cal said. "And her leg. But she's okay."

Okay seemed relative. I was pretty sure Jennifer didn't think she was okay, but it could always be worse, I supposed. I held back the darkly inappropriate "break a leg" joke that my coping mechanisms had come up with.

"She tripped," I said instead. "Or that's what I was told."

Cal nodded.

"Just a mistake," I said. "An accident. It's no one's fault."

That got a laugh out of Cal. Hoarse. Harsh.

"No one's fault?" he asked. "I'm the fucking director, Kathleen. It's *my* fault."

"No," I said.

"You kept telling me the number was too hard. You kept saying it was too complicated," he said. "Did I listen?"

"Yes," I said. "You did. You changed it."

But he wasn't listening now.

"I just had to have my big showstopper, didn't I?" Cal's words were mocking as he paced my dressing room. "Couldn't just do something good and safe, could I? Nope. I *needed* this big fucking ridiculous number."

"Stop," I said. "It was an accident."

I put my hand on his shoulder and he spun toward me. Backed me right into the vanity.

"I thought it was you," he said.

"What?"

"I saw your costume. Your wig."

I didn't move.

"I saw you lying on the stage. Completely still."

My palms were against my dressing room table. I had nowhere to go and nowhere I wanted to go. Cal's feet brushed against mine. I could smell sweat and his cologne. Oranges.

"I'm okay," I said. "I'm not hurt."

His eyes were focused on mine, as if he wasn't quite sure he could believe me.

"If you had been—"

"But I wasn't," I said. "Look. I'm fine."

I lifted my arm. My hand was trembling.

"Kathleen," Cal said.

"I'm okay," I whispered.

"I'm not," he said. "The thought of something happening to you . . ."

He put his head down.

"Cal . . ."

When he looked up, his gaze was intense. Unwavering.

"I can't pretend anymore," he said. "I need you, Kathleen."

My breath stopped in my throat.

"Tell me it's just me," he said.

"Cal . . ."

"Tell me this is inappropriate," he said.

"You're in shock," I said.

"Tell me to leave."

"You're my boss," I said.

"Tell me that bothers you," he said.

I couldn't. It didn't.

"I really think I might die if I don't kiss you right now," he said, "if I don't touch you."

"So dramatic," I said, even though I felt exactly the same way.

"Kathleen." Cal's voice was so low.

He was begging.

And yet he hadn't touched me. He was standing there, his hands fisted at his sides, his entire body tense. He was waiting.

He had been waiting.

Both of us, all this time, all these months. Fighting and not fighting. It had all been leading up to this and we were complete idiots for thinking there was any other possible outcome.

We were trouble together, and yet.

"Yes," I said.

I hooked my fingers into the neck of his shirt and pulled his mouth down to mine.

CHAPTER 29

expected another collision.

Instead, Cal's lips were soft on mine. Gentle.

His hands cupped my face, and he kissed my mouth, my cheeks, my nose, my chin, my eyelids. He kissed me with such gentleness and care that I felt a knot tighten in my throat. His touch was tender, but I could feel his desire building underneath it. The way his fingers pushed back into my hair as I leaned against him, into him. His hips pressing against mine, trapping me—willingly—against the vanity.

He kissed my throat. The base of it. He took my hand and kissed its palm. He took the other and left it pressed to his face, his eyes closed as he nuzzled his cheek against my skin. The stubble scratched me, but it felt good. So good.

"Cal," I murmured.

He lifted his head, eyes meeting mine. And I saw the banked desire there. All that need, all that want, just waiting for permission to be released.

"Yes," I said. "Please, god, yes."

Cal's hands gripped my ass and lifted me onto the dressing room table. His mouth was hot on mine, my hands cupping his face. I wanted to devour him, wanted to be lost in his scent, his touch, everything.

It had been so long.

I was so ready.

I released him so I could drag my fingers down his torso, undoing buttons as I went, pushing his shirt aside, my palms flat on the rough hair spread across his chest. My legs were around his waist, one of his hands clutching my hip, the other fisted in my hair.

He bit my throat as I undid his jeans. Growled as I touched him.

"Fuck, Kathleen," he said, thrusting against my hand.

"Yes," I said. "Let's."

I stroked him as he drew his hands down to the hem of my dress and then up, up, up, displacing fabric as he went, baring my knees, my thighs.

"I don't have a condom," Cal said.

His forehead was damp as he pressed it against mine.

"My place or yours?" I asked.

He kissed my cheek. My eyelids. The corner of my mouth. My mouth.

He couldn't stop kissing me.

"Here," he said. "Now."

I was about to correct him when he dropped to his knees, pushing mine wide.

My underwear was gone in a second, my hands braced back against the vanity, my ass in Cal's hands.

"Yes," I said.

His mouth on the inside of my thigh.

My head hit the mirror as Cal's tongue made wicked circles, one of my hands clutching his hair, the other scrambling for purchase until I white-knuckle gripped the edge of the table. One of his palms was on my leg and I looked down to find the other one wrapped around his cock, stroking slowly as he licked me.

It was so hot. So right. So good.

His touch was everything. I closed my eyes, focused only on the sensation, on the pleasure he was giving me. I braced my feet against his shoulders, my toes curling as my entire body shuddered. The release I felt was instantaneous and took me by surprise. If anyone had still been in the theatre, they would have heard me in the rafters.

I slumped back against the vanity, feeling boneless and brainless.

Cal drew the back of his hand over his mouth as he stood, tucking himself back into his jeans.

"Taxi," he said. "Now."

＊ ＊ ＊

I wasn't sure how we made it from the theatre to a taxi and to my place without ripping each other's clothes off, but somehow we managed to keep it together until we were in the foyer of the apartment.

Fish didn't even look up from her bed as we crashed into the living room.

The bedroom was close, but the couch was closer. The backs of my legs bumped against it, but we remained upright, still focused on our clothes and removing them.

His hands were on my waist, moving upward, fingers tracing the straps of my bra. They had been digging into me all night, and when he reached behind me, unhooking the beast with one go, I let out a sigh of relief.

Cal looked down and tsked.

"Poor skin," he said, dipping his head down to run his tongue along the red imprint the bra's straps had left on my shoulders and beneath my breasts.

I clutched him, my fingers in his hair as he soothed the painful line.

When he straightened, he kept his hands at my sides instead of bringing them up to cup my breasts, which were now aching for his attention. I kept waiting for him to push me down on the couch, to press his big, strong body on top of mine.

He kissed me, fingers aligned with the knots of my spine, as I undid his belt and pushed his pants off his hips and onto the floor. He kicked off his shoes, pulled off his socks. I did the same until we were both wearing nothing but a few pieces of stretchy cotton.

"It must have driven you crazy," Cal said, kissing my neck.

"Hmmm?"

"All this time," he said. "Taking direction. From me."

"I can take direction," I said.

"Yes," he said.

"I'm very good at taking direction," I said, drawing my palm down his chest.

"Oh, I know," Cal said.

He put his hand over mine.

"But so am I," he said.

My mouth went dry as he stripped off the rest of his clothes.

"Tell me what you want," he said, linking his fingers with mine. "Direct me."

It was quite possibly the sexiest thing I'd ever heard. Or maybe that was just Cal.

"You might regret this," I said.

The offer and everything else.

"Not a chance," Cal said, leaning closer. "Come on, Kathleen. I dare you."

Oh, he was a wicked, wicked man.

My hands on his hips, I turned both of us, so he was the one with his back to the couch. With a push, I sent him down, his body now reclined against the cushions, waiting for me. Ready for me.

All for me.

I slipped my underwear off.

"You're fucking gorgeous," Cal said.

Doubt and guilt tickled at the back of my mind, but with Cal looking at me like that, it was easy to push everything else aside.

I climbed onto the couch, onto Cal, my knees on either side of his hips. With my hands on his shoulders, I kissed him deeply. I lost myself in the kiss, in the heat of our mouths, our tongues. The scratch of his stubble against my cheek.

It hadn't been like this before.

Cal kept his hands at his sides, our bodies touching, but not in the most interesting places.

"Cal," I murmured into his ear.

"Mmm?"

"Put your hands on me," I said.

"Where?" he asked.

"My hips," I said. "My ass. My breasts. Touch me."

He did, following instructions precisely, sliding those big, rough palms along the backs of my legs, curving over my hips, squeezing my ass, and coming up to cup my breasts, his thumbs brushing against my nipples.

My head went back, and I sank onto his lap, my body coming into contact with his. He was hot and hard between my thighs, and I dragged my hips forward and then back, teasing both of us with the friction.

"Kathleen," he breathed, his head pressed against the cushions.

His mouth was wet and lush, his eyes hooded.

His hands lifted and pressed my breasts together before he leaned forward and pressed a kiss in the damp hollow at my throat and then lower, along the curve he had created. My nails dug into his shoulders as his tongue tasted the salt on my skin, drawing one nipple into his mouth, and then the other.

"More," I said.

He took direction *very* well.

"Here," I said, taking one hand and dragging it down my stomach, down between my legs where I still ached to be touched.

Cal slid his fingers against me, gentle at first. I leaned forward, pressing my hips down, my body, against his hand.

"More," I said.

He pressed his knuckles against me, dragged them up and down, creating friction exactly where I wanted it. His other hand left my breast and curled over my shoulder, cupping the back of my head, which had swooned backward again.

Cal kissed my throat as I rode his hand, the tease of release peaking and falling with each movement of my hips. I was close, so close, but I needed more.

"Harder," I said.

His hand tangled in my hair and with a sharp twist of his wrist, he pulled—the sensation sending me over.

I collapsed, gasping and damp, onto his chest, Cal's hands at my back, holding me tight against him. I could feel his heart racing.

Once I'd caught my breath, I raised my head.

"Condom?" he asked. "Lube?"

"Bedroom," I said, with slight apology. "So far away."

"If I were younger, I'd carry you there," he said.

"Old man," I teased, my fingers in his chest hair.

He closed his eyes, smile curved with pleasure.

With great reluctance, I lifted myself off him, then offered a hand to pull him off the couch. He rose and met me with a kiss. Deep and wet. We nearly tripped over our shed clothes as we tried to make it to the bedroom without breaking contact. This time Fish lifted her head, yawned, and went back to sleep.

The bedside table held everything we needed. With both in hand, I pushed Cal onto the mattress and climbed on after him. Onto him.

He hissed out a breath as I touched him, his body stretched out on the bed.

"Still want me in charge?" I asked.

"Fuck yes," he said.

I wrapped my palm around him, feeling the smooth slide of skin as I stroked him. His eyes were closed, red heat high up on his cheeks. He was completely at my mercy, and he'd never been more gorgeous.

"Have you thought about this?" I asked. "About us? Together? Again?"

"More times than you can imagine," he said.

His voice was hoarse. His hands clenched.

I unwrapped the condom and rolled it on him. He remained still, perfectly still, though his very skin seemed to vibrate with anticipation. Mine felt the same way, that hot, shaky, wonderful pulse of desire. Despite my release, I was far from satiated.

Pouring lube onto my hand, I got us both very slick, Cal's knuckles going fully white. With heat building from my belly and spreading everywhere, I rose up and straddled him, palms on the insides of Cal's arms, pressing them down and out.

His jaw clenched as I tilted my hips forward, drawing my body against his. He didn't move, he just let me use him this way, this slow, delicious drag of skin and heat.

I released one hand as I lifted myself onto my knees, reaching between his thighs, between mine, discovering how we fit together now. As I sank down on him, my hands found his, our fingers linking together as I pressed his wrists down hard into the mattress.

The groan he let out when my hips met his again was one I felt all the way to my toes.

"Kathleen." It was a blessing. A curse.

I leaned toward him, my hair curtained over us.

"I am going to *ruin* you," I said.

"Yes," he said. "*Yes.*"

I began to move, our fingers still linked together. I rose and fell, my body a wave, his the shore. Everything was about this moment, this connection. I lost myself in the rhythm, taking what I wanted. What I needed.

Cal arched up to meet me, his palms pressing back into mine, but never taking control. Never taking. He gave, and I braced my body against his as I sank deeper, rocked harder.

His fingers gripped mine as pleasure lashed through me, my release a surprise. A relief.

My thighs were still trembling as Cal dug his fingers into them. I didn't even remember letting go of him, my hair damp against my forehead as he thrust upward and found his own release with a guttural groan.

I all but melted off him, lying flat until he rolled and gathered me against him.

His breath was hot against my hair, our bodies slick with sweat, but he held tight.

"I love you," he said.

He kissed my temple, and I knew he was waiting for me to say it back. I opened my mouth, but the words got caught in my throat.

Instead, I turned and wrapped my entire body around him, holding him until we both fell asleep.

CHAPTER 30

I was going to tell Ryan tomorrow, I decided.

Cal was curled up behind me, his arm draped across my hip. I could feel his chest hair tickling my back, the warmth of his body, the press of his thighs against mine.

We'd had sex.

We'd had sex.

I'd had sex with Cal Kirby.

It had been a little awkward, a little uncomfortable, but then it had gotten good. Like, *really* good.

We had a show tomorrow—our last show of the tour. I would tell Ryan afterward. Tell him that it was best that we broke up. I wouldn't tell him about Cal. That would be too much, and now that the sweet, satisfied glow was fading, guilt and shame rushed in to take its place.

I'd had sex with Cal Kirby.

While I was still dating Ryan.

I'd done it all wrong, I knew that. I hadn't been able to help myself.

Isn't that what men said all the time when they were caught doing something inappropriate or wrong? That they'd lost control?

But I knew that wasn't an excuse. And that it would be best if I left.

I shifted, but Cal's arms just tightened around me.

"Don't go," he said.

His voice tickled my ear.

He'd put his tongue there before. It had felt incredible. I shivered a little at the memory.

"I should go back to my room," I said.

"Not yet," he said.

I didn't really want to leave, so I didn't.

We lay there together, and I snuggled even closer to him, wanting to be touching him in as many places as possible.

I felt full of emotions, most of them unnamable.

"I love you," Cal said.

I wasn't sure if that was one of the emotions, so I said nothing and pretended I'd fallen asleep.

* * *

"Wow," Harriet said. "You look happy."

"Tell me about it," my makeup artist said. "I barely need to put anything on her today—she's glowing."

I looked at myself in the mirror. They weren't lying. I looked amazing. So. Damned. Happy.

It was a little ridiculous.

"I'm just glad we're getting a break," I said. "And that we get to start working on your album soon."

"*Your* album," Harriet corrected.

I snorted. "Please. I'm doing the easy part—you're the one writing all the songs." I reached my hand out—her fingers found mine and we intertwined them. "I can't wait for everyone to hear your music."

She grinned at me in the mirror, but her smile faltered a bit.

"Is that really the reason you're so happy right now?" she asked.

My smile dropped off. Harriet was too observant for her own good.

"Yep," I said, but didn't look her in the eye.

She waited until the makeup artist was done and we were alone. Then she dropped down into the chair next to mine, swiveling it so she was facing me.

"What is going on?" she asked.

I tried to ignore her, leaning forward to check my eye-lashes. My lip liner. Anything.

"Kathleen," she said.

"It's nothing," I said.

But she grabbed the arms of my chair and forced me to turn toward her.

"It's not nothing," she said. "I haven't seen you this happy since . . . I don't know . . . since you got your first record deal."

That couldn't be possible. I'd been happy other times. Really happy.

Ryan had made me happy. Sometimes. Most of the time.

"Did something happen?" Harriet asked.

I didn't say anything, but of course, that was enough of an answer.

"Oh my god," she said. "What happened?"

I gestured for her to be quiet.

"Nothing," I said. Lie.

She knew it.

"I'll figure it out," she said. "You're terrible with secrets."

Was that true? The thought scared me. Would Ryan be able to know what had happened the moment he looked at me? Maybe I should tell him now, before the show.

But no. That would guarantee a bad performance. Plus, I still hadn't decided exactly what I was going to say.

"Kathleen," Harriet whined. "Tell me! Come on! I'm your best friend!"

"Fine," I said.

I *had* to tell someone.

I scootched my chair and leaned over, bringing my forehead close enough that it could touch hers. I took a deep breath. She took a deeper one.

"Cal and I—"

"Omigod!" she screeched before I could say anything else. "Did you? You didn't! You did? You did!"

"Shut up!" I grabbed her hands. "Shhhhh."

"Omigod," she whispered. "You did."

I nodded. "Last night."

Harriet's eyes were the size of spotlights.

"Oh wooooooooow," she said. "What did Ryan say?"

I hung my head.

"You're kidding," Harriet said.

I could hear the disappointment in her voice.

"I didn't plan it," I said.

"Yeah, clearly," she said.

"Hey!"

She wasn't wrong, but it hurt anyway.

"It was a mistake," I said.

Harriet raised an eyebrow, and I blushed, thinking about last night. About Cal's mouth. His throat. His hands.

"Okay, not a mistake," I said. "Just. Not good. Not good planning."

"Definitely not good planning," she said. "What are you going to do?"

"I don't know!"

We both sat there. The show would be starting in thirty minutes. One more show and then the tour was over. One more show and then I could sit down with Ryan and talk to him. Explain to him.

Hopefully.

Harriet leaned even closer toward me. Our foreheads did touch.

"And Cal?" she asked, the question barely above a whisper. "Was he . . . ? Are you guys . . . ?"

"I don't know," I said.

Harriet frowned. I knew she was on Team Cal, and I was too, but it was all really confusing and overwhelming. I wanted to be with Cal. I *did*. I just wasn't sure what to do next—I didn't *want* to hurt Ryan. I didn't want to hurt anyone.

I was such an idiot. I'd done this all wrong.

"Kathleen," Harriet chided.

"I *know*," I said. "It's just . . . it's just complicated."

She gave me a look worthy of that understatement. I deserved it.

I pulled back and checked my hair in the mirror.

"I'll figure it out," I said. "It will be fine."

I tried to sound more confident than I felt.

"Okay," Harriet said.

"I just have to get through the show," I said.

"Okay," Harriet said.

"Okay," I said.

* * *

It was an incredible show. The crowd loved every second of it and so had I. It was the perfect ending to a very, very long tour, giving me a necessary burst of excitement and pride. I'd done it.

I chugged almost an entire bottle of water as soon as I got offstage. My skin was soaked with sweat, my extensions sticking to the back of my neck and my temples. I needed a shower, a bath, and a massage. And chicken fingers. With fries.

"Got them ready for you," I told the guys as they gathered in the wings.

Mason and LC were warming up, one of them rubbing the other's shoulders before swapping. Wyatt had a water bottle that I was pretty sure didn't have any water in it from the way he was drinking and wincing and drinking and wincing with each swallow.

I couldn't look directly at Cal. I'd left while he was in the bathroom that morning, just snuck out, which I knew wasn't cool, but I didn't want to get caught in his room.

"A good luck kiss?" Ryan asked.

He pulled me close, arms wrapped around my waist, holding me there in front of him.

"Sure," I said, and gave him a quick, smacking kiss on his lips.

He frowned. "That's no good luck kiss," he said, and

planted a good one on me, even bending me back until my hair swept the floor.

"Get a fucking room," Wyatt muttered, and belched.

It was definitely not water in that bottle.

"Last show!" Ryan said, releasing me so he could pump his fists in the air. "Let's fucking do this!"

The other guys looked exhausted in the face of Ryan's overwhelming energy.

"Hey." He grabbed my hand before heading out onstage. "Don't go anywhere, okay?"

"I'll watch the show," I said.

"I know," he said. "But stay here and watch it, okay?"

I'd planned to watch the first number from the wings and the rest in my dressing room while I took off all the accoutrements that made me into Katee Rose.

"Okay," I said, but I was tired, my performance high rapidly fading.

Ryan nodded, gave me a kiss on the cheek, and headed onstage. Cal was the last one there. He lingered, but didn't look at me. I didn't look at him either.

"Break a leg," I finally said.

"Yeah," he said, and got in place with the rest of the guys.

I could feel his disappointment like another layer of sweat on my skin. Things were a mess, but I'd fix them. After the show, I'd sit down with Ryan, and I'd talk to him. He'd be upset, but we'd figure it out. We'd work through it. After all, we were all friends. We all cared about each other.

As promised, I stood in the wings, waiting for the curtain to go up on the final half of our final show. I didn't mind that I'd started opening, that the crowds were attending more and more to see them. I was happy for them. Proud.

Harriet joined me in the wings.

"Great show," she said.

I grinned at her. "Thanks," I said. "Ryan wants me to watch from here."

Her eyebrows went up. "For the whole show?"

I shrugged. "As long as I can," I said, but I was fading fast.

I'd used up all my energy and adrenaline to get through this last performance, and now I was on the verge of crashing. I couldn't wait to go back to my room and sleep for a week.

"Hello, New York!" Ryan said to a thunderous applause. "We're CrushZone!"

The guys all assembled in perfect unison for their first number with Ryan in the center, like the point of an arrow. I waited for the music to start, but it didn't.

"Hold on! Hold on!" Ryan said.

I could see the guys look around at each other with confusion. Clearly whatever was happening right now, they hadn't rehearsed. Or they were all becoming very, very good actors.

"I know you're excited to see us," Ryan said. "But I hope you won't mind if I bring back our opening act, just for a moment."

What?

"Did you know about this?" Harriet asked.

I shook my head.

"Katee Rose!" Ryan called. "Come out here."

I felt a queasy sensation in my stomach, one that only intensified when Cal glanced my way, his expression inscrutable beyond the general bewilderment. What was going on?

"Katee! Katee! Katee!" Ryan had started up a chant and the entire crowd was repeating it.

"You'd better get out there," Harriet said.

I didn't want to. I knew, deep in my gut, that nothing good would come of me doing that. But what else could I do? They wouldn't stop cheering until I did. The show would never end.

"Fuck," I said.

Fixing a smile to my face, I squared my shoulders and walked back out onstage.

The crowd went nuts. I waved and grinned and came to stand next to Ryan.

"What are you doing?" I asked him, voice low, thankful that I'd taken my mic off.

But he didn't answer me. Instead, he turned to the crowd, one hand taking mine. My heart was rat-tat-tat-tatting around my chest like a dizzy, chattering weasel. I felt sick.

"Katee Rose," Ryan said. He was still facing the crowd. "There's something I want to ask you."

No. Oh no, no, no.

I glanced over at Harriet, whose look of horror no doubt matched my own.

Please god no.

"Katee"—Ryan turned toward me—"I love you so much."

No. No. No, no, no, no, no, no.

He got down on one knee.

I thought I might throw up.

"Will you do me the honor of becoming my wife?"

I couldn't even hear myself think, the cheering in the stadium was immense. It was like being buried under a sound, my eardrums ringing.

This wasn't happening.

Except it was.

I looked at Ryan. He was still kneeling there, still smiling up at me, though the smile was now a little bit forced.

"Katee?" he asked, before turning to the audience. "I guess I surprised her, huh?"

They all roared with laughter.

And I looked at Cal. He was looking at the floor.

Ryan cleared his throat. Loudly.

When I glanced back it was clear that Ryan hadn't missed me staring at Cal.

Fuck. Shit.

"Come on, Katee," Ryan said. "I think you owe our fans an answer."

I. Was. Fucked.

"Uh," I said.

"Yes! Yes! Yes! Yes!" shouted the crowd.

Harriet had her head in her hands.

I looked down at Ryan. He was now holding a ring. A big one.

"What do you say, Katee?" he asked.

"Yes," I said. "Yes."

NOW

CHAPTER 31

"Kathleen?" Cal mumbled.

His face was smushed against the pillow, and I could feel his breath on my neck. It was early, but I didn't mind. Just like I was sore and didn't mind that either.

I felt good. So good. Really good.

"Hmmm?"

"Your cat is on my butt," he said.

I lifted my head.

"So she is," I said. "You're welcome."

He let out a grunt but didn't move. Fish sat with her tail wrapped around her feet, right on top of Cal's magnificent ass. Smart cat.

Shifting carefully, Cal extracted his arm from underneath his pillow and wrapped it around my waist. With a tug, I was pulled right up against him, his nose coming to nuzzle at the base of my throat.

"Good morning," he said.

"Good morning," I said.

I was smiling. A big, bright smile. It was still mostly dark in my room, but I was pretty sure my smile was strong enough to power the entire block.

I waited for the fear to set in, for the flight impulse to set my heart to hummingbird, but it didn't come. I felt safe. Comfortable. Happy.

"She's on the move," Cal said.

I opened one eye to see Fish move from Cal's butt to his back, riding the rise and fall of his breathing like a surfer waiting for her wave.

My heart was so full that it felt like it would crack.

And yet. . . .

"I can feel you thinking," Cal said. "Everything okay?"

"Mm-hmm," I said.

Because it was. And it wasn't.

Just like back then, we hadn't really thought this through. And yes, circumstances were different now, and I highly doubted that Ryan would show up at the theatre this afternoon with a camera crew and get down on one knee in front of the entire world, but there were still consequences to consider.

Harriet was going to be pissed.

I'd promised her that I wouldn't sleep with Cal.

I stared up at the ceiling, wondering what I was going to do.

"Are you worried about what people will say?" Cal asked.

He'd turned over onto his back as well, with Fish curling up in the middle of his chest. Of course she'd warm to him immediately. She was a glutton for a good man. Just like her mom.

"I don't know," I said.

I hadn't thought much about "people," but I should have. Because it wasn't just Harriet that would feel strongly about the news. Cal and I weren't headline makers anymore, but if the karaoke night in Rhode Island had proved anything, it was that I could still make a splash. I'd weaponized the press that time, had maintained control of the narrative, but there was no guarantee I could do it again, especially in this case.

No one would be talking about the show. They'd be talking about me and Cal.

Did it matter? We were grown-ass adults. We were both single. What was the problem?

Well. He was still, technically, my boss. And even though I'd auditioned for the role, even though I'd earned it, the assumption would be that I slept my way into it.

Plus all that messy history.

"We don't have to say anything," Cal said.

I looked over at him. He was looking at the ceiling.

"It can be just between us," he said. "For now."

I was surprised. But things were different. We were older. More mature.

"You'd be all right with that?" I asked.

He glanced over before reaching for my hand and linking our fingers together.

"Do I wish we could just be together? Yes," he said. "But it's more complicated than that. I get it."

I was relieved.

"Let's just get through opening night," I said. "Then we can figure out how to tell people."

Cal nodded, but there was something in his expression that gave me pause. He smiled, but didn't look at me. Didn't say anything else. Just petted Fish and looked up at the ceiling.

I told myself it was fine. He was fine. We were fine.

Everything was fine.

CHAPTER 32

"'m not in the theatre for one day and everything goes to hell," Harriet said.

"Yes," I said. "This is all your fault."

She reached over and hit me on the arm. "That's not funny."

"Sorry," I said.

We were having lunch at Aardvark and Artichoke. I was trying to be very, very normal. Cal had left earlyish this morning and Harriet had called soon after.

"Why didn't you call me?" was the first thing she demanded.

I'd sputtered and stuttered, not sure how she could have figured out that Cal and I were sleeping together unless she had supersonic slut-sense radar. (I apologized to myself after thinking that. It wasn't very nice.)

But she just wanted to know about what had happened

with Jennifer and the accident. Her question was legit. I should have called her. Cal should have called her.

Thankfully, she didn't question the lack of communication any further than that.

"Do you think this is bad luck?" Harriet asked.

I'd been thinking about how Cal had pulled me into his embrace when he kissed me goodbye that morning, lifting my feet off the ground. How safe I'd felt in his arms. How I couldn't wait to see him again.

"Kathleen?" Harriet nudged me with her fork. "What is going on over there?"

I blinked. "Sorry," I said.

"Guess yesterday really freaked you out," she said.

"Uh-huh," I said, looking down at my scrambled eggs.

"Must have been intense," she said.

"Very," I said. "So intense."

She gave me a strange look.

"I think she'll be okay," I said. "In a cast for a while, but everything should heal fine."

At least that's what Cal had texted me. He'd gone to visit her after leaving my place.

"Poor girl," Harriet said.

"Yeah."

"Probably not the best time for a 'break a leg' joke, huh?"

I lifted an eyebrow. Great minds thinking alike and all that.

"How was Cal?" Harriet asked.

I nearly choked on my tea.

"When the accident happened," she clarified.

"He was good," I said. "Very take-charge."

"Good," she said.

I ate my toast, cramming as much as I could into my mouth without looking like a total weirdo. I figured the more food I had in my cheeks, the longer I had to chew and respond to any further questions.

"But you really don't think it's bad luck?" Harriet asked.

I shook my head before swallowing.

"No," I said. "It was just an accident."

Harriet didn't look convinced, gnawing on the edge of her nail. I supposed it was better that she was distracted by the possibility of bad luck—always a fear in the theatre—rather than paying too much attention to me. I'd checked my neck for any hickeys—thankfully Cal and I were *not* kids anymore—but I was still half convinced that if Harriet looked at me carefully enough, she'd figure out what had happened last night.

And then she'd kill me.

I hated lying to her. Hated keeping things from her. And this was all just too much déjà vu for it not to end as poorly as it had last time.

"I can't believe it's almost here," Harriet said.

We were starting previews next week. I tried not to think about it too much. Tried not to think about fulfilling a life-long dream and possibly failing miserably at it. Because nothing on Broadway was guaranteed. Reviews could make or break a show. We could open—and then close the following month. The following week. The next day.

It happened.

"The show is great," I said.

"Since when does that matter?" Harriet asked.

"Fair," I said.

For the first time I noticed how fucked-up Harriet's nails

were. It looked as though she'd been chewing on them—and around them—nonstop. I couldn't remember the last time I'd seen them all red and raw like this.

"Hey," I said. "It's going to be fine."

She paused, her pinkie halfway to her mouth. I lifted my eyebrows, and she sheepishly lowered her hand.

"I know," she said. "I'm *trying* not to freak out."

"We're all freaking out," I said. "We're about to be on Broadway. It's a big fucking deal."

Harriet nodded. "It's one of the reasons I wasn't there for the accident," she said. "I've been going to therapy three times a week for the past month."

"That's smart," I said.

Why couldn't I have done that? Upped my therapy visits instead of, I don't know, sleeping with my director.

"Is it?" Harriet extended her hands, which were trembling. "I'm still freaking out."

I put my hands on top of hers. "It's okay," I said. "This is a totally normal reaction to an extremely exciting—and terrifying—series of events."

Harriet took a few deep breaths, and I could feel her hands begin to steady.

"What about Cal?" she asked.

I tensed. "What about him?"

"He's not freaking out, is he?" Harriet asked. "Or is it better if he *is* freaking out? Because if it's normal, then he should be freaking out, right?"

She put her head down on the table.

"It doesn't seem like anything gets to him." Harriet's voice was muffled.

I remembered his own trembling hands against my face, the desperation of his kiss, the worry in his eyes.

"He has his own way of coping," I said. "But he's freaking out. In the way you want your director to be freaking out—a normal, healthy amount."

Harriet lifted her head and took several deep breaths.

What will happen if I tell her? She's my best friend. She'll understand.

"I've been such a jerk," she said.

"What?"

"In Rhode Island," she said. "Accusing you of sleeping with him. Or wanting to sleep with him or vice versa."

"Uh," I said, "thank you?"

I didn't like where this was going.

Harriet drank some more coffee, which was most certainly cold by now.

"I was just so stressed," she said. "And jealous, honestly."

"Jealous?"

She nodded. "You were getting all the attention in the trades."

I'd suspected that had been the root of it, but being right about that didn't make me feel any better.

"The trades are stupid," I said. "It's your show. It wouldn't exist without you."

"I know," she said. "It's just hard sometimes."

"Yeah," I said. "I know."

"I should have talked to you about it," Harriet said. "Instead of being ridiculous and acting like Cal's nice deed was some nefarious plot to get in your pants."

I didn't say anything. Harriet burst out laughing as if something extremely hilarious had just occurred to her.

"I mean, can you imagine?" she asked. "After everything you and Cal have been through? You both barely got through rehearsals in one piece and all of a sudden I'm worried about you sleeping together? I should have been more concerned that one of you would murder the other and try to get my help hiding the body."

"Ha," I said.

It was not funny at all.

Harriet put her head in her hands. "This production has made me nuts," she said. "I can't promise I'll be normal after opening night, but I'm hoping the fever lifts."

"You're fine," I said. "You're great."

Harriet gave me a fond smile.

"You're amazing, Kathleen," she said. "What would I do without you?"

"Probably chew your nails less," I said.

My stomach churned with guilt.

"I'm so glad we're in this together," Harriet said.

"Me too," I said.

THEN

CHAPTER 33

"What the fuck did you do?" Harriet asked me the moment I came offstage.

"I . . . I don't know," I said.

I felt like I'd been hit by a bus. Somehow, I was standing and then I was sitting on an apple box while Ryan and the rest of CrushZone started their set.

"You said yes?" Harriet all but shrieked.

I looked down at my hands. There was a giant fucking ring on one of my fingers so apparently . . . I had—

"Oh my god," I said. "Oh my god."

Harriet was pacing in front of me. "Are you going to marry Ryan?"

"No!" I said.

Everyone backstage froze, and turned to stare at me. Harriet grabbed my arm and pulled me to my feet.

"Come on," she said.

We made it to my dressing room, where she kicked everyone out and shut the door behind them.

"I thought you and Cal . . ." she said.

"I know!" I said. "Oh my god. Cal."

"He did not seem pleased," Harriet said.

I gave her a look. She put her hands up.

"This is such a mess," I wailed, feeling like everything was spinning out of control.

I wanted so badly for all of this to be a horrible dream, but I looked down at the ring again, felt its weight on my finger, and knew that it wasn't a dream at all. I'd just been proposed to—onstage—by the very person I'd planned to break up with.

And I'd accepted.

"Why did you say yes?" Harriet asked.

I stared at her. "What else was I supposed to say?" I held up my hand, the ring. "Thanks, but no thanks? In front of *that* crowd? In front of our *fans*?"

Harriet chewed on her nails.

"Shit," I said. "Fuck. Fuck! Fuck, fuck, fuck, fuck."

Because what else was there to say?

How was I going to get out of this?

"What do I do?" I asked.

Harriet looked panicked. "I don't know," she said. "How would I know!" She was pacing again. "I mean, I don't know anything about this kind of stuff. I haven't even had one boyfriend, let alone two."

"I don't have two boyfriends," I said, but she was still going.

"I mean, I would say that honesty is the best policy, but it's not like *I've* been completely honest."

"What?"

I wasn't even sure she heard me. Her hands were gesticulating madly, and it almost seemed like she was in a trance, talking to me, but mostly talking to herself. In the brief moments when her hands stilled, I could see that all of her nails had been chewed to the quick.

"I've been trying to tell you for months," she said. "Months! And I'm just too much of a coward."

I got up and grabbed her by the arms. Stopping her. "Harriet, what are you talking about?"

Her eyes were wild and unfocused. I waited until she seemed to see me. Actually see me.

"What are you talking about?" I asked.

"I'm gay," she said, and then put her hands over her mouth.

"Okay," I said, waiting for her to tell me what she'd been so afraid to share.

We stared at each other, each of us waiting.

Finally it sank in.

"*That's* what you've been trying to tell me?" I asked. "You're gay?"

She nodded, eyes wide.

"That's great!" I said, pulling her into a tight hug.

"It is?"

"I mean," I said, "it's not bad. Is it?"

"No," she said. "I just didn't know if you'd—"

"You're my best friend and I love you," I said.

"You're not disappointed?"

"Why would I be disappointed?"

"Because of stuff and LC . . ." She looked down at the floor. "You wanted us to get together so badly."

I shook my head. "I just wanted you to be happy. I want you to be happy. That's all. That's all."

I could see relief wash over her. And there was a little sadness in knowing she'd been so scared to tell me, but I was glad that she finally had. It was good enough news that for a moment I completely forgot about the massively fucked-up mess I was currently in the middle of.

My hand felt so heavy.

Both Harriet and I stared at the ring.

It was enormous. Beautiful. Not my style at all.

"You could pull the moon out of orbit with that thing," Harriet said.

"What am I going to do?" I asked.

We sat. I wanted to take the ring off, but I was a little afraid I'd put it down somewhere and something would happen to it.

"You have to talk to him," Harriet said.

"Cal or Ryan?"

"Both," she said.

I nodded.

"Ryan first, probably," she said.

I nodded again, but when the show ended, the first person at my door was Cal. Harriet made a quick but awkward getaway, leaving us alone.

"Nice ring," he said.

It was in a tone I'd never heard him use before. Mean. Cruel. That wasn't the Cal I knew.

"I had no idea it was going to happen," I said.

He gave me an incredulous look. "Really," he said. "This is all just some insane coincidence."

"Yes!" I said.

"You just happened to follow me to my room the night before your boyfriend proposed to you onstage in front of thousands of people?"

He was making it sound like I'd planned the most elabo-rately cruel prank.

"It came out of nowhere," I said. "We haven't even spo-ken about marriage."

That was all true. Mostly.

Every so often Ryan would mention it, but it was always around fans and in some casual "maybe we'll get engaged, wink-wink" way that I'd always assumed was to keep the rumor mill talking about him.

I realized now that I probably should have taken it more seriously. Probably should have taken Ryan more seriously.

"I'm so sorry," I said. "I was going to tell him after the tour was over."

Cal crossed his arms. "And now?"

"I'm going to tell him," I said. "I just . . . I just need some time."

He nodded, not in an "I understand, that makes perfect sense" way, but in a tense "well, if that's how you want to handle it" way. He was so angry.

"How much time?" he asked. "Should I come back on your one-year wedding anniversary?" His face was twisted into a sneer. "Or should I just show up the night before and sneak away in the morning after you've had your fun?"

"*My* fun?" I couldn't believe what he was saying. "As if you haven't been obsessed with me for years. For years!"

"Don't flatter yourself," Cal said, but his face was red.

"You wanted it," I said. "Wanted me."

"Yeah, well"—he gave me a long once-over—"everyone makes mistakes."

We were trying to hurt each other and damned if we weren't succeeding.

"Fuck you, Cal," I said.

"Been there, done that," he said.

I wanted to slap him.

"Get out of my dressing room."

"I'll do you one better," he said. "I'm out. Period. We're done."

"We never even began." I was angry and heartbroken as I watched Cal harden into something—someone—I didn't know anymore.

"Good," he said. "Because this was all a *big* fucking mistake."

"Get out!" I shouted. "Get! Out!"

He did, jerking the door open to reveal Ryan on the other side. The expression on his face indicated he'd heard us.

"Perfect," Cal said. "Just fucking perfect." He stepped aside with a flourish. "She's all yours, *bro*."

And then he was gone.

"Katee?" Ryan asked, his voice hesitant, his expression confused. "What's going on?"

I sat down at my vanity, my head in my hands. I wanted to cry. I didn't know over what.

"I'm sorry, Ryan," I said. "I'm so, *so* sorry."

He came and knelt in front of me. "It's okay," he said.

"No, it's not," I said, looking up at him. "I cheated on you. With Cal. That's extremely not okay."

I could see a muscle twitch in his jaw.

"It doesn't matter now," he said, taking my hand. The one with the ring on it.

We both looked at the sparkling stone.

"Ryan," I said. "I can't."

He dropped my hand immediately.

"What?"

"We can't get married," I said, certain he would understand.

"You already said yes," Ryan said. "In front of everyone. You can't take it back."

I was startled. Did he think that a marriage proposal was a binding contract? Did he just want to pretend that nothing had happened between me and Cal? Did he just want to act like it wasn't real?

Did I?

He was giving me an out. A chance to keep everything the same.

"I cheated on you," I told him, in case there was some possible way he hadn't really understood what had happened. "I slept with Cal."

This time, the muscle in Ryan's jaw jutted out like he had a piece of gum stuck in there.

"It was a mistake," he said. "You said so yourself."

I hadn't. Cal had.

"I can get over it," Ryan said.

It wasn't what I expected. And a part of me was tempted to take the easy out. To accept Ryan's permissiveness. To agree that it was a mistake.

And it had been, just not in the way that Ryan thought.

"I'm sorry," I said. "I can't."

He stared at me.

"Are you fucking kidding me?" he asked. "You're seriously going to throw away everything because of one night with *Cal State*?"

"It's more than that," I said. "I can't—I don't think we're good together."

His mouth hung open like a broken puppet's.

"How can you say that? We're great together. We've been on the cover of *People,* like, three times!" he said. "They'd probably pay for our wedding. Or maybe *Rolling Stone.* Everyone would want to be a part of it. You and I could make an album—a whole record of love duets, or something. It would be huge."

I was staring at him.

"You don't care about Cal?" I asked.

"I care," he said, and the way he was balling his hands into fists indicated that was true. "But, like, I don't know. Give me a free pass or something. Where I can do whatever, whoever, I want. Then we'll call it even."

I was horrified.

"That's what you want our marriage to be?" I asked. "What about love?"

Ryan snorted. "Come on," he said. "This would be incredible for our careers. Isn't that good enough?"

"No," I said.

It was the loudest silence I'd ever heard.

"No," Ryan repeated. "Are you fucking joking?"

I shook my head.

"Wow," he said. "Wow. Okay. Well, I'm not going to make this offer again."

I looked down at my ring. At the heavy, beautiful, sparkling diamond.

"I'm sorry, Ryan," I said.

And I was.

I pulled off the ring and handed it to him. He took it, rolled it around in his palm, and put it in his pocket. The look he gave me wasn't unlike the one I'd gotten from Cal. Stone-faced. Bitter. Rageful.

"Yeah," he said. "Yeah. You will be."

NOW

CHAPTER 34

It was the perfect spring day. Fragrant and bright and sunny and wonderful. The kind of day where every breeze seemed to sound like Tom Hanks murmuring, "Don't cry, Shopgirl."

I sat across from Cal on the A train. We'd gotten on together, but were acting like we hadn't. I was on my phone—the beret I'd bought during our ride to Rhode Island had been surprisingly versatile and I was looking for a warm-weather one—while Cal had a book. Every so often I'd glance up at him, and always catch him watching me. I pretended not to notice, but I loved it.

We rode to the end of the line, got off, and—still keeping our distance—walked to the Cloisters. At some point, Cal came up next to me.

"How long are we going to do this for?" he asked.

"Aren't you having fun?"

"Oh, sure," he said. "I love spending a day with someone by pretending I'm not spending the day with them."

We were smack dab in the middle of previews with opening night rapidly approaching. Performances had been solid, and while they weren't selling out, the rumblings were that we were getting good word of mouth. All of which would be fairly meaningless if the actual reviews were garbage.

I didn't want to think about it. I couldn't think about it. All I could do was work my ass off during each show and then take my frustration and excess energy out on Cal afterward. So far, there had been no complaints from either of us.

Today was different though. Today was our day off—a glorious show-free Monday—and Cal wanted to spend actual daylight in public with me. My conversation with Harriet had made me skittish—or rather, more skittish than usual—and I'd compromised by going to one of the places all New Yorkers claimed to want to visit, but never did.

"I can't believe you've lived here all these years and haven't been to the Cloisters," Cal said.

"That just makes me a true New Yorker," I said.

He put his arm around me and planted a kiss on my temple. No one was around, but still, I tensed. Cal released me almost immediately.

"Sorry," I said. "It's just—"

"Yeah," he said. "I know. It's fine."

But it wasn't. I could tell that Cal understood—on a rational level—that it was best to keep this *arrangement* to ourselves. It was the smart thing for both of us to do. Yet, I knew he was frustrated.

"They really liked unicorns, didn't they?" I asked as we looked at the famous tapestry.

"They're just narwhals of the land," Cal said.

I laughed. "Narwhals of the land?" I repeated. "I don't think anyone calls them that."

"Well, yeah," he said, tapping me on the nose with his program. "Because they don't really exist."

"Ha," I said.

"Learn something new every day," he said. "You're welcome."

"What would I do without you?" I asked.

He smiled and took my hand in his, lacing our fingers together. It was a test. We both knew this, and I was pretty sure I passed because I didn't flinch or pull away. I let my hand be held and then as soon as it seemed appropriate, I pretended to need that hand and pointed at one of the exhibits in the case.

From the expression I caught in the reflection of the glass, I hadn't really fooled him. I just got a raised eyebrow as he put his hands in his pockets.

It was a nice day. A perfect day.

We had lunch. We walked around. We talked.

We were a normal, average pair of people spending their day at a museum together.

A part of me didn't want to go back to Brooklyn, or back to the theatre, or back to the real world. I wanted to stay in this bubble of happiness with Cal, where our relationship was just between us. Where it wasn't hurting anyone. Where it wasn't *a thing*.

"They're just not interested," I told him.

"In what? Theatre? Music? Art?"

We were talking about my family.

"Entertainment, I guess," I said. "I mean, they're kind of

Luddites. Or Luddite-aspirational. Always the last to get whatever new technological advance is improving lives. My dad got an iPhone last year."

Cal let out a whistle. "And they're not coming to opening night?"

I shrugged. "I didn't ask, actually," I said. "But I did offer them tickets for the show in general and they said what they always said when I was touring as Katee—thanks, but no thanks."

Cal shook his head. "That sucks."

"It is what it is," I said. "At least, that's what my therapist and I agreed on when I accepted that I could love my family and not like them very much."

"That seems very freeing," he said.

"Sure," I said. "Still sucks occasionally, but that's life."

"Life sucks?"

"Sometimes," I said. "Don't you agree?"

Cal looked at me. "Not lately," he said.

I blushed. "Stop," I said.

He grinned. *All* the dimples.

"You're very bad at accepting compliments," he said.

"Oh, and you're so good at it?" I asked.

"Touché," he said.

"It's weird," I said. "Compliments. I both crave them and distrust them at the same time."

Cal nodded. "I know what that's like."

"Because you're supposed to be proud of your work," I said. "But also, modest about your talents."

"Life of an artist," Cal said. "You need a thick enough skin to withstand the criticism, but also be vulnerable enough to do your job right."

"Exactly," I said. "Curtain Call definitely helped with the thick-skinned part."

Cal grimaced. "Abuse is not the best way to build calluses."

"I'm sure Ms. Spiegel would disagree," I said.

The eye roll could have been seen from space.

"Are you saying you didn't get anything from that summer?" I asked. "Or any of the other summers you were there?"

Cal thought about it for a moment.

"Well," he said, "there *was* this one night on the roof of my bunk."

It shouldn't have made me blush, but it did.

"That can't be the highlight," I said.

"Oh, but it is," he said.

I gave him a shove. "Please," I said. "It wasn't even that big of a deal."

Except it had been. And Cal's raised eyebrow indicated that he knew exactly why.

"Are you saying you don't remember?" he asked.

"Of course I remember," I said. "You don't forget your first—"

"Duet partner?" Cal finished dryly.

"Exactly," I said.

The air smelled incredible, like the most perfect bubble bath, fragrant and warm.

"I knew it was your first time," Cal said.

"You did not," I said.

He laughed.

"How?" I asked. "It was good."

"Sure," he said. "It was great. But the way you basically

leapt off the roof and ran for the woods immediately afterward kind of tipped me off that it was new to you."

"It was not a leap," I said. "I had somewhere to be."

"In the middle of the night?" he asked.

"Yes," I said.

"Okay," he said, clearly humoring me.

We walked. I could practically feel his residual mirth.

"Was it your first . . . ?"

He burst out laughing, and then stopped at my expression.

"Uh. Yes?"

I shoved him in the shoulder.

"I was a straight guy at a theatre camp, Kathleen," Cal said. "What do you think?"

"Ew," I said.

He just stood a little taller and walked ahead. I jogged to catch up with him. And then, with a glance to make sure that we were alone, I reached out and took his hand. I could feel him pause, could feel him take in the moment. Then he gave my fingers a squeeze, and we walked back to the train station.

CHAPTER 35

I was impressed with myself. We were halfway through previews, Cal and I were spending every night together, and no one suspected a thing. We wouldn't know what the consensus was until opening night when reviews were released, but the whisperings had been good. And so had the sales.

"Explain to me again," Cal said. "Which one is Trixie and which one is Katya?"

We were in my dressing room. He was behind me, rubbing my shoulders, his thumbs against the knots in my neck, his fingers spread out, warm and comforting across my clavicle.

"Trixie is on the left, Katya on the right," I said.

"And their show is about . . . ?"

"Whatever they want," I said.

"Right," Cal said.

I could tell that he still didn't really get it, but considering he'd gotten a crash course in drag queens since we'd started—

Sleeping together? Dating?—whatever we were doing, he was doing pretty well keeping track of all the new information I was throwing at him.

"You were great tonight," Cal said, leaning in to kiss the line of my jaw.

I loved watching him in the mirror.

"I'm almost done," I said. "Want to meet me at the subway station?"

Cal didn't say anything, just let out a breath and kissed me again. I knew he hated all the sneaking around. All the pretending.

"It will be over soon," I said, and patted his hand.

He gave me a smile, but no dimples.

"I know," he said.

"We can order milkshakes when we get home," I said.

The diner around the corner from my apartment was one of the few places still open after curtain call, so we'd made it a little routine to get dessert when we stayed at my place.

"Sure," Cal said.

I wanted to kiss that worry wrinkle in the middle of his forehead away.

There was a knock and Cal moved back from me just in time.

He was on the other side of the room when Harriet entered.

"Hi," she said.

"Hi," I said.

"We can go over the rest of my notes later," Cal said.

"Notes?" Harriet teased. "We're in previews—the show is great. What notes do you have to give?"

"I'm just doing my job," Cal said.

"I know," Harriet said. "But jeez, Cal, give it a break and stop riding your leading lady."

Well, fuck.

My cheeks flamed red, and I caught Cal's expression in the mirror before I ducked my head. He couldn't have looked more guilty if he tried.

Harriet's smile disappeared as she looked between the two of us. Her mouth went lax.

Cal cleared his throat.

So much for keeping it a secret. I should have known better.

"I'm . . . I have to . . ." He gave up. "Bye."

The minute the door closed behind him, Harriet was facing away, arms crossed.

"You swore to me that nothing would happen," she said.

"I know," I said.

There was a long, heavy silence. Harriet lifted her head and looked over her shoulder at me. I was taken aback by the anger in her eyes, and yet, it was still easier to face than disappointment.

"You lied," she said.

"I know," I said. "I'm sorry."

She let out a breath, closed her eyes, and shook her head.

"No," she said. "No, you're not."

I knew that arguing with her was the worst thing I could do.

"You feel bad," she said. "But you're not sorry."

The room seemed to fill to the brim with her disgust.

"I never ask you for anything, you know?" Her fists were clenched. "In all our years of friendship, I've been there for you. The loyal little follower, going from place to place with you—being your support system, being your friend, your assistant, your family."

"Yes," I said. "You have."

"And how do you repay me?" she asked.

I hung my head.

"It was one thing to lose the record deal all those years ago," Harriet said. "I stood by you, even when you took down your career and mine in the same fucking night. When you ruined the best opportunity I'd had in years to make it as a songwriter. And now?"

She was so angry.

"I am not going to let your bullshit drama and inability to keep it in your pants ruin this production," she said.

"No one knows," I said. "You're the only one."

She looked at me with disbelief and disgust.

"Are you joking?" she asked. "You think you can keep this a secret?"

I lifted my chin stubbornly, but she just laughed.

"This will get out," she said. "And that's all anyone will be talking about. Not about the show, certainly not about my music, but you. It will all be about you and your foolish, stupid romance with Cal."

"I didn't plan for this to happen—"

"No, of course not," Harriet said. "You never plan for any of this, Kathleen, and that's the problem."

She pinched the bridge of her nose between her fingers.

"I feel like I'm stuck in the worst déjà vu of all time." She pitched her voice up, wrists limp. "I don't know how this happened. It was a mistake. I'm sorry I've just ruined your career because I couldn't stop fucking Cal."

I reared back at the cruel imitation.

"The first time was bad enough," Harriet said. "But you were young and stupid."

I flinched at her assessment.

"But now? What's your excuse now?" she asked. "Are you seriously that horny that you couldn't have fucked literally any other guy? It had to be Cal? It had to be the director?"

I wasn't sure how much more of this I could take.

"You're pathetic," Harriet said. "But I'm not letting you drag me down with you. Not again."

"I'm dragging *you* down?" I asked.

My voice was soft, but hard.

I'd lied. I didn't deny that. I'd made a mistake. Mistakes. But I'd had enough of being blamed for things that weren't my fault.

"Your lack of opportunity is your problem," I said. "Not mine."

Harriet pulled back.

"Excuse me?"

"Don't blame me for the fact that it took this long for someone to take an interest in your work," I said.

It was a low blow, and I knew it.

But this was a fight a long time coming, and like a night of too much drinking, sometimes you just had to get it all out before you could feel better.

Harriet and I had kept our anger at each other locked up tight, but that never made it go away. It just made it fester. Grow. Expand. Distort.

"At least I earned my success," she said. "It's not due to my tits and ass."

"No," I said. "It's due to *my* tits and ass. Because we both know I'm the only reason this show is getting made. My name. My reputation."

The worst part was that there was truth in every single word we were saying, and that was the thing about being friends with someone for as long as Harriet and I had been. You knew exactly where to strike. How to wound.

"I don't buy your surprise," I said. "You've been testing me. From the very beginning."

"I don't know what you're talking about."

"No?" I stood. "You lied about Cal approaching you. Kept that whole fucking thing a secret until you could spring it on me."

"Right," she said. "The opportunity of a lifetime. That I *sprung* on you."

I ignored her. "You knew how I felt about Cal and you still went to *him*." My fingers wrapped around the back of the chair. "And all this time, it's like you've been watching me. Waiting for me to make a mistake. Waiting for me to fuck up."

Harriet's arms were crossed, her chin up. Defensive.

"This whole thing was like a big fucking test," I said. "That night at your place. Where you *forgot* that you'd invited both of us over? Tell the truth, Harriet, did you actually forget or were you trying to prove something?"

"I didn't have to prove anything," she said. "You proved it for me."

I was exhausted.

"What do you want, Harriet?" I asked.

I was tired. I was hurt. Sad.

"It doesn't matter what I want," she said. "You clearly don't care."

She slammed the door when she left.

CHAPTER 36

We didn't say anything on the subway ride back to my place. We didn't get milkshakes.

"Do you want to talk about what happened?" Cal asked.

I'd dropped onto my couch like I was a stone. Fish climbed up onto my lap, but I didn't feel like I deserved her attention or her purrs so I pushed her off. She went to Cal—smart girl—rubbing against his legs until he picked her up.

"Harriet knows," Cal said, stating the obvious.

"Yes," I said.

"Okay," he said.

I shook my head. "No," I said. "Not okay. This is a problem. This whole thing is a problem."

Cal didn't say anything. He was still holding Fish, scratching her neck, and even from here I could hear her purring. She adored him.

She was going to be so mad at what I needed to do.

"We can't do this, Cal."

He put Fish on the ground.

"No," he said. "Not again."

My eyes burned.

"I'm sorry," I said. "It's just . . . it's just too complicated. It's too much."

"Right," Cal said. His hands were on his hips. He was looking at the ground. "Right. Right."

He was angry.

"Okay then," he said. "I'm going to go."

My heart felt like it was breaking.

"I'm sorry."

I'd said that a lot in the past few hours. And I was sorry. I just didn't know what else to do.

"Are you?" he asked. "You're both grown-ups. Why do you care what she thinks about your love life? Is it any of her business?"

"We are all *literally* in business together," I said. "And she trusted me to keep my personal life out of our professional one."

"Maybe that was an unrealistic request," Cal said.

"Right," I said. "Because this is all *my* fault. You had nothing to do with any of it. Just poor innocent Cal stuck in my wicked web of sluttiness."

"You're being ridiculous," he said.

"I just feel *so* sorry for you," I said. "Clearly, I've taken advantage of you. Again."

"Let's not do this," Cal said. He reached toward me. "I'm sorry. I shouldn't have said those things."

"You meant them," I said.

"No," he said.

"Let's stop lying to each other," I said.

"What are you doing?"

"This is for the best," I said. "This was always a mistake."

Cal winced, and I regretted my choice of words.

"There's too much anger," I said. "Too much bitterness. We're past forgiveness. It's too late."

"You're giving up," Cal said.

"There's too much history," I said. "I hurt you. I didn't mean to—not this time and not then, but it doesn't matter. It seems I'm only capable of hurting the people I care about."

Cal was silent for a moment.

"I'm not going to argue with you," he said. "I'm not going to try to convince you that you're wrong, but I don't think I'm the one who needs to forgive you."

Tears brimmed in my eyes, making everything blurry.

"I think you need to forgive yourself," he said.

We looked at each other. I knew it was over, and yet.

"If I leave, I'm not giving you another chance, Kathleen," he said. "Two is more than enough."

"I know," I whispered.

We just stood there staring at each other. I knew he didn't want to leave. I didn't want him to leave either.

But what could we do? I'd just hurt him. Again. And again. And again. Because that's what I did.

"I am sorry," I said.

"Me too," Cal said.

CHAPTER 37

The only time I didn't hurt was when I was onstage. I lost myself in Peggy, in the show. Buried myself in that character. It wasn't until I got to my dressing room and took off my wig, washed off my makeup, that I was forced—once again—to confront the reality of what I'd done.

Harriet had been avoiding me for a week. Cal was polite but wouldn't look me in the eye. I smiled too big and spoke too loudly.

After each performance, I left as quickly as I could. I was usually the first one out, and then it was the wall of fans at the stage door. I didn't want to linger and sign autographs, but it was also hard to resist the requests of the only people who seemed happy to see me these days.

I signed as many as I could, smiling but not looking up as I scrawled my name over decades-old headshots and magazine covers. I tried not to look too closely at who I'd been.

Someone shoved an old copy of *People* magazine into my hand. There was a picture of Ryan and me on the cover with the headline "The Prince and Princess of Pop: Their Happily Ever After."

"Hiya, Katee," Ryan said.

It was like seeing a ghost. A very tanned, subtly botoxed, well-manicured ghost.

"Oh, come on," Ryan said when it became clear that all I was capable of doing was staring at him with my mouth wide open. "Give your old friend a hug."

He pulled me into his arms—he was a little damp, but it was also kind of nice? I wasn't sure. I was probably still in shock.

"They're taking pictures," he said in my ear. "A smile might be a good idea."

I did my best, letting Ryan take the lead, putting his arm around me.

"Isn't this great?" he asked the group of fans gathered at the stage door. "I love reunions!"

Everyone cheered.

"What are you doing here?" I muttered out of the side of my mouth, while he waved at the sea of cellphones turned in our direction, capturing every second.

"I was in town and thought I'd stop by," he said.

"Bullshit," I said, still smiling. "Were you in the audience tonight?"

He laughed. "Come on," he said. "The show's like three hours long."

"I figured," I said. "Okay, nice seeing you. Bye."

"Don't be that way," he said. "Let's go somewhere, okay? We should talk."

Of course, Ryan took me to the fanciest, most exclusive bar in Midtown. I spotted at least three other celebrities as we were led to a table in the back.

"Was that Jacinda Lockwood?" I asked.

"Probably," Ryan said.

We sat.

"So, Katee Rose," Ryan said. "How have you been?"

I gave him a look. "It's Kathleen," I said. "And it's been over ten years. What are you doing here?"

He grinned at me, and despite everything, that smile still brought back a lot of memories. Good ones. Complicated ones.

"You look great," he said. "I can't even tell what work you've had done."

I just sipped my drink, knowing he wouldn't believe me if I told him the truth.

"Ryan," I said, "spit it out. What do you want?"

He looked sheepish, but purposefully so. He'd always been good at that look—that "who, me?" sad, confused puppy dog look. Then again, a lot of the time it had been genuine—he *was* confused more often than not.

"I'm hearing great things about the show," he said.

"You want tickets?" I asked.

He laughed. "God no," he said. "Musical theatre? No thanks." He gave a full-body shiver as if he couldn't imagine anything worse.

"Well, this has been lovely," I said.

"Wait, wait, wait," he said. "I just wanted to see you. Is that so wrong?"

"Ryan," I said slowly, patiently, "you told the entire world that I cheated on you."

"Well, you did," he said.

Touché.

"We haven't spoken since then," I said. "So I'm sure you can understand my confusion as to your sudden reappearance."

Ryan was silent for a moment, and I watched him weigh the pros and cons of telling me the truth. God, this was all so familiar that it hurt a little. Not that I wanted to go back in time—especially not to that era of my life—but it was still this tender, bittersweet feeling, remembering how long ago it had been and how far away I was from that girl now.

"Okay," Ryan finally said. "Ever since you and Cal announced the show, my manager has been getting all these calls about us. About the band."

"Your manager?" I asked. "Diana?"

It should have felt more like a betrayal when I found out that my manager had left me to go work with Ryan, but I'd been so exhausted and worn out by the lashing I'd gotten from the press that I'd been numb to it.

And I supposed I wasn't really surprised. Then or now.

"And we just thought it would be a good idea for you and me to be seen together," he said. "You know, to show there aren't any hard feelings."

"Your hard feelings or mine?" I asked.

Ryan shrugged. "Both, I guess," he said. "Apparently the internet is divided on what happened between us. Some people think I wasn't very nice to you."

I sipped my drink, saying nothing.

"I mean, you did cheat on me," he said. "That's pretty uncool."

"Yes," I said. "Yes, it was."

"Apology accepted," he said.

I'd apologized multiple times—before and after Ryan

had gone public with the scandal—but I guess now was as good a time as ever to have that apology accepted.

"Are we done?" I asked.

"Diana thought we could do a photo shoot or an interview or something," he said. "I bet we could get on, like, *Good Morning America.*"

"I don't want to be on *Good Morning America,*" I said.

Which was partially a lie. I didn't want to be on *Good Morning America* with Ryan.

"It would be great publicity for the show," he said.

"And for you too, I'm guessing."

"Well, yeah," he said.

I looked at him for a long time. He fidgeted. Looked away.

"Why?" I asked.

"Because we're old friends," he said.

I laughed. "What's the role?" I asked.

He deflated a little. "It's a really good one," he said. "And I'd be perfect for it."

"But . . ."

"But people are kind of angry at me, I guess," he said. "They think I threw you under the bus and used you to help my career."

I didn't say anything.

"I didn't," Ryan insisted. "I'm a nice guy."

"Sure," I said, thinking of all the calls and emails he ignored when I asked him to call off the attack dogs—all the press—he'd sicced on me. When I begged him to stop sharing details about my private life, like that I'd lost my virginity to him and that I waxed my upper lip and stomach.

"Just an interview," he said, "or two. Showing that we're friends."

"We're not friends," I said.

"Oh, come on, Katee," Ryan said. "You can't still be mad about what happened."

I stared at him.

"Do you mean the entire destruction of my career?" I asked. "Can't imagine why that would still bother me."

He squirmed.

"You forgave Cal," he said. "It's not like he stood by you."

He had a point, and that was annoying as fuck.

"That's different," I said.

Ryan was watching me.

"Are you two together?" he asked.

"No," I said.

He didn't look convinced.

"I just think you owe me," he said.

I'd spent the last ten years agreeing with him. That I was the villain, that I was the one to blame. But maybe Cal was right—maybe it wasn't about Ryan's forgiveness or his or even Harriet's. Maybe it was about forgiving myself.

"No," I said.

"No?"

I'd made mistakes, but I'd paid for them. I'd learned from them. Mostly. I'd continue to learn from them. But not if I kept punishing myself over something I couldn't change. I'd done a bad thing, but I wasn't a bad person. I wasn't beyond salvation. Wasn't beyond love.

"No," I said. "I don't owe you anything."

"Wow," Ryan said. "Guess nothing has changed."

I looked at him. Stared him down. "Guess nothing has," I said.

"You cheated on me," he whined.

"We were kids," I said. "And it was a mistake and I apologized. However, I'm still waiting for your apology."

"Mine?"

"You didn't have to do what you did," I said. "I know you were hurt, but you didn't just lash out, Ryan, you did everything you could to destroy my career. You wanted to ruin me."

He crossed his arms tightly over his chest and pouted.

"And don't pretend that you didn't have control of the narrative. I know you chose not to tell people it was Cal—you wanted to keep the band together until you had your out, until you had your big break."

"I was the only talented one in the whole group anyway," he said.

"So you've claimed," I said. "And yet, you need my help to keep your name in the press."

"I don't *need* it," he said. "*You* need it."

It was a bit like playing "I know you are but what am I?" Like interacting with a child.

"I know what you and Cal used to say about me," Ryan said. "You thought I was an idiot, but I knew that you guys were getting closer."

I didn't say anything.

"Come on," he said. "It's just one interview."

But I didn't trust Ryan.

"Sorry," I said. "You'll have to get that role on your own."

"You're being unfair," he said.

I stood and put a hand on his shoulder.

"You know, we had a good thing for a while," I said. "But that was over a long time ago. Fuck off forever, Ryan."

CHAPTER 38

"What is this?" Harriet shoved her phone in front of me.

It was Wednesday, a two-show day—which meant I'd have to be back in the theatre in a few hours. Not enough time to go back to Brooklyn and I didn't feel like hiding in my dressing room.

I'd gotten myself two chocolate rugelach from the Breads kiosk and was sitting eating them in Bryant Park when a picture of Ryan and me slid across the table.

It was the most Harriet had said to me in days.

"Are you hanging out with Ryan now?" she asked, sitting down.

That was the Harriet I knew. No more small talk.

It was a stage door photo from a few nights ago. Big smiles on both of us, but only someone who knew us would be able to tell that they were fake.

"He stopped by for a chat," I said, pushing her phone away.

"A chat?" Harriet's eyebrows rose.

"We had a drink," I said. "He wanted me to do a talk show with him."

"And?"

"And what, Harriet?" I asked, feeling frustrated and angry. "If you want to know if I slept with him, just ask, okay?"

"I know you didn't," she said, but she didn't look convinced.

"Look," I said, "I know you're angry and you have reason to be. I lied to you—I said I wouldn't get involved with Cal and I did. But I made that promise before I knew . . ."

I stopped talking.

I didn't want to do this. Didn't want to fight with someone else I loved. Didn't want to risk damaging this relationship any further.

"Before you knew what?" Harriet prompted.

"It doesn't matter," I said. "We broke up. I'm not sleeping with him, I'm not sleeping with Ryan, I'm not even sleeping with Fish these days because she apparently hates me too."

"I don't hate you," Harriet said.

I felt like crying with relief, but I just took a deep breath.

"Well, that's good," I said. "Because I love you. You're my best friend and I'm sorry this happened—I'm sorry I messed up—again—but I can't take this. If we're done, then just tell me. It will break my heart, but at least I'll know."

Harriet looked stricken.

"You think I don't want to be your friend anymore?" she asked.

"I don't know what I think," I said. "I just know that I can only apologize so many times before it starts to feel like you're only interested in punishing me."

Harriet was silent.

"I was," she said.

That much was obvious.

I passed her the remaining chocolate rugelach.

"Really?" she asked.

They were probably my favorite baked good in the entire state. Harriet knew this.

I nodded. She took a bite. Gave an appreciative little moan, which was necessary and appropriate. I watched her eat the rest of it in three quick bites.

"You've got a little something here." I gestured.

She brushed the crumbs off the corner of her mouth.

"You were right," she said. "And I didn't like hearing it."

Her hands were folded in her lap.

"I *was* jealous," Harriet said. "I've been jealous."

The wind picked up around us, brushing leaves from the ground, sweeping them up into a brief paso doble.

"You wrote an amazing show," I said.

"For you," Harriet said.

I shook my head. "You wrote it for yourself. I've just been lucky enough to tag along."

Harriet spread her hands wide on the table. Her gold rings caught the light filtering through the trees.

"That's always how I felt," she said. "Back then. Like I was lucky that you were letting me tag along with you."

"Harriet." I reached over and put my hands on hers. "I was the lucky one. I don't know what I would have done if I hadn't had you." I gave her fingers a squeeze. "I'm so sorry

I fucked everything up. Then and now. I'm so sorry I let a guy get in my way. Get in *our* way. Your album would have been amazing."

Harriet wiped her eyes.

"I shouldn't have pinned all my dreams on you," she said. "That was wrong of me."

I didn't say anything.

"You know what I did when I saw those pictures of you and Ryan?" she asked.

I didn't.

"I read the comments," she said.

"Oh no," I said. "Why would you do that? Never read the comments."

"I know!" Harriet said. "I'd just been so mad about the attention that you and Cal had been getting. How every article was about you or him or both of you. And I just knew that if people found out that you were together then that's all anyone would be talking about, and I was so angry and jealous."

"I'd be mad too," I said.

"But then I read the comments," she said. "Do you know what they said about you?"

"Probably that I looked older and fatter," I said.

She nodded.

I shrugged. "So what? I am."

"They're so mean," Harriet said. "The things that people say. That strangers say."

"I'm not a person," I said. "I'm a rich bitch pop star who cheated on her boy band boyfriend and thinks she deserves a second chance. I'm not normal. I'm a *celebrity*."

I gave her jazz hands. She laughed, but it wasn't funny. Not really.

"I watch the show every night," Harriet said. "Sometimes from the orchestra. Sometimes from the back of the theatre, sometimes from a seat."

"Cal too," I said.

Harriet nodded.

"Last night I was sitting next to this group of four. It was two women our age and their kids. I could tell that they were old friends—the women—and that the daughters had been brought against their will."

"Love that for an audience," I said.

Harriet smiled.

"By the end of the show, all four of them were spellbound. Your number made them cry—it made teen girls cry."

"Teen girls cry at everything," I said. "I remember."

"Not if they don't want to," Harriet said. "Nothing more powerful than a teen girl who wants to hide her emotions from her mother."

"True," I said.

"I listened to them during intermission and after the show," Harriet said. "I might have followed them into the lobby."

"Creepy."

She gave me a look. "They couldn't stop talking about how great you were," Harriet said.

It was nice to hear.

"But it wasn't just that," she said. "The daughters had no idea who you were."

"The mothers were fans, I'm guessing."

Harriet nodded. "And they kept trying to explain who you were, but the girls didn't care. All they saw was their new favorite Broadway star."

I bit my lip. It was too much.

"It doesn't matter what the press writes," Harriet said. "It doesn't matter if people come to the show because they remember you. It doesn't matter if people come because they've heard of all the drama between you and Cal. What matters is that they'll be in the audience when you show everyone exactly how fucking talented you are."

"*We* are," I said. "It's your show."

"It's *our* show," she said.

"Does this mean we're friends again?" I asked.

"Please," Harriet said. "We're family."

"Oh, thank god," I said.

Harriet pulled me to my feet and into an embrace I'd been waiting weeks for. Months even. I'd missed her. I'd missed her so much.

"I'm sorry I was a jealous monster," she said.

"I'm sorry I can't keep it in my pants," I said.

She looked at me. "You and Cal?"

"We're over," I said. "I swear."

She bit her bottom lip.

"What?" I asked.

Harriet looped her arm through mine, and I followed as she led me away from the table, taking us around the park.

"What?" I asked again.

"I'm sorry," she said. "That you broke up with Cal because of me."

I shook my head. "It wasn't because of you," I said. "It was because of me. I'm no good for him. I think we both know that. I think the whole world knows that."

"That's utter bullshit," Harriet said.

"Hey!"

"You *are* good for him," she said. "He's good for you. I couldn't see it because I was so jealous and stupid, but honestly, it doesn't even matter that I see it now. It doesn't matter what I think. You're adults. You love each other. You shouldn't be making decisions based on my opinion."

I stared at her.

"I'm getting whiplash," I said.

"I know," she said.

"It doesn't matter," I said. "There's no way Cal would give me another chance. Even if I asked for one."

"Would you?" Harriet asked.

"No," I said. "I can't."

She raised her eyebrows at me.

"You love him," she said.

"Stop," I said.

"You do."

"I thought you just said that I shouldn't make decisions based on your opinion," I said.

"That's not my opinion," she said. "That's fact. You love him and he loves you."

It was getting colder. I buttoned my jacket up under my chin.

"It's too late," I said.

"He said that?"

I nodded. "I don't blame him. I've jerked him around enough for one lifetime. He deserves someone better."

"No, he doesn't."

"Thanks," I said dryly.

"You know what I mean," she said.

"I do," I said. "And thank you. But this is just the way things are going to be."

Harriet leaned her cheek on my shoulder. I could tell she wanted to say more, to argue with me further, but she didn't, and we just walked on.

CHAPTER 39

The standing ovation lasted ten minutes.

Of course, it was opening night, which meant the audience was packed with friends and family and supporters, but I savored every single second of that applause. I'd earned it. We'd earned it.

Backstage the energy was electric. We all were aware that our jubilant moods could change once reviews were released, but at that moment, it didn't matter. We had opened on Broadway.

Harriet met me in my dressing room, where we exchanged nearly identical bouquets of roses.

"Can you believe this?" she asked.

I'd taken off my costume and wig, and joined her on the small couch in my robe with my hair still pinned back. She poured me a glass of champagne.

"We're a triumph," I said.

We clinked our glasses and drank.

"How was it being in the audience?" I asked. "Watching *your* show premiere?"

Harriet let out a deep, satisfied sigh.

"It was incredible," she said. "If only I could bottle this feeling and take a tiny sip of it whenever I felt bad about myself."

I squeezed her hand.

"To your *first* Broadway opening night," I said. "I can't wait for the next one."

"And to you," she said. "Not that you're allowed to leave the show anytime soon."

"Speaking of." I got up and went to my bag. "I found your next project. *Our* next project."

"Are you kidding me?" Harriet asked. "The last thing I want to do is start something new. It's time to bask, not work."

"I don't know if you'll consider this work," I said, holding her gift behind my back. "But if you don't want it . . ."

Harriet was trying to see what I was hiding, but I kept turning away from her.

"Fine," she said, holding out her hand. "Let's see what this new project is."

I gave her the package.

"Is this . . . ?" She turned it over.

"Open it," I said.

She tore the paper off.

"Kathleen . . ." she said. Her voice was thick with tears.

"I'm ready," I said. "Aren't you? We've waited long enough."

It was the demo we'd recorded all those years ago. All of Harriet's beautiful songs.

"You think we can do it?"

"Why not?" I said. "Why not try?"

She stared down at the CD, and then pulled me into a hug.

"Let's do it," she said. "Let's fucking do it."

We poured some more champagne. Drank.

"Was Cal happy?" I asked.

I couldn't help myself.

"With the performance," I clarified unnecessarily.

We'd been completely professional since our split, polite and respectful but also keeping our distance.

Every time I looked at him, it hurt.

"He's happy," Harriet said, her fingers still tracing the label on the CD.

"Good," I said.

She gave me a long, searching look.

"Are you?" she asked.

"I just made my Broadway debut," I said. "A lifelong dream. How much happier could I be?"

"Have you spoken to him?" Harriet asked.

"He's given me his notes like he does with every other actor," I said.

"You should tell him."

"Tell him what?"

"That you're in love with him," Harriet said.

I nearly snorted my bubbly through my nose.

"Why would I do that?"

"Because it's true," she said.

"So?" I stood and went to the mirror to begin unpinning my hair. "It won't change anything. Besides, he knows."

Harriet joined me in the reflection.

"Does he?"

"Of course he does," I said.

But had I actually ever said it? He had. He'd been brave enough to. Twice.

Harriet put her hand on my shoulder.

"I'm not going to tell you what to do," she said.

I gave her a look.

"But that man has been in love with you since we were kids," she said. "And I think you've been in love with him too."

I stared down at my hands, unable to look her in the eye.

"Tell him," Harriet said.

"I think that's literally the opposite of not telling me what to do," I said.

Harriet laughed. "Well, I'm your best friend," she said. "And I'm right."

She gave me a hug from behind and a kiss on the cheek.

"See you at the after-party," she said.

* * *

I looked incredible. My dress was long and slinky and sexy, and I felt amazing in it. I'd never been much for the step-and-repeat red carpet photo-calls, but tonight, I was brimming over with pride. If these people wanted to take my picture, well, they were going to get the biggest smile on this side of Manhattan.

The production had rented out a gorgeous space along the Hudson River near Hell's Kitchen. It was decked out like a USO bar from the forties, including waiters and waitresses done up to blend in.

It felt like stepping back in time, and it was pure rib-sticking magic.

I spotted Harriet and Whitney across the room and waved at them. Harriet, subtle as ever, pointed to her left where Cal was standing with the producers.

My heart caught in my throat. He looked so good in his suit.

I missed him.

And I loved him.

Tell him.

Tell him.

Tell him.

I could hear Harriet's voice echoing in my ears, but it slowly morphed into my own. Because I knew deep down that she was right. That I needed to tell Cal how I felt.

He'd been honest with me. He'd been brave.

I owed him that. At the very least.

I saw him duck behind a curtain along the wall of the space, and I hurried to catch up to him. My heels were high, but my legs were long. I pushed back the curtain, nearly out of breath, and spotted him standing alone. He was looking out at the water.

"Cal!"

He spun at the sound.

"Kathleen." He put his hand on his chest, over his heart.

I didn't know what it meant. Had I startled him? Was it a protective gesture?

"What are you doing here?" he asked. "Go back and join the rest."

"I need to tell you something," I said.

I moved closer.

"This isn't a good time," Cal said, eyeing the curtain to his left.

"Just give me a moment," I said.

I saw him debate arguing with me, but in the end, he just closed his mouth and nodded. His hand was still on his chest.

"You don't owe me anything," I said. "You don't even owe me an answer or a response, but I just had to tell you that I love you."

"Kathleen, I—"

"I know," I said, holding up my hand. "I know. You already gave me a chance. Two chances. I blew both of them. I screwed up. Big. Huge."

"That's not—"

"I'm not asking for another chance," I said. "I just wanted you to know. That I love you. Harriet thinks I've been in love with you since we were kids and I think she's right. I think I've loved you since that night on the roof. Probably before, but definitely then."

"Kathleen—"

He looked sad, and my heart broke.

"It's okay," I said. "It's over. You were right. I just wanted you to know. Okay?"

Cal looked down, gave a small huff of a laugh, and glanced back up at me.

"What?" I asked.

His expression was inscrutable.

"I'm mic'ed," he said.

He lifted his hand to reveal that he had been covering a small microphone pinned to his jacket.

Suddenly a huge roar of applause came from the other side of the curtain. It lifted to reveal the entire cast, crew, press, and guests cheering and hooting at the announcement I'd just made over the speakers.

"Oh my god," I said.

"I hope you weren't planning to keep it a secret this time," Cal said.

He reached out and grabbed my hands, pulling me to him.

"Kiss her!" the crowd shouted. "Kiss her! Kiss her!"

I wouldn't have been surprised if Harriet had started it.

"I'm so embarrassed," I said, Cal's hands on my waist.

"You've always done your best work in front of an audience," he said.

"Surely not my best," I countered, eyebrow raised.

The crowd whooped and continued their chant.

Cal gave the microphone a yank, detaching it from his jacket, and dropped it onto a nearby table. He pulled me offstage, to the audible groan of the crowd.

Once we were alone, I pressed my face into his chest.

"Oh my god," I said. "I can't believe I did that."

Cal put his hand under my chin and lifted my face to meet his.

"It was perfect," he said.

"Really?"

"Well," he said, "perfectly you. Perfectly us."

I put my arms around his neck.

"Us?"

"I've loved you forever," Cal said.

I felt faint with relief. With joy.

"Everyone is going to think I slept with you to get this job," I said.

"Probably," he said. "Until they see you perform. Then they'll know the truth."

"Which is?"

"That this is where you've always belonged," he said.

I didn't know if he meant the stage or his arms, but it didn't matter. Both were true. Now, and forever.

◇ FINALE
◇

"Is it safe to be up here?" Cal asked.

I shrugged. "It's a roof," I said. "I don't think it's going to break."

I could tell he wasn't very comforted by my response, but he followed me up anyway. We sat next to each other, arms wrapped around our knees, close enough to be touching but not touching at all.

It was cold, but the best kind of summer cold—with the heat of the day still lingering on the skin. I pulled the hem of my sweatshirt down over my bare legs, probably looking a bit like a sweatshirt blob with a head and feet.

Cal was wearing a T-shirt and plaid pajama bottoms. In the moonlight, I could see goose bumps on his arms, but he didn't say anything and neither did I.

"Do you ever wish you could just freeze time?" I asked.

Cal didn't say anything for a while.

"Not really," he said.

"Oh," I said.

"I wish it would speed up," he said.

"What are you waiting for?" I asked.

"To be an adult, I guess," he said. "To have freedom and be able to make choices of my own."

I turned toward him, resting my cheek on my knee.

"I feel like I'm just waiting for something to happen, I guess." I nodded.

"Sometimes you have to make it happen," I said. "You can't wait."

He was staring up at the sky.

"What do you like about it?" he asked. "Performing."

"I like how it makes me feel," I said.

"Which is?"

I thought about it. "Powerful, I guess," I said. "Because when I'm onstage, when I'm really in the moment, everyone is watching me. I'm going to tell them what to feel—how to feel. At least, if I'm doing it right. That's pretty powerful."

"I never thought about it that way."

"There's nowhere else I'd rather be," I said. "What about you?"

"It's fun," he said. "I like that it's kind of a surprise, you know, telling people you can dance or sing or whatever."

"Yeah," I said.

We looked at the stars.

"I wish I could come back next summer," I said.

He shifted. "You're not coming back?"

"Can't," I said. "This was my chance. At least until I'm eighteen."

He nodded. "Well . . ." He thought for a moment. "Maybe you'll get a call when you get home. Sometimes that happens—scouts and agents—they get in touch."

"Maybe," I said.

I'd been good. I'd been great. But no one had come to speak to me after the showcase.

"Someone will call," he said. "You're really talented."

"You are too," I said. "And Harriet."

"I don't think I'm that good," he said.

"You know what you like," I said. "What looks good. What works."

"I guess," he said.

"Maybe you should be a choreographer or a director or something," I said.

He laughed. "Okay," he said. "Sure."

"What?" I gave him a shove. "If scouts are going to call me, then why can't you be a director one day?"

"I guess I could try," he said.

"Promise me that you will."

I held out my hand, pinky extended.

Cal looked like he didn't really think this was necessary, but linked his pinky with mine anyway and followed my lead as I blew on my thumb.

"This was the best summer," I said. "Despite everything."

"Yeah," he said.

I looked at him. He was really cute.

"Cal?"

"Yeah?"

"Can I kiss you?"

He turned to stare at me. "What?"

I should have said "nothing" or "never mind" but instead I just repeated myself.

"Can I kiss you?"

He looked gorgeous in the moonlight.

"Yeah, sure," he said.

I shifted my body toward him. I didn't know what to do with my hands. Or my knees. Or anything really. I kind of just sat there, my torso twisted in his direction. Then I put my palms on either side of his face.

And kissed him.

It was a short, smacking kiss. So short that I didn't even really process anything besides the softness of Cal's lips. I felt disappointed. I'd expected more. I'd wanted more.

But I'd asked for a kiss and that's what I'd gotten.

I was about to turn away when Cal's hand came up and cupped my jaw. He pulled me toward him and pressed his mouth against mine.

This time I felt everything.

The stroke of his thumb underneath my chin. The press of his lips and the taste of ChapStick and toothpaste. The way my entire body felt like it was humming. My knees trembled, knocking into each other beneath my sweatshirt, which was still pulled over my legs.

We drew apart and I opened my eyes.

"Okay," I said. "Thank you."

"Thank you?" Cal asked.

I untangled myself from my clothes and hurriedly climbed down off the roof.

"Kathleen?"

"I gotta go," I said.

"What?"

I took off before he could follow me down. I ran back to the girls' bunk, that cool summer night against my hot face. I'd been kissed. I'd been kissed. I'd been kissed by Cal.

And I had a feeling that nothing would ever be the same again.

THEATRE REVIEW

RIVETED! IS RIVETING!
BY SHAUNA MILLER [EXCERPT]

Cal Kirby, previously known for choreographing *that* scene in *The Hildebrand Rarity* as well as directing numerous concerts and live performances, takes to Broadway like he was born for it. Doing double duty as the director and the choreographer, Kirby seems poised to join the ranks of Fosse, Kidd and Robbins with this debut. His direction is inventive, confident, and most importantly, fun.

There are no weak numbers in this show. Harriet Watson's music is catchy and bright. She builds her score around a brassy, big band sound, and her lyrics are heart-wrenching. It's the perfect balance of familiar and new—songs that you feel you've always known and loved, but still completely fresh and unexpected. Let's hope they are working on a cast album, which will become a must-have for any and all theatre fans.

Everyone is already buzzing about Kathleen Rosenberg's performance. When she takes to the stage to sing "I've Never Been Seen," you won't be able to take your eyes off her. She's astonishing. Anyone going to the theatre expecting Katee Rose is going to be disappointed, because this is not the pop star we knew.

Or maybe we never really knew her at all.

ACKNOWLEDGMENTS

There are few things more tragic than a theatre kid who can't sing, dance, or act.

When you're the opposite of a triple threat, sometimes you have to find another way to express your adoration. That's what this book is. A love letter to one of my first loves—musical theatre. I'll never get the chance Kathleen gets—to perform on Broadway!—but writing about it has been a pretty fantastic and fun substitution.

I am indebted to the incredible team at Random House, both past and present. Courtney Mocklow and Morgan Hoit, who worked on *Funny* and continue to be the best cheerleaders, even from afar. Taylor Noel and Corina Diez, marketing duo of my dreams, and Melissa Folds, queen of publicity. I am so grateful for you all. Chances are, if you're holding this book in your hands it's because of the work these incredible women did.

Thank you to everyone at Penguin Random House for

your support. Thank you, Kara Welsh, Kim Hovey, Jennifer Hershey, Cara DuBois, Belina Huey, Ella Laytham, Elizabeth Eno, and everyone else who touched this book. I am grateful for every one of you.

To Kasi Turpin for another absolutely gorgeous cover, and Cassie Gonzales for making it shine.

Mae Martinez—assistant magnificent—who keeps everything in order and gives killer notes to boot.

My amazing editor, Shauna Summers, who held my hand throughout this entire process, always patient, always kind, always supportive. Writing books is *SO* hard, but worth it when I get to do it with you.

Elizabeth Bewley. How can I even begin to express my gratitude for you? You've literally changed my life and I love you. We are at the beginning of a very exciting adventure.

My most wonderful writing group, Zan Romanoff, Maurene Goo, Sarah Enni, Doree Shafrir, and Kate Spencer. I adore you all. Thank you to Dyan Flores, Lauren Cona, and Gregory Bonsignore for the at-all-hours brainstorming text sessions (and especially to Dyan for coming up with the name for CrushZone, among others). Thank you to Morgan Matson for creating *Riveted! The Musical* with me instead of watching the baseball game we were attending.

Thank you to Robin Benway, Katie Cotugno, Brandy Colbert, Anna Carey, Veronica Roth, Margot Wood, Alisha Rai, and anyone else I might have forgotten in my post-drafting brain fog, for being the writing community I've always dreamed of. Thank you to Mike Hanttula for building me the best website and being the best pal. Thank you to my teacher Kellie Wells, who gets complete credit for "the manly dangle," one of my favorite euphemisms of all time (to improve upon it, imagine it in an Irish accent). Thank you to

Laura Hankin, Emma Straub, Mady Maio, and all the other booksellers and readers that brought me here. Thank you to my dear friend Tal Bar-Zemer for being my big-boobed, theatre-loving, New York–living beta reader. All mistakes are mine and mine alone.

Thanks to my therapist. To the workers at Baja Fresh on Riverside Drive. To all my plants (even the ones I accidentally maimed). To On Broadway radio on Sirius. To Solvang. To edibles. To Costco blueberry muffins. To Pilates and scented candles. To Sondheim. To all the things that helped make each day just a little bit easier.

Thanks to my mom.

To my brother and my sister. To Tim and Amy. To Feivel.

To John. My favorite human.

To Mozzarella and Geordi and Susannah (dog and dog and cat).

To Basil (my heart).

To you.

PHOTO: © JOHN PETAJA

ELISSA SUSSMAN is the bestselling author of *Funny You Should Ask, Once More with Feeling,* and several YA novels. Her work has been praised by NPR, *The Washington Post, Cosmo, Publishers Weekly, Booklist,* and others. She lives in Los Angeles with her husband and their many pets.

elissasussman.com
Instagram: @Elissa_Sussman